# SAVING DELLA-RAY

## GEORGIA LE CARRE

# ACKNOWLEDGMENTS

Many, many thanks for all your hard work and help:

Leanora Elliott
Elizabeth Burns
Nichola Rhead
Kirstine Moran
Tracy Gray

Saving Della-Ray

ISBN: 978-1-910575-93-2

# DELLA-RAY

"*What?*" I croaked.

The cashier pulled my MasterCard out of her card reader, and stopped chewing gum long enough to repeat loudly, "I said, your card has been declined."

My face burned with embarrassment. I could feel the gaze of everyone in that store on me. I wanted to run out of there and never go back, but this was now my local. Tightening my hold on my niece's warm sweaty hand, I swallowed the shame crawling up my throat and said, "It can't be. I just got paid. Can you please try it again?"

Her bored eyes were a dull amber as she held my card out to me. "There's a bunch of people waiting behind you, ma'am. I know a declined card when I see one."

I forced a smile. "Please. Sometimes it doesn't go through on the first time, but if you try it again, it does. I work at the diner down the road and it happens to my customers occasionally."

She stared blankly at me.

I let go of Jess and leaned towards the cashier. "Just one more time, please. I'm pretty sure it will go through."

"Go on. Give her card another try. We haven't got all day," the woman behind me said.

I turned to meet the queue of eyes watching me with various expressions, impatience, annoyance, curiosity, and outright pity. "Sorry about this," I said with an awkward smile to no one in particular.

With a long-suffering sigh, the cashier slid my card back in. My paycheck should have cleared, but as I tapped in my pin number, I could feel the sweat begin to gather under my arms. Silently, I prayed the card would go through. Otherwise, Jess would be eating peanut butter sandwiches for dinner tonight.

The cashier turned the face of her machine in my direction. "Declined," she said loudly, as if she was pleased to have proved me wrong. "Martin!" she bellowed. "Can you come here for non-payment re-shelving?"

"Coming," a male voice answered from somewhere at the back of the store.

I didn't bother to wait. I picked up my card from the cold steel counter, straightened my back and gave Jess the sweetest smile I could muster. "Let's go, Sweetie."

# GAGE

https://www.youtube.com/watch?v=KiN4L16sMH4
-Knocking On Heaven's Door-

I looked at the blonde child's head bobbing innocently. Then I looked again at the girl. Her face was flushed with embarrassment, but that smile which she gave the child. There was something majestic and noble in it. I saw that self-less smile once when I pulled a woman out of a burning car. "My baby. Is my baby safe?" she'd asked. When I said yes, she had smiled like that just before she breathed her last. I stared at the girl in fascination. She was too thin. Her clothes were clean, but well worn.

*Let it go. Let it go.*

She wasn't my problem. Her check would clear in a couple of days and she would come back for the groceries. Not the end of the world. I definitely shouldn't get involved. No way. Not with a girl like that. One look at her and I knew she would be a big complication. I didn't need even a small complication.

"What about the groceries for our nice dinner, Della?" the kid asked innocently.

The girl took the child's hand in hers with such infinite tenderness that something happened inside me. I felt a tug in my chest. Like the first time I looked into the big, bottomless eyes of a child whose father I had just killed. He didn't cry. He didn't scream. He just stared at me with blank empty eyes. I knew I had destroyed him. As I'd turned and walked away, something inside me shattered. I was never the same again. Sometimes I still dream of him.

I didn't consciously plan it, but suddenly I had pushed my way to the front of the narrow aisle.

She looked up at me, frowned, and pulled the little girl to her.

I put my carton of milk on the counter and dropped some twenty-dollar notes next to it. "This should cover both bills."

The cashier's eyes widened. "You want to pay her bill?"

I didn't answer her. I didn't even wait for my change. I needed air, even if it was the suffocating hot noon air outside. I grabbed my carton of milk and walked away without looking at the girl. I couldn't look at her. I couldn't get involved. There should be no blowback from this moment of weakness. It could mean the difference between life or death for her and me.

# DELLA-RAY

https://www.youtube.com/watch?v=eSbxJMkI-tI
-I need some sugar in my bowl-

I watched his damp cascade of dark hair, the black T-shirt that showed his strong back; the tightly muscled and inked arms, and the stone washed black jeans that hugged his lean hips as he strode out of the store.

"Ma'am, take your groceries, please," the cashier prompted.

I was bright red as I turned around. "I-I ..."

"He paid for it all, so can you just take it and leave? There are a lot of people waiting."

"Just fucking take it," someone spat from the line.

I snatched the $62.30 worth of groceries and hurried out of the store. Jess pulled on my hand and I looked down at her.

She was smiling happily. "There he is," she sang.

I followed her pointing finger to see the biggest monster of a bike I'd ever seen, parked on the curb. It was jet black and the polished chrome was blinding in the sun. The rear lights were blood red. My eyes were riveted to the man who sat on it. As I watched he tipped his head and downed the 500ml carton of fresh milk he'd just bought, I felt my brain turn to mush.

"Big bike. Can I go on it?" Jess squealed excitedly.

The man pulled back his head, and with the back of his tattooed hand, he wiped the milk off the light dusting of dark stubble across his face.

His gaze met mine. There was no friendliness, no smile. In fact, it was a do-not-approach look.

It had the opposite effect on me. I was immediately jolted into motion. "Wait here," I said to Jess, and marched across the sidewalk into the parking lot. I stopped a safe distance away from him. "Excuse me, but ..." I nudged my head towards the full plastic bag in my hand. "I can't just accept this. I have to pay you back for it."

His gaze darkened with displeasure.

"I—I mean, I truly appreciate it. Thank you so much for helping us, but ..." I glanced down at the bag once more, then backwards at my niece. She was watching the man with unbridled interest. When I turned back to him, I saw that he was watching Jess too. I stiffened defensively, out of habit as I usually did, ready to tear his head off if he made any snide comments whatsoever about my angel.

"I have to pay you back," I said more loudly.

Completely ignoring me, he bent his leg, fired up the beast of a bike, and revved it. Thunderous noise filled the hot air.

Seeing that he had no intention of responding to me, I moved closer. I was determined to pay him back. Only when I was this close did I notice the ocean blue of his eyes, the slight scar that was hidden in the stubble along his left jaw and the wild, untamed beauty of the man. He was so, so, so beautiful.

"My paycheck was supposed to have cleared yesterday. Something probably went wrong, but the moment I'm able to resolve it I'll immediately transfer your money. Can I please have your bank account details?"

For a moment, he regarded me without expression, then, the rude brute started to reverse back.

Before I could stop myself, my hand shot out.

He broke his gaze from mine and let it slide to the pitiful hold I had on his thick, tattooed forearms.

I snatched my hand away as if burnt. I hadn't even realized I had done that. "I'm sorry."

He gave me an, 'I-thought-so-look' and continued his prep to leave.

"Look, I'll leave the groceries here if you don't allow me to pay you back," I cried.

"Do what you want with them. They're yours." His voice was deep, gravely with something dark and dangerous running underneath.

"Don't you see? I cannot accept them," I replied. I was getting frustrated. "Especially since you refuse to give me a way to pay you back?"

"I don't want money, sweetheart … but if you really insist on paying me back, you could let me fuck you," he drawled, his eyes so blue and piercing it was as if he was trying to look into my soul.

The bag fell from my hand.

He held my gaze as I stared wide eyed at him. I felt my lips begin to tremble and I saw his unspeakably beautiful eyes drop to my mouth. Some strange expression flashed in them. I should have said something rude. Something cutting, something to put him in his place. The arrogant bastard thought I would have sex with him for $62.30 worth of groceries, but I couldn't. For the first time in my life, I wanted to—I wanted to fuck a total stranger.

Without a word, I turned around and headed back to my niece.

As I reached her, I saw the empty carton of milk fly in an arc and land inside a rubbish bin by the side of the road. Then I heard his engine roar harder and zoom away into the distance. I couldn't help turning around to glance back to the spot he had occupied. The bag was on the ground where I had dropped it.

Together with my niece, we retrieved the cherry tomatoes that had rolled out of the pack.

Jess spotted one that had rolled underneath a vehicle parked nearby and she immediately got down in the dirt and belly-crawled under the car after it.

I should have told her not to, but my heart was pumping in

my chest and I could still feel my palm tingling where it had touched his warm skin.

"Got it," she shouted happily, and jumped to her feet.

"Good girl," I said automatically, and stroked her sweet angel shaped face.

He had ridden off into the sunset, but I had every intention of finding him and paying him back. This was Arnault, a small desert town on the way to the Sangre de Christo mountains and there was no way a man like that wouldn't be known by absolutely everybody.

# DELLA-RAY

"He said what?" Nichole, my best friend and roommate, screeched from where she stood scrubbing a pan in the sink. She sounded like I had startled the life out of her.

Nichole and I left our hometown and moved out here to Arnault, Texas looking for change and a new life. We came because we heard it was a special place, a haven for artists, writers, and creatives.

I wanted to leave our dead-end town and reach for something different, so this was supposed to be our great adventure. We were full of excitement. I was going to write in my free time, and she was going to paint.

Nichole managed to secure herself a dream job as an apprentice with a painter she admired, but to my dismay, I realized I couldn't write a single word. Every time I found a minute to sit down with my laptop, the words simply didn't flow. Forget about words flowing, my page stayed completely blank.

I knew it had to do with the fact that I was physically exhausted and constantly harassed with the thoughts of all the bills and debts I'd acquired from the last time Jess fell ill. I told myself the words would come back once I had finished paying my debts, once I had more time to myself when Jess was old enough to go to school.

Jess noisily sucked another strand of spaghetti into her mouth.

I turned my head so she couldn't see my face, and calmly mouthed to Nichole, *"He said he wanted to fuck me."*

"How dare he?" Nichole gasped, the pan clattering into the sink.

I hid my smile at her offended, incredulous expression. Nichole's morals were set on the very traditional, or maybe even on the Amish dial. She did not approve of sex before marriage, let alone fucking for fucking's sake. I'd known her since we were both fifteen and in school together and she'd only ever had one boyfriend. She dropped him like a hot potato when he hinted at sex without putting the all-important ring on her finger first.

"What? All because he bought you some milk?" she demanded, utterly furious on my behalf.

"Well, he bought *himself* some milk. He bought *us* the groceries."

She looked at me quite speechless.

"He was extremely hot, Nichole," I said teasingly, to scandalize her further.

Her mouth tightened. "How in God's name do you manage to attract these creeps?"

I pretended to glance around the room and then back at Jess. "Umm ... I must have missed something here. How exactly did I, who was minding my own business in a grocery store, become the problem?"

She sighed and shook her head, making her blonde curls bounce wildly. "Please, Della-Ray. Just stay away from him, okay."

"What makes you think I'll run into him again, or have anything to do with him?"

"Because I know you. Admit it. You're itching to pay him back, aren't you?"

"Well, there is that." I grinned. "And his hot body."

She snorted. "Stop trying to wind me up by talking like that. I know you don't mean it, but you're not from these parts and if you're even slightly tempted, I should tell you that those kinds of men are lethal. They *always* break your heart. And if he indeed took a liking to you, especially in—in that way—then he will find you and—and have you. So you make sure to stay away from him at all costs. If you see him again, just immediately run away."

"Well, if he's as dangerous as you say, then what will running away solve?" I teased.

If I were honest, I felt a little discouraged by her crushing words. I'd hoped it would be a giggly, girly conversation between us, something that brought us closer, but it was clear that wasn't to be. Ever since we moved out here, she seemed to have lost not only her sense of humor, but also her smile.

She turned her back to me and continued washing the pan, but much harder, her curls bouncing with how much pressure she was exerting. Suddenly another thought occurred to her, and she whirled around to face me again. "Was he just a regular dude with a motorbike, or did he seem like one of those biker gang type?"

"Wow, you didn't think to ask that before you started blasting me?"

"I didn't blast you," she countered calmly. "I was looking out for you. As it happens, they're both equally dangerous to a woman like you so everything I said stands."

I raised my eyebrows. "A woman like me?"

"A woman with a big heart who thinks everyone else lives by her high standards too. Now answer me. Was he a biker or a regular dude?"

I shrugged and turned back to Jess.

She grinned innocently at me, a thick ring of tomato sauce around her lips.

I smiled back at her, before turning back to Nichole. "I have no idea. How can you tell?"

"By their patch. You know, the symbol of their club, they usually wear it on their clothes or sometimes they even tattoo it onto their bodies."

"Well, I don't remember seeing any patches on him. He was just in a black tee and a pair of faded jeans."

Nichole put a soapy hand on her hip. "And why couldn't you afford to pay?"

"I have no idea. My paycheck should have cleared the night before, so I didn't even bother checking my balance before I went to the store."

She frowned. "Have you got some installments other than your loan payment coming out?"

"Not any more, I took them all off my card ... even the phone contract. It was becoming a nightmare to even have money on the card."

Her face filled with anxiety.

"Please don't worry about it, Nichole. I've got it all figured out. I've called all my creditors and agreed to pay them all in small installments. By the end of this year, I should be debt-free. And I'll sort my paycheck out when I get to the bar tonight. Perhaps Karl just forgot to bank it."

I saw her mentally bite back whatever she wanted to say and return to her dishes in silence.

I was sorry I had brought up the issue of my debts. "Are we going to at least talk about how hot he was?" I asked lightly.

She turned back, one eyebrow raised. "You want to say all that in front of Jess?"

I turned to my little niece, my heart aching just a little bit when her face broke into another huge smile of pure trust and love. I threw a teasing look at Nichole. "I don't think Jess will mind if Nichole and I indulge in a bit of girl talk."

"I'm not in the mood for girl talk," Nichole shot back. "I'm not happy."

"Well, I am. So ... just back off."

"Are you really?" Her eyes moved to Jess.

I instantly grew defensive. I knew what she was thinking. "Yes, Nichole," I replied firmly. "I'm incredibly, deliriously happy."

"I'm not," she stated firmly.

"For Pete's sake, what's wrong with you today?"

"I saw your shoes at the entrance." Her frown dug deep into her forehead. "They look battered."

"Of course, they are. I've had them for almost two years and worn them almost every day."

"Exactly!" she said. "You need new shoes."

"And?"

"You need to buy them."

I blinked at her. "All this harassment was because I need to buy some new shoes?"

"No, all this is because that is not the only thing you need."

"Nichole ..." I softened my voice trying to understand her. "What is wrong with you today? Did something happen at work?"

She made a frustrated sound. "No, nothing happened at work. I'm just tired of seeing you this way. You have two jobs and everything else you can get your hands on in between. This is not the first time your card has been declined. You've stopped going to the mart by your work because you're sure now that they've labeled you and

15

now, you go all the way to Walmart to get bits and pieces."

"That's because it's cheaper." I shrugged.

"Of course," she replied. "You go thirty minutes away from home to get milk because it's a dollar cheaper. You're not living, Della-Ray and I can't breathe. Watching you ... I just can't breathe. I've known you for ten years now, and you weren't like this. You had dreams and plans even. More than any of us. You wanted to be a writer, remember? You used to write all the time. You wanted out of that forsaken town we lived in. You dreamed of going to New York ... You wanted to live and create. Instead, look where we've ended up. When was the last time you wrote anything other than a food order?"

I pushed so angrily out of my chair that it fell back behind me.

Jess jumped and made a surprised O with her mouth.

Controlling myself, I looked down at her and brushed her hair away from her face. "I'm sorry, sweetie. Did I startle you?"

She shook her head.

"I tell you what, why don't you go and wash your hands and face and we'll go and play on the swing for a while."

"Yay," she agreed happily.

The silence in the room was palpable as she slid out of her chair and walked out of the room. I closed the door and leaned against it.

"Della-Ray," Nichole said into the deadly silence. "Listen to me. For once, freaking listen to me. You can't keep doing this. The years are going to go by and one day, you'll wake up and not be able to recognize yourself."

"What do I fucking do then?" I exploded, my chest constricting with pain at her words. "What do I fucking do? You want me to abandon Jess?"

I thought she would back down, but she didn't. "You want me to tell you what I really think?"

"Obviously."

"All right, I will. I'm not going to pussyfoot around this situation anymore. I'm going to be the friend I've always been and be dead honest with you." She took a deep breath and went on, "I want you to give Jess up for adoption. Before you say anything, my brother is adopted and my parents have loved him as much as they have me. With the right people, they could be a better option than you struggling to take it all upon yourself. I honestly do think the best thing you can do for her is to find her a good home, where they will love her and give her the best medical attention she needs."

I stared at her in disbelief. "You really think that's possible?"

She nodded firmly. "Yes, I really do."

"In that case, you're crazy. To start with, I would never ever abandon her, and also you think there are people who will take in a child with down syndrome and a cardiovascular heart disease by choice, huh? The last time she ended up in hospital, I used up every bit of savings I had and then some."

"You don't know that no one will take her," she argued. "You haven't tried. There are people with money and kind hearts."

17

"Nichole, let's get one thing straight. I'm not putting her up for adoption. Over my dead body. Can you see Jess in some other home, without me? It would break her heart."

"She's only four. She'll get over it."

"I wouldn't." My voice was shaking.

"Oh, Del. What about you, though? What about *your* life?"

"She is my life and I can't believe that you can't see that."

"All I know is that Denise wanted to give her up as soon as she was born, but you stepped in and stopped it."

"I'm the bad guy now? For not abandoning the child my sister gave birth to?"

"You are," she shot back.

I stared at her, taken aback.

"To yourself," she continued. "Okay, so you gave up on the idea of living in New York as a writer, but at least if you were in some way working towards becoming a writer, I wouldn't mind so much. We came here so we could both pursue our artistic dreams, instead every dime you make and every free hour you have goes into Jess's care. You pay absolutely no attention to yourself. To the things you want or even need. You can't even get a boyfriend because no guy wants to be saddled with the kind of baggage you're carrying around with you. Even that shitbag, Michael, that you hooked up with was only pretending to like Jess. You're not *living* and you're going to regret it."

"As for Michael, I have to be grateful to Jess. If not for her, I might have wasted more time on that loser. And as for being an author, I promise, I'll start writing again. Soon. When I'm debt-free."

Her voice rose. "Then let me help pay off your debts … please."

"I can't let you do that, Nichole. If I did, you won't be able to carry on with your apprenticeship. Please, just trust me … I've worked it all out. By the end of this year, I should be in the clear again."

She looked at me with sadness in her eyes. "What happens if Jess gets sick again before that, or even after that?"

A wave of horror swept over me.

She saw the shudder I couldn't conceal and pounced, "You can't even get insurance for that girl, can you? What will you do if she gets sick again like she did last winter, Della?"

I pushed away the fear that kept me awake at night and answered her quietly, "I don't know, but I'll cross that bridge when I come to it."

"You can't keep avoiding this, Della. You're not doing Jess any favors keeping her when you can't afford to take care of her properly."

I dropped my head in guilty silence. It was true that I couldn't provide Jess with the best health care, but no one could give her more love than I could and maybe that would be enough … if we were lucky and she didn't get sick again. After all, the doctor said he had never seen a healthier child during our last visit.

When I didn't respond, Nichole continued with her rampage,

"Give Jess up, Della. You cannot sacrifice yourself for her, and as much as you hate to hear it, she really does deserve better."

I lifted my chin. "I'm sorry you feel that way, but Jess is mine and I won't give her up. Ever."

"I know you love Jess, but you can't give up your own happiness for her. How do you think she'd feel when she grows up to know she was the reason you lost your greatest dream? Would that make her happy? Would you wish that kind of life where she put everyone else before herself for her? Would you?"

I was out of the room before she could finish her sentence, but her words were still ringing in my ears. My heart felt as if it was being crushed in my chest. Nichole called me to come back and stop being a coward, but I ignored her.

I found Jess in the bathroom standing on her pink plastic stool almost done with washing her face and hands. Her almond shaped eyes focused on me and immediately a big smile split her face, but it faltered and changed to one of confusion. "What's the matter, Della?"

I shook my head and knelt next to her. "Nothing, honey. Nothing is the matter."

She frowned at me, her little pink tongue sticking out slightly. "Then you gotta smile."

I forced a smile and she immediately smiled back happily.

"You know, I'll always take care of you, right," I said to her as I brushed the thin blonde strands of hair away from her face.

Her answer was simple and without hesitation, "Yeah."

My sister's blood ran in her veins, but she was as much a part of me as my hands were. She didn't choose any of this, and I'd be damned if I let her suffer any more than she needed to. No matter what happened, I would never give her up.

21

# GAGE

https://www.youtube.com/watch?v=s43FpUG9uxQ

I felt like I was flying.

Going a hundred and twenty on the Harley, the highway wide open and the looming trees zooming past like ghosts. It was the only time I breathed deeply and felt my lungs fill with clean, smoke-free air. It was wonderful to leave behind the rage that usually consumed me. Here, I was one with earth.

I could forget the lying cheating human beings in my path.

In these moments, little else existed, but the possibility that it could all come to a crashing end … and then nothing would matter. The thought excited and terrified me and at the same time, a perfect adrenaline fest. So I sped on, until I tore past the county's Chief Deputy's vehicle. His sirens began to blare into the still summer evening. I thought about ignoring the interruption, but I knew better.

I slowed down.

Pulling up by the side of the road, I watched him drag himself out of the vehicle in my mirror. He came over, the swagger of authority was evident from his black shoes to his slicked back hair. I guess he was one of the good guys.

"You were going over the limit there—" He stopped suddenly as I pushed my sunglasses onto my head. There was no smile on his face. "Breaking the law on my turf, Miller?"

"It's one of those days," I responded.

Yeah, he understood. Nothing more needed to be said.

I slipped the glasses back over my eyes, and revved my bike back to life. Something that looked suspiciously like pity flashed in his eyes and instantly it turned my mood sour.

"Take it easy," he said to me. "I'll let you off this time."

With a nod, I lifted my feet off the ground and was on my way. Something about the expression in his eyes had spoiled my mood permanently. Even the wind in my hair didn't feel good anymore. I felt restless and angry. I could die tomorrow. And for what? My life was one long, lonely shit fest. Every day, I wallowed in the stink and the disgusting slime. What was there for me?

Easy, Gage, a little voice in my head warned, but I wasn't listening.

Damnit, I needed something for me too. A little taste of sweetness.

23

Do you want to get both of you killed, you fool? the voice asked.

I hit the pedal hard and the bike shot forward. The world around me became a blur. Adrenaline poured into my blood. It calmed me right down. The weak moment passed away. Of course, I would never endanger her. The twist in my gut remained, a physical pain. I knew I had to see her again. Not to start anything. I wasn't stupid. She was trouble. That much was clear. I just ... I just wanted to look at her face again. One fucking look and then I'd be on my way. Maybe one day when all this was over, I would go back for her.

I knew exactly where I'd find her. I'd heard her tell the cashier where she worked. In less than half an hour, I was back in town. I stopped across from Good Eats, a diner downtown I'd never been in before, on account of its wholesome family vibe. Places like that weren't for me. I'd stick out like a sore thumb, but that was okay, since I wasn't planning on going in.

I brushed my hair, matted from the wind, out of my eyes and looked through the windows into the bright red decor. A corny sign on the wall said, *'Pie fixes everything.'* My eyes swept around looking for her. When I spotted her I felt like a lost, condemned man whose heart is accidentally touched by the tip of an angel's wing. Something inside me burst open and flooded with brilliant color.

She was wearing a canary yellow uniform. Her hair was tied back, and she was wiping down a recently vacated table. Her movements were quick and fluid. It was as if she had cleaned a thousand tables in her young life.

Someone must have called out to her, because she lifted her

head, then started to make her way towards the kitchen. I watchèd her walk away and Jesus, the girl was so fucking thin I wanted to take her back to my place and feed her for a week.

As she disappeared out of sight, my boots landed on the ground. The soft thud reverberating in my head. I didn't question my actions as I disembarked. Chasing after trouble was what I was doing, but I told myself all I wanted was a bit of pie. After that, I would leave. Maybe pie would fix what ailed me. I walked through the door, I found myself walking towards the table she had cleaned.

It was no big deal. A bit of pie, then I was walking away.

## DELLA RAY

"Della-Ray! Della-Ray!"

I was sitting on the corner stool of the kitchen, my mouth filled with a less than graceful bite of buckeye pie.

"Hmm," I sounded out, but it was more than enough for Gloria to locate me.

She bounced over, her eyes enormous in her heart shaped face, and almost crashed into me.

I blinked in surprise and waited for her to catch her breath with a hand over her full chest. I somehow managed to chew fast enough and swallow before she could get herself together. "What's wrong?"

"One of your tables," she began.

"Are they leaving?" I asked, immediately putting my plate aside and started to hurry of.

She grabbed my arm and stopped me.

I couldn't understand what had gotten into her. "What's up, Gloria?"

"Here's the thing. There's a new customer in," she explained in a rush, "but I want to take him."

Gloria wanted one of my customers? I stared at her curiously. "Why?"

"Consider this a favor," she said. "He's ... let's just say he's what I need right now."

Confused, I headed over to the kitchen door to peep out through the round glass cut out, but I could see no one. She pulled me forward for a better view and then I saw *him*.

Everything stilled.

I couldn't believe my eyes. I stared, dumbfounded as he pulled his phone out of his pocket and began to browse through it. Almost in a shocked daze, my eyes drifted towards the window. Through it, I spotted his big black bike. The devilish machine and its devastatingly sexy owner hadn't left my mind since I had become the object of his charity yesterday.

"Let me take the table, please?" Gloria pleaded, pulling on my arm.

I snapped out of my daze and focused on her.

"After my break-up with Al, this is exactly the kind of man I need right now. All that leather and ... tattoos ... and big, rippling muscles. Damn, I usually don't fancy bikers, but he is the good kind ... all dark and tormented ... aaand he's looking over here. Shit, move!"

She pulled me backwards so hard we almost stumbled and landed on the floor.

I moved away from her. "Actually, I know him."

Her expression turned hostile. "You do? How?"

"Uh ... we've met at the grocery store ... so I need to take his table. Sorry."

She scoffed in disbelief.

"Sorry," I said again.

"Whatever," she muttered sarcastically and flounced off.

Quickly, I wiped whatever traces of peanut butter and chocolate was left around my lips. Taking a deep breath, I pulled myself out of hiding and headed over to the man who looked like a dark overlord in our small friendly diner. "Hello! May I take your order?" I asked brightly.

A whiff of his dangerous scent assaulted my senses, as he lifted his intensely blue gaze to mine. I found myself holding my breath for absolutely no reason. It was plain silly, but it just didn't seem logical to breathe in that moment. I waited for recognition to flash through those incredible eyes, but he only regarded me coldly for a few seconds before looking down at the menu again.

"What's the special for today?" he asked, his gaze on the menu spread in his hands.

I stared at his dark head, shocked at how disappointed I felt that he didn't remember me at all. Or if he had decided I was too unimportant to acknowledge. From the corner of my eye, I could see Gloria watching us and felt my cheeks go red with embarrassment. "Breaded chicken cutlet," I responded, my voice small. "It comes with mashed potatoes and the Chef's special chicken gravy."

"I'll have that," he responded, and shut the menu.

Our pitiful three-fold menu was tossed across the table and I felt a sort of kinsman-ship with it.

"Coming right up," I muttered to the back of his head and turning away, I made my way back to the kitchen. I didn't miss the gloating look Gloria shot me from the table she was wiping down at the end of the aisle. She could see I had been utterly dismissed.

It was a slow afternoon so I was able to remain in the kitchen until the Chef, Allan had his plate ready. When I carried it over to his table, he was on his phone. As I put the plate down, I realized I hadn't been so flustered to see him that I hadn't even asked him what he wanted to drink.

I hovered over him for a few seconds waiting for his gaze to meet mine so I could ask his choice of refreshments. He raised his eyes to me, and the two, ocean blue balls of sheer beauty regarded me. He was watching me, but listening to whomever he was talking to, and I shifted from one foot to the other, wondering if I should just leave him. But he kept watching me, his face expression-less, and the intensity of his look made my mind go blank.

I began to sweat. When I couldn't take it anymore, I turned around to take my leave.

His hand shot out suddenly and captured my wrist.

I froze.

"Sure," I heard him say, but I couldn't turn around. "I'll update you soon."

He let me go when he was done with his call. The part of my skin he had encircled with his touch felt like it had been seared. Fighting the urge to hold it with my other hand I turned around and gave him a polite smile. "I forgot to ask earlier. What can I get you to drink?"

An odd expression passed in his eyes and it reminded me of a line from a song about tombstones in someone's eyes. Every hair on my skin stood up to attention and my throat was suddenly parched.

"I'll have what I had the first time we met," he said.

"So you do recognize me?" I asked in a hushed voice.

## DELLA RAY

"**D**oes anyone ever forget you?"

Once again, my brain got scrambled. What did he mean by that? Perhaps it was solely in reference to the humiliating incident at the store. "I suppose it must be particularly hard to forget someone who owes you money."

"Forget the milk. I'll have water. Make it cold," he responded, his eyes boring into mine.

I blinked at the sudden change in topic. "Uh, sure," I replied, slightly offended. I went to fulfill the order and wondered if he was aware that he'd made me this flustered. His words the last time we had met about wanting to fuck me had rattled my peace. I had replayed the scene again and again in my head. To be honest, I had been completely and truly unable to get him out of my head.

I returned with his glass of iced water.

He was already well into his meal, fork digging into the

cutlet and knife cutting it into neat pieces which ended up in his wonderful mouth.

I wanted a reason to linger, but he gave me none. He didn't even lift his head to look at me as I placed the glass on his table. It irritated me that he could so easily turn me on and off again. I glared vindictively at the head of dark hair before taking my leave.

Whilst in the kitchen, I continued with the rest of my buckeye pie, but I had lost my appetite. Chewing despondently, I thought about how I was going to pay him back his money.

I had no cash on me and his meal wouldn't even be up to twenty percent of the amount he paid to settle my grocery bill. I resolved then to come to some sort of agreement with him. Maybe I could pay for his meals here so he could eat here for free until he reached $62.30.

At that moment, an elderly couple in matching blue Hawaiian t-shirts took a table in my section and I quickly busied myself serving them. So much so that I only realized he had finished his meal and was leaving when the whiff of his scent called all my senses to attention as he walked past.

I turned to look at his table and saw the bill on it.

"Please excuse me," I said to the couple in the midst of taking their order and hurried over to see what trouble he had stirred up this time around. I found a crisp hundred-dollar bill on the table. Annoyed, I sprinted out of the diner and caught him just as he was about to kick start his big bike to life.

"You can't keep doing this," I said.

"Doing what?"

I held up the hundred-dollar bill. "Why would you leave a hundred-dollar bill for a meal that isn't even fifteen bucks?"

"Okay," he responded calmly. "Your diner has a policy against tips?"

I was stumped for a moment, then I took the bull by the horns. "Of course not, but a hundred dollars? Are you trying to make me more indebted to you than I already am? I'm not a charity case."

With his eyes narrowed, he folded his hands across his chest.

I tried my very best not to notice the clench and flex of his thick biceps as they strained against the leather. One did not need too much of an imagination to conclude that beyond the layer of clothes he had on was a hard body, sculpted with slabs of muscle and intoxicating virility. There was absolutely nothing tender about this man.

"Help me understand what the problem is," he stated quietly.

"I already owe you. I should be paying for your meal. Instead, you're leaving me a disproportionately massive tip."

"So?"

There was no winning with this man, so I stepped forward and placed the money on the seat of his bike, but a gust of wind caught it and carried it away. If I had thought about it for even a moment, I wouldn't have chased after it like a mad woman. When I returned, my face was flushed with embarrassment and rage at myself for being so unladylike.

He was in the exact same position I had left him in, his gorgeous eyes filled with amusement.

I wished I could tear up the bill. That would wipe the sarcastic smile off his smug face. "Just freaking take the money," I yelled.

For the longest time he simply watched me, his expression veiled, then to my surprise, he reached out and accepted the bill from my hand.

I jumped back like a cat coming upon a cucumber when his skin touched mine.

Luckily, he caught the bill before it could be sent on another flight up the street. "I thought you'd abandoned the groceries," he said as he tucked the cash into the pocket of his jeans.

My eyes innocently followed his hand but when it got close with the one part of him I definitely did not want to be caught staring at, I shot my gaze back up to his face. I could have sworn his eyes flashed with a glint of cruel amusement. He seemed to be mightily entertained by my lack of sophistication.

I straightened my shoulders. "Well, it would have been a shame to just leave them there ... wasted."

"Hmm," was all he said in response. Then his gaze lowered to rev his machine to life.

At the deafening sound, I took a step backwards and tried to ignore the panic that was arising at his early exit when we were still yet to come to an agreement. "After deducting your meal, I still owe you ..." With my eyes raised to the sky I rushed to make the calculation in my head and to my surprise he waited. "I still owe you about forty-eight dollars. Would you like to keep coming for some more free meals?"

"Nah, this is not my kind of place, after all."

For some weird reason that hurt. It meant he didn't want to see me again. "So how do I get the rest back to you?"

"What's wrong with now?"

My cheeks burned. It was horrible being poor. "I don't have any cash on me."

"No problem," he responded.

Instantly, I felt the sting of my situation. Whether unintended or not his aloofness made me feel like a beggar before him. "I will pay you back," I said through clenched teeth. "I'll get it to you the moment I'm done with my shift. Send me your account information."

He laughed. "All that for forty-eight dollars?"

I blinked. "Well, how else am I going to pay you?"

"You'll have to figure that out yourself, lady." Now he just sounded bored.

My eyes narrowed and I gave him a dose of his own derogatory medicine. "Fine. I work late night shifts at Sinkhole. It's on East Main Street, close to the pawn shop. If you stop by tonight, I'll have your cash ready for you."

"I'll be there," he said quietly.

I watched as he slipped his aviator sunglasses on the bridge of his Roman nose, completely shielding me from whatever was lurking in those blue eyes of his. I wanted to walk away as if I didn't care, but my legs wouldn't move. I stood there like an idiot and watched as he backed out of the lot and zoomed off into the late Saturday afternoon with a frightening speed.

It was almost a few minutes later before I was shrieked back to my senses. I turned to see Gloria angrily calling out to me from the door of the diner. "You damn well have customers to attend to!" she screamed, green with resentment.

"I'll be right there," I answered, and hurried back to work.

## DELLA RAY

I had always considered waiting tables at the diner to be a decent enough gig to fill out my days, but as the clock ticked with excruciating slowness towards the end of my shift at 5pm, I started to feel restless and irritated.

As I slammed my notepad on the pickup counter, Allan arched his eyebrow at my aggression. "What's up? You exhausted?" he asked, surprise in his tone.

"Yeah," I lied.

"Already? What about your gig at Sinkhole? You have at least five more hours of grinding before you can call it a day."

"More like six or seven, but I have energy for that I'm just tired of ... *here*. The time drags, doesn't it?"

His mouth filled up with air as he debated on how to respond to me. He decided on teasing amusement. "Well, you have been working here for almost two years and you've never commented about the time dragging. You have something to look forward to tonight?"

"Rest. A long hard rest," I lied again, and turned my gaze to the red clock on the wall as it crawled its way in seconds to the strike of five.

The moment it struck the hour, a big smile spread across my face. Heck, my heart was fluttering with uncontainable excitement. First, I would go home and see my little angel, have a shower, put on some make-up then I was off to the Sinkhole.

"See you guys tomorrow," I sang out, as I untied the little white apron from around my waist.

An hour later, I was hurrying into Sinkhole with more zeal than was normal to feel after just completing an eight-hour shift at the diner.

"Hey, Nick," I greeted the boisterous, broad, bald bartender I worked with as I strolled into the back-alley club just off East Main Street.

"Della-Ray," he bellowed and for once, I matched his level of energy, with a huge smile.

I headed to the back room to change and minutes later I was out in my black polo shirt uniform and tight, black jean shorts to begin my six-hour shift as a cocktail waitress. The low serenade of Paul McCartney filled the air as I followed the four women who strolled in just then and subtly cajoled them into sitting in my section.

"What can I get you?" I asked brightly.

It was almost three hours later before I had the chance to

take a proper break. The place was filled with the din from the chatter of its patrons winding down after the long and hard work day. Everyone was relaxed except for me.

Nursing a glass of ice cold cranberry juice I stretched my neck and looked towards every dimly lit corner I could see from where I stood behind the bar, and still there was no sign of him. I couldn't remember him giving me a time for his arrival, but still it was nearing midnight and I had to face the fact that he was most probably, *not* coming.

The adrenaline of wanting to see him again died away and suddenly, I felt exhausted. I noted a group of businessmen walk in. They were laughing and had obviously been drinking elsewhere before they came here. I quickly downed my drink and went after my bread for the day. Soon, they were seated and I was at their service.

One of them asked why I wasn't part of the menu, and I gave the same answer I always gave to their incredibly unoriginal and banal question, "Because you wouldn't be able to afford me."

"Oooo … feisty," they cackled, elbowing each other like they were teenagers.

Obviously, they were more inebriated than I'd first thought. "So what'll you have this evening, gentlemen?" I asked crisply.

They gave their orders between snorts of amusement and suggestive noises.

"Be right back," I said with my usual dazzling smile.

But as I turned to leave, one of them tapped my ass and the smile instantly faded from my lips. Any other day, I would have turned around and told him where to get off, but that day I was disappointed and a bit blue, so I carried on walking towards the bar.

As I arrived at the bar, Lena the other waitress was walking away with a tray of six Sex On The Beach cocktails.

"You feel like taking over table fifteen?" I asked.

She glanced towards the promising businessmen, and looked back at me surprised. "That's going to be a big tip."

"I know but I can't deal with that today, not even for the money. I might smash one of their heads."

With a smile, she handed the cocktails over to me, and I took it over to the young group of women.

I served them their drinks and went on with the rest of the night, my mood becoming gloomier and gloomier as the minutes passed. The bar would be closing by one and by midnight, I'd given up on him ever showing up. After handling what I hoped was my last table for the night, I headed over to a corner of the bar with my tray and plopped down on one of the seats.

Plopping my elbows and hands on the counter I rested my head on my hands and tried to catch some rest. I felt utterly defeated and tired.

"Rough night?" I heard someone ask. I'd intended to ignore the inquiry until I realized ...

My head shot up to meet the hot blue gaze of—I didn't even know his name.

Even with no name, he had become important enough to cast such a shadow on my evening just from not turning up. I couldn't think of anything to say as I took him in. His hair had been slicked back neatly. I followed the clink of the ice swirling around in his glass.

"When did you get here?" My voice was an exhausted whisper.

"What?" he asked, and leaned forward so I could whisper my question into his ear.

"When did you get here?" I repeated, dazed by the scent of him.

He leaned away and looked into my eyes. "A while. This is my second drink."

"Why didn't you look for me?"

"You were occupied," he stated. "I didn't want to intrude."

I wanted to be furious at him, but just like that, he had taken the logic out of my annoyance. "I'll go get your money," I said and walked away. A few minutes later, I returned with the envelope. Whatever excitement I had nursed for so many hours had completely dissipated. When I returned, his glass was sitting at the bar, but he was no longer there. I looked around, wondering where he had gone off to, but I couldn't see him.

Suddenly, I felt a hand slip around my waist just as I was pulled roughly against a body.

My heart instantly seized at the sudden intrusion. For a fraction of a second, I wondered if it was him, but the disgusting reek of tobacco and beer hit my nostrils, and I immediately tore the hand away and spun round to face the last person I ever wanted to see.

M ichael!

Wearing a wide smile. He had replaced the broken part of his premolar with a gold tooth. "Angel," he said in that insufferably patronizing voice.

How I'd ever been able to stand his voice, was still beyond mysterious.

"Missed me?" he asked.

I was helpless to stop my eyes from rolling up towards the ceiling, but his gloating expression didn't falter. Hell, the man had a rhino's hide. My first thought was how long would it take to get rid of him. I definitely didn't want biker guy to think I was with him. *Ugh.*

"No, I did not miss you. I'm working now, so please can you leave me alone?" I turned to walk away.

He reached out to grab a hold of my hand.

I had anticipated that move and in response, I swung my arm away.

It appeared he had this figured out, because a second later, his other arm circled tightly around my arm. He yanked hard and my body slammed into his.

I lost my temper. Using all my strength, I jerked away and turned on him furiously. "How dare you?" I spat.

He swung his head around us to see if anyone had seen the rejection he had suffered. When his eyes returned to me, the amusement had faded from his face. "How dare I what?" he snarled.

I rubbed the place where he had gripped me and stared at him silently.

"Touch you?" he asked nastily.

Damn, why did I let him get to me? I shouldn't have reacted to him. Clearly, I had given him the very ammunition he was looking for.

"Are you kidding me? You poverty-stricken bitch? You still have that air about you, don't ya? As though you're worth more than that sour slit between your legs. You turn anymore guys away and that hole is going to dry right up and wither away. Hell, I can't fucking believe I wasted my time on a frigid little bitch like you." His voice was deliberately loud and his teeth were clenched with fury at what he considered to be disrespect from a mere woman. People were starting to look at us. The last thing I wanted was a scene.

I worked here, so I really needed the job and my reputation intact. "Great. If you feel that way then keep away from me from now on," I said, and immediately tried to hurry away, but he caught me again. I faced him and tried to unclench his fingers from round my arm.

"Look at me!" he ordered as he shook me like a rag doll.

Red hot rage bubbled up in me, but before I could throw all caution to the wind and slap him hard right there in middle of my workplace, a large fist came out of nowhere and ploughed into his face. The blow hit Michael so hard he went flying to the floor. It all happened so fast I was still standing shocked. For a second, all I could do was stare at the pile of trash he looked like on the floor. Then I turned and met the eyes of the other person I didn't want to see at that moment.

I still didn't know his freaking name.

He stood staring down at the prone man with an expression that was begging him to get up so he could knock him right back down again.

"It's alright. He's just drunk. Don't worry about it," I said quickly.

He didn't even look at me. His gaze remained on Michael as he struggled to peel himself off from the floor.

"Honestly, it's okay. I know him," I tried to explain. "Well, we used to date. He's not troubling me. Just … just let it go. This is where I work. I don't want any trouble. Come on. Let's go."

Suddenly, Michael recovered his senses, jumped to his feet with a roar and before I could say another word, the biker pulled me out of the way.

"You fucking bast—" Michael drew out his clenched hand to land a punch, but then froze mid-air the moment his brain registered the biker. It would have been comical if it wasn't so damn embarrassing.

At first, I thought it was fear at his imposing presence since Michael was at least a head shorter than the biker.

Then he smiled, his golden tooth once again appearing. "Bone? Why the fuck are you here?"

I turned towards my savior. His name was ... Bone? And he was acquainted with Michael? Well, that made sense since they must operate in similar circles, but ... why did he have a name like Bone?

"McCarthy," was all Bone said, not answering his question.

Michael regarded him a while longer and then the suspicion flashed in his eyes as his gaze roved from the biker to me behind him. "You're - you can't be ... You're fucking with him?"

When neither of us responded, Michael burst out into hysterical laughter, but the absence of humor was almost painful.

I didn't understand why we were still indulging him as he fought all on his own to put an end to his fake mirth.

I wanted to leave but the biker didn't move and instead waited patiently for Michael to get over himself.

"She used to be mine," he began.

My head fell a little at this announcement.

He went on, "Did she tell you? For a while, we had quite the romance going, didn't we? Have you tasted her? She's juicy, isn't she? You're going to have quite the ride with her." He leaned forward toward Bone to say in a conspiratorial whisper, "Just between you and me, she especially loves the reverse cow girl. She goes even wilder when she can't see your face and all she has to take along for the ride is a big cock."

I felt the tears sting my eyes. He was lying. We never got past first base, but no matter what I said, some of the large audience around us was enjoying the show and would spread that piece of gossip.

"You're a pathetic liar and a pig, Michael," I snarled. I couldn't meet the biker's eyes. I couldn't meet anyone's eyes as I turned around and walked away.

A round of gasps rang out behind me a split second before the sound of a table breaking and glasses smashing as women's screams filled the air.

I whirled back around to see Michael sprawled on the floor and it all made me even more furious, at the embarrassment, the attention, and the spectacle. I would now be the talk of the town for a long time to come. I went past the bar into the backroom and decided to stay there until it was closing time.

I would have left straight away, but my ride home was Henry, the barman. The longer I stayed at the backroom fuming, the more the shame dissipated and all that filled my thoughts was the checkup I had to take Jess to next month. I began to calculate the tips that were falling into Lena's pocket because of my decision to wallow in self-pity and not work in my section.

So I rose, straightened my shoulders and returned to the floor. The usual flow of the night had resumed, as though absolutely nothing had happened.

Lena hurried by then, but stopped and backtracked when she saw me. "Hey, I thought you left."

"Nah, Henry's my ride, remember? How's it going?"

"I'm going crazy. It seems the little fight over you boosted the morale of the damn place, the drama thirsty bastards. There's practically an unspoken consensus for a round of new drinks. I'm dying, come back and take over your section. I can't do this."

"Alright," I replied and tapped her arm with gratitude for her kindness. I knew she could manage very well on her own, but she knew I needed the money and she was just trying to help me without wounding my pride. I moved into the room to find new orders, but it looked like she had taken care of everyone already. To my horror, my eyes kept darting about looking for him. Was he still around?

My eyes found him and my heart caught in my throat.

He was sitting at the bar a drink in hand ... and his gaze was on me, hooded, heated, and unblinking.

## DELLA RAY

https://www.youtube.com/watch?v=JF8BRvqGCNs
-if you dare come a little closer-

I felt like I couldn't breathe. I stopped in my tracks and felt as if I was frozen in time. My heart was beating so fast I thought I would faint. Then someone pushed into me and in the process of them apologizing knocked me out of my trance. I remembered my debt to him, so I checked to confirm that the envelope was still in my pocket and made my way over to him. I pulled the battered envelope from the pocket of my shorts and laid it on the counter. "Here's what I owe you," I said unable to meet his eyes.

"Sit with me," he invited.

"I'm not really supposed to," I croaked. I did not know why I even responded. Perhaps my body was already pre-programmed to respond to the anticipation I had nursed all day about him.

He pushed the envelope over to me and said quietly, "Will this cover a drink for both of us?"

I nodded. "But—"

"I'll also cover your tips till the bar closes," he added.

Okay, I was sold. I took the much-needed rest and sat down.

"What do you drink?" he asked.

I stopped for a moment to think about it and when I returned my gaze back to him, I could see the ghost of a smile tugging at the corners of his mouth.

"You don't know?" he teased. "You work in a bar, and you don't know?"

"I'm not much of a drinker," I responded, almost hypnotized by his direct gaze. "You don't blink much, do you?"

He blinked then, just as his set of perfectly gorgeous teeth flashed at me.

Something warm burst open from my chest then and began to trickle into every nook and hidden place in my body. I couldn't take my eyes off him.

He took a sip of his drink. Strands of hair had escaped from the slicked style and hung around the sides of his face. They softened his look considerably, but I knew that was all a deception. Everything about him said, *tread carefully*. From the strong jaw to the veiled, hooded eyes, to the strained vein that ticked restlessly down the side of his strong neck, and the thickness of his biceps straining against his plain black T-shirt. He radiated a quiet strength that very few would be oblivious too. As a matter of fact there was absolutely nothing soft about this man. It made me wonder why I had been invited to sit down next to him.

"Why? Why did you help me out at the store?"

He drained the last of his whiskey. When his tongue shot out to lick his lips, I clenched my thighs to stop the painful arousal he was effortlessly invoking in me. I had never ever been so physically attracted to someone. I wanted nothing but to taste him.

"I was in a rush," he answered.

"What?"

He never took his eyes off me. "I was in a hurry that day. I didn't want to wait."

"Oh," I responded and looked away, my gaze fluttering over to the racks of glistening bottles of liquor that lined the bar before me. It was just what I needed. I looked at Bone, then at his empty glass. "Same again."

"Same again," he echoed.

"Nick?" I called out. "A long island iced tea for me, and same again for … Bone, please."

Nick's eyes widened not just at my order, but also at the man I was sitting by. With a kind smile he delivered our order. "I added a bit of juice to sweeten things up for ya," he said.

My heart went out to him in gratitude. I pushed the money I had extracted from the envelope towards him.

Nick shook his head. "This one's on the house."

"Thanks," I said.

He winked at me and walked away.

I took a long, long sip of my drink and glanced at the man I knew was watching my every move. "Thank you," I said. "For your help that day."

"The little girl you were with," he began.

Then like a habit, I felt everything inside of me tighten in defense. "Jess," I whispered my baby's name.

"Is she yours?" he asked.

My answer was prompt. "Yes, she is."

He looked away. "Must be tough," he said with a sigh.

My back was ramrod straight with defensiveness. "It's not. She's the loveliest little girl in the entire world. She's made my entire life a million times better."

"Probably," he said and lost himself to deep contemplation.

I didn't know whether to continue being offended by his pity, or if something else entirely was going on.

"Tracy was definitely a light in mine," he said quietly. "But sometimes, I'm not entirely sure if that was true. It wasn't her fault, I know but she still left, and destroyed me. I don't know if I can ever forgive her for that."

My eyes narrowed in confusion. "Tracy?"

"My daughter," he replied. "She had down syndrome just like Jess. She left a day before her fifth birthday."

Something cold and painful struck me so hard in the middle of my chest, it took my breath away.

He swung his body towards me. So fast, I was surprised how in tune he was to me. "You okay?" he asked, his voice soft, but edged with concern.

"You had a daughter like Jess," I gasped in shock. It was the last thing I could have ever imagined hearing from this man.

"I did ..." he responded, his voice taking on a wistful, yearning quality. "A lifetime ago."

I wanted to know more, much more, but I didn't know if it would be appropriate to prod any further. Even revealing what he already had, it felt like I'd somehow pried into something very, very private and horribly painful.

"Jess is actually not my daughter," I explained softly. I hadn't planned on telling him that, but I hated seeing the pain buried inside him, and I just wanted to take the conversation away from his girl and his pain. "My sister had her, but because we'd just lost both of our parents she didn't have much to live by and she couldn't cope with how much attention Jess needed. She's not a bad person. She just got terrified that she wouldn't be able to do it. You know, care properly for Jess."

"And you?" he asked, staring at me. "You're not terrified?"

In that moment, brutal reality hit me. Maybe Nichole was right. I was the cruel one here. Denise had enough brains to give up Jess, so she could find a family who would be able to give her all the care she needed. I had been adamant that we shouldn't put Jess up for adoption, but now I could barely feed us and I'd definitely, massively underestimated the intensity of the medical care she would require for the heart disease that came with her condition. At the time, I had been so full of naïve enthusiasm I had been ready to do whatever it took to keep her with me, but I was beginning to doubt the wisdom in my decision.

"Hey," he prompted softly. "I'm not criticizing your decision."

"I am terrified," I replied. "I'm terrified she needs more than I can give, but—I can't trust that anyone else would love her more than me or give her what she deserves either."

For the longest time, he didn't speak, just stared at the surface of the bar as if he was a statue.

I waited until I couldn't anymore, then I leaned a bit closer to him. He was more than just the hunk I couldn't get out of my mind now. He had become a person whom had been through the same deep waters I was currently trying my best to stay afloat in, but he had drowned. More than before, I could appreciate the sadness in his eyes. Something told me that his pain went much deeper than I would ever be able to comprehend.

"What do you think? Do you think I should give her up?" I asked. "Bone?"

He turned to me, his gaze so full of pain, regret and fury I felt my chest constrict.

"Keep going," he growled. "Keep going until you absolutely cannot anymore. Because if you don't, and she gets hurt. God! The guilt that you could have done much, much more for her, if only you'd tried just a little bit harder will forever haunt you. You might never recover from it."

I wanted to ask about the mother of his child, but I reckoned that we had gone a little further than I had anticipated tonight. Yeah, it was time to stop.

I drained what was left of my drink and rose from the stool with a mixture of exhaustion, emotion, or maybe it was just the drink, I couldn't tell, but it made my knees buckle under me. I stumbled and staggered backwards, my arms flailing.

His reaction was lightning quick. He caught me, one strong hand snaking around my waist and the other on my arm.

I looked up into his smoldering eyes. "I'm sorry," I apologized, breathing him in as much as I could just before my feet were completely stabled on the ground.

"You okay?" he asked, his voice husky.

"Yeah, I'm fine," I croaked, staring up into his eyes. My heart was beating so fast it felt like it was fluttering.

He let go of me.

I needed to know his real name. That mattered. "What's your name?" I asked. "Your real name."

He cocked his head. "I have many names. Which one do you want?"

It should have been a funny comment to make, but as we gazed at each other, we both knew that there was nothing amusing in what he just said. He wasn't joking and I had a feeling that I didn't want him to already have an answer to that question. "The name your mother gave you."

I waited with bated breath.

He shook his head. "Not that one."

"Okay," I said softly, "we'll stick to Bone."

I suddenly realized neither of us had brought the issue of

Michael up yet. "Uh, thanks for what you did ... with Michael, I mean."

His eyes hardened suddenly. "It was a pleasure."

"By the way, those things he said ..." I swallowed hard. The way Bone was watching me made me feel lightheaded. "It was all lies. I—uh, we never—we never got that far."

A flash of something crossed his eyes. It was only for a second, but it was fierce and primal.

"I have to go ... round up for the evening," I said, my voice suddenly breathless.

When I turned around to leave, he caught my hand and pulled me softly back into him.

I wanted to move away, but my body went spineless and weak, unable to fight against the intoxicating draw of him. The strangest thing happened then. He slid his hand around my waist and without thinking, I leaned my head to the side of his body as he cradled my face in the crook of his arm. It wasn't a sexual thing. It was as if we were the scarred, war torn survivors of a holocaust blindly turning to each other for warmth and comfort. If he hadn't been holding me up, I was certain I would have collapsed right there. The scrape of the hairs down his arm wreaked shivers down my skin.

"Have you ever flown through the quiet night on the back of a Harley?" he whispered hoarsely.

I couldn't speak. I could only shake my head in response.

"Let me give you a ride home."

Both of us knew it wasn't a ride home that he was offering. I wanted with all my heart to go, but he had been drinking all night, and I was the guardian of a girl who very much needed me. I couldn't make foolish decisions like blasting off on the back of a very dangerous motorcycle with a very dangerous man, in the middle of the night.

I found the strength to pull away from his scent, from his warmth, from the fire he was igniting throughout my body. I still couldn't speak, so I cracked a smile and forced myself to walk away, my hand resting on the emptied bar stools along the counter to keep me stable. When I arrived in the staff room, I sank down on a chair. I needed to get my wits back on track.

This man ... was far too dangerous for me.

## DELLA RAY

"Hey, aren't you ready to go?" Henry asked from the door.

I looked up from the sneaker laces I'd been tying. "Oh, no need," I said to him. "A friend of mine will drop me off."

"Cool. See you tomorrow, then," he said and closed the door.

I was left alone in the changing room. In the silence of the room, I began to doubt my sanity. I had just given up my only ride home, almost half an hour away and for what? What the hell was I thinking? I had already even said no to the biker whose name I still didn't know. Why did I think that he would still be outside and waiting? I was truly losing it!

I grabbed my backpack and without even putting on my jacket, I ran into the bar.

"Bye, Della," Nick called out from polishing a glass.

"Bye," I called back and ran out of the bar.

Henry's car was pulling out of the lot, so I ran after him. "Henry!" I screamed, but the audio system in his car drowned out anything but the sound of his rickety engine as he sped it onto the road.

"Henry!" I shouted once more and watched as his tail lights disappeared into the dark night. "Shit," I cursed and wondered how I would get home now. I turned to head back to the bar so Nick wouldn't lock me out when I heard the loud rev of an engine.

I jumped with my hand flying to my chest in fright. Turning around, I watched as the Harley rode up to me, its driver putting his booted foot on the ground.

Some crazy part inside me had hoped he would wait for me, but seeing him here. Now. Wild joy thrilled through my veins. I felt as if I was standing on top of a mountain, the wind snapping at my hair.

"Do you want a ride?" he asked.

I put my trust in God. "I do. How do I get on?"

"Grab my shoulder," he responded.

My eyes shot up to his. He waited too long before breaking the stare and motioned his head towards his shoulder.

I didn't hesitate I placed my hand on his rock-hard shoulder.

"Put your left leg here." He indicated to the pedal. "And then swing your right over the seat."

I did as I was told, my grip tightening on both of his shoulders as I settled myself on the seat behind me. "What now?"

"You put your arms around my waist." Amusement echoed in his voice

I slipped my arms lightly around his waist. Up this close, I could smell the scent of him. Leather, a bit of whiskey and all man. It made me feel giddy with excitement.

"Where do you live?" he asked.

"Olivesburg Road. Do you know it? It's just behind the Presbyterian church."

"Yup. Sit tight."

I kept my grip as loose as I could.

"I'm going to be blasting through the night," he warned. "Are you sure you want to hold me that lightly?"

I didn't need a second warning. I wrapped my arms so tightly around his waist my breasts were pressed into his back.

He was right.

Blasting into the darkness on a Harley was the closest thing to flying that existed … a wonderful, exhilarating sense of freedom. I held tightly to him and wished the ride would never end, but to my surprise, we arrived back at my home less than fifteen minutes later. Even when Henry had put his foot on the gas, it took the best part of half-an-hour!

He shut the engine off, and the deafening noise came to a sudden stop, but I wasn't sure whether to let go yet, until I heard him announce, "We're here."

In the new silence, I was suddenly aware of the intimate way I held onto him, my thighs pressed to his and my body glued to his back. I immediately jerked away and began to disembark from the Harley. It was quite a feat to do it gracefully, but somehow I had my feet on the ground.

Unable to look into his eyes I let my gaze roam across the beast of a machine and the man that sat upon it in wonder. I still couldn't believe I had accepted the ride home from him. I looked behind me to our front door and the windows, slightly paranoid she might be watching. If she were, I'd never hear the end of it. I turned back to see him studying the small detached house set in the quiet street.

"So this is where you live."

It suddenly occurred to me that I might have made a huge mistake by allowing him to know this. After all, I didn't know who the hell he was. Not even his real name. His talk about his dead daughter had softened me towards him, but still ... "I live with my roommate Nichole and Jess," I said quickly.

He swung his gaze back to me and suddenly, I couldn't look away. Neither could he, I realized.

"Do you just own this bike just for fun?" I found myself asking, simply to break the hypnotic trance he was putting me under.

It was too dark to see properly, but his eyes glittered as he shook his head.

"Are you part of a gang?"

"I belong to the Blood Knights MC," he murmured.

Nothing about the name struck a chord. The only club in this county I'd ever heard of was the Death's Hand Motorcycle

Club and that was only because Michael spoke of them admiringly. "I've never heard of it."

"We're yet to achieve infamy compared to the rest?"

If I had sensed his comment was without humor I might have withdrawn from him, but the lightness of his tone seemed to suggest he didn't take any of the gang stuff seriously. So perhaps his club was actually a motorcycle club and not a behind the scenes drug trafficking, murdering bunch. "Do you all—I mean, does your club—do you do dangerous stuff?"

His eyes never left mine as he shifted his weight and slipped his hands into his jacket. "What do you classify as dangerous?"

I wasn't sure if I should answer that. All I really wanted from the guy was an earth-shattering kiss since there would absolutely be no future here. I shrugged. What was the point anyway? It was clear there would be absolutely no future with him for me. "It doesn't matter," I responded, feeling a bit sad about the fact.

His brow shot up. I think he thought I was trying to dismiss him.

"I wasn't trying to be rude," I rushed to explain. "I don't need to know any of these things. I don't want you to think I'm prodding and getting into your business."

He said nothing. Just stared at me with those mind-blowingly intense eyes.

*Kiss me.* I wanted to say, *Kiss me so hard that I lose my mind and collapse into you. Incoherent, unaware.* I bit my lip to stop myself from saying it out loud.

As if he'd heard me, his gaze instantly drop to my mouth. Slowly, his eyes travel back up to my eyes. His remained dark, completely veiled of all expression, and hooded.

"What?" I whisper.

"How are you going to repay me," he asked, "for the ride?"

## DELLA RAY

"Y ou want me to pay for the ride?" I gasped.

"You've rejected everything I've offered, so surely you have to be consistent. You can't suddenly be willing to receive a favor, can you?"

I frowned. "Sure, I'll pay," I responded. "How much do you want for it?"

"I've already told you what I want," he responded. "From the first moment I met you."

My brain screeched to a halt. "That's an incredibly rude thing to say to a complete stranger."

He glanced briefly away in boredom. "Well, you're not a complete stranger and anyway, I'm not one for propriety."

"Well. I'm going to reject that request."

His eyes narrowed at me. "Why?"

"Because I don't know you." I hated the primness in my voice, but I couldn't help it. My heart was beating hard with excitement.

"Do you need to?"

"I imagine you could have almost any woman you wanted, so why ask me?"

"I don't know," he said. "I haven't been able to get my mind off you. Maybe you just have something I need right now."

My breath stuttered in my chest. I knew exactly how he felt. Suddenly, I didn't care if Nichole was watching. I took a deep breath. My voice was barely a whisper. "I'll give you a kiss. Will that be enough? It's all I'm able to do."

He smiled then and even though it didn't reach his eyes, it was still powerful enough to set my blood racing. He got off the bike and stepped forward. "I'll take it."

Reflexively, I stepped backwards. After that everything happened too fast for me to comprehend but by the time I could grab onto the reigns of coherence, my back was against the tree in our yard. We were hidden away from the street, and facing the empty little park where I took Jess to play on the swings.

In the darkness, his eyes gleamed as they roved all over my face searching, for what, I didn't know. I felt as if I was breathing loudly enough to awake the entire neighborhood, but I was powerless to stop it—to stop him.

Not that I wanted to.

He gripped my waist and leaned into me.

I was too overwhelmed to say or do a thing. I just stood there like a damn statue.

Burying his face in my neck, he breathed me in as his hot hands traced my body, shaping my hips and then going around to grab my ass. He pressed me hard into his groin so I would know exactly what I had said no to.

"I reek of sweat and exhaustion," I rasped out unsteadily. "Don't inhale me in too hard."

I felt his smile on my skin as I shuddered while his tongue slipped out to taste the skin over my pulse. A whimper escaped my lips.

"You reek of goodness and hard work," he said huskily. "There's no sweeter perfume."

Whatever control I possessed dissipated right then. I grabbed the back of his head, lifted myself onto the tip of my toes and slipped my tongue into his mouth.

He tasted of whiskey, and heat ... delicious smoldering heat that took my breath away.

Up till this point, I had kissed a few guys, some pleasant, some not so, one or two even quite exciting, but after this kiss I didn't think that there would ever be any need to kiss anyone else. The way this moment felt—with my throbbing body pressed hard against his, the warmth of him surrounding me, and the force of the arousal he'd provoked in my every sense, made me feel like I had been dead all these years. Only now, I had come alive.

His tongue danced sensually against mine, teasing, stroking and sucking. The pull between my legs became torturous. When he pulled away slightly, I grabbed a hold of one of the hands grabbing my ass. I didn't even realize what I was doing until I placed that hand between my legs and raised a leg to grant him better access. His hand rubbed at my mound greedily. The relief made me groan into his mouth, but frustrated by the barrier of my jeans I rocked my hips in desperation.

Suddenly, my legs left the ground.

I encircled his shoulder for stability, as the pace of his kiss grew feverish. I was helpless against him as he bit down on my lower lip and pulled.

My fingers slipped into his hair to pull him further into me.

He let go of me to focus his attention on my jeans. My button was snapped open. My heart was pounding in my ears as he yanked my zipper down. I knew I shouldn't. I wouldn't see him again after tonight anyway. The thought saddened me so much I felt the pain in my heart.

I shut my eyes as he gained complete access. My face remained buried in his neck as his calloused hand slipped into my panties and connected with the light dusting of hair that covered my groin.

I gasped when he splayed his hand over my soaking wet slit.

"You're dripping," he growled in wonder, and pulled his hand away from my panties to hold it up in front of me. His fingers were glistening with my arousal.

I watched in a haze of heat as he held it to his face and spread a hard lick across his hand.

"I was right." His breathing sounded ragged. "You taste like a fucking dream." He kissed me hard once again and I tasted the smoky sweet taste of me on his tongue. "Let me give you what you want," he said as he drowned himself in my taste and his hand slunk back into my jeans. He began to stroke the painfully swollen bud of my sex.

Pleasure completely blinded and deafened me from then on. I shut my eyes to the sensations. All I could see, feel and hear was … *him.*

A gasp tore from my throat as he pushed a long, thick finger into me.

"Fuck, you're so tight," he swore, as he savored the tightness of my walls clenched around him. Another finger joined the assault. Only when a third stretched me to the maximum that he began to finger fuck me ferociously.

I cried out, and couldn't believe what was happening, right outside the house, and in the middle of the night. Something like this had never happened to me before.

Never.

He muted me with his lips and ravaged my mouth. I felt as if my bones were melting into nothing. I couldn't even stand up straight, my spine was curved with the torrent of ecstasy surging from his hands into my body. I didn't even realize that he had pushed my shirt up and one of the cups of my bra until his mouth left my mine then descended on a bare nipple.

A light suddenly shone on my shut eye lids and I dragged it open to see that someone had been alerted. There was no doubt that it was Nichole, but I wasn't going to stop him from what he was doing to me. I couldn't. Not even if I wanted to.

My body jerked and writhed in sweet agony.

The lights went off in the living room, but I know that she hadn't given up. Then I saw the curtains to our living room move slightly aside, and I knew I had been busted.

I didn't care. She couldn't really see me. I was well hidden behind Bone's big body.

He went after my release then. With equal wild abandon, I met the thrusts of his fingers as he pushed me into oblivion. His palm caught the high-pitched whimpers that tore through my mouth at the build-up.

Just before I exploded on his hand, he moved his lips from the suckling kisses he had been giving to my breasts and covered my mouth with his again. I grabbed his hair as my orgasm shook me to my very core.

I fought against him to breathe. Through the leaves of the tree above us, I could see the sky and the stars. They felt so close. I felt as if I could reach out and touch them. The stars twinkled and winked as this earth-shattering climax went on and on.

I was shaken for longer than I wanted to admit and when he pulled his fingers from me, I felt what remained of my orgasm roll shamelessly down my legs. I was suddenly filled with an embarrassment I couldn't explain. I had fallen apart in his arms. Shown him how vulnerable I was to his minis-trations. Now he knew what an easy lay I was.

I zipped my jeans back up, arranged what I could of my appearance. He was watching me intently and I couldn't for the life of me find even a single sentence to say, so I grabbed my backpack from the ground. It had fallen there at the base of the tree ages ago.

He didn't say anything and neither did I. I took a sideways step, then another, as I headed towards our house. It took everything in me not to run from him like the coward I so obviously was. Only when I shut the door behind me, did I lean against the wood, take a deep breath, and begin my descent into normalcy. I heard footsteps approaching but I didn't even bother to look up.

"What the hell happened out there?" Nichole whispered fiercely to me.

Just then we heard the rev of his engine as he brought the machine to life and we both listened as he zoomed it dangerously off into the night.

"Della-Ray!" Nichole called out again. "Are you all right?"

I managed to nod.

She opened her mouth to say something else, but I raised my palm at her, before peeling myself away from the door and staggering back to my room.

# GAGE

https://www.youtube.com/watch?v=0SZbJpbVRzo
-this is the road to hell-

Fist clenched as I watched her hurry into the house. If she only knew the state she'd just put me in. My whole fucking body throbbed like a fresh wound. All I wanted in that moment was release, and not from anyone else but her. Only her. I felt like the man who had been wandering around for weeks in an endless desert with only bitter water from his camel skin bags to slake his thirst...then he stumbles upon a spring of fresh, cool water.

My phone kept vibrating in my pocket, but I ignored it. Like desert sand slipping through my fingers she slipped through the door and it closed behind her.

Aggravated and frustrated, I pulled the phone out of my pocket, placed it to my ear and barked, "What?"

"Bone," Skippy said. "Where are you? There's trouble at the house."

The haze of lust dissipated into vapors of sweet nothing. "What trouble?"

"RJ crashed into Death's Hand's bar and did a burnout."

"What? Shit," I swore, as I began to stride towards my bike.

"I know," Skippy responded. "He's a fucking moron. They pounced on him, but he managed to get away. They tore off his vest though before they sent him on his way."

I exhaled. "Fuck."

"Exactly," Skippy responded.

"Snake?" I asked, the club's president's deathly gaze and chilling tone coming to mind. "Is he aware yet?"

"Yeah, they're in the den now. I'll be surprised if RJ makes it out of there alive."

Shit. Reaching into the seat of my Harley, I grabbed my gear then kicked my bike to life and hit the gas. I arrived at the three-storied house in Glenwood to see the driveway already packed with bikes.

I headed inside, my weapon hard against my skin. Nodding at the brawny men idling in the hallway I made my way down to the basement. I walked in to see twelve of the club's members grouped around the brazen and most moronic fool that ever lived: RJ, a red-haired lout who had long established his reputation as a mad man with no boundaries.

Some of his escapades included almost burning the house down along with every member inside it, continuous overdosing to his near death, jumping up on the counter of every single bar he'd ever visited nearly intoxicated to stupor, but still somehow coherent enough to boast of the power the club's patch had granted him. He believed he could own the bar and the town if he wanted to. No questions asked.

He insisted we all call him mayor. Vermin was a more appropriate name, but it would have started unnecessary fights, so we all just stuck to how he had been introduced to us from the very beginning, with his initials RJ, standing for Reynolds Jordon.

His clothes were dirty and messy. His face was bloody while he was on his knees, his lumpy shoulders curved as if he was cowering with fear and respect for his betters, but I knew different.

"I say we quarter him and deliver his body to Death's Hand," Tank growled. Brutal looking features and bald, with a yellowish-white face and granite gray eyes which were hidden by a pair of steampunk sunglasses. He rarely took them off. Not even now in the middle of the night in a damn basement. He wore an armless vest as his tattoos of demons and naked girls shone a sickly blue in the fluorescent light.

"I'll chop him up," Shotgun offered. He was Tank's equally brutish distant cousin, but with a penchant for thick silver chains. They dangled around his neck and made delicate tinkling sounds. It was the most disconcerting thing about him.

"Rooster and I will make the delivery," Tattoo Man contributed.

I regarded the men perched on the bar's stools, as they

nursed tumblers of Glenfiddich, their eyes boiling with disgust at the offender who knelt in the middle of the room.

"No one is fucking asking what exactly led to the argument," Dobson, an edgy, long-haired coward, spoke up in his defense. His hands were shaking with uneasy excitement. He was afraid of danger and yet fascinated by it as some people are fascinated by a venomous snake. "RJ could have a good—"

"Shut the fuck up, you pathetic bastard!" He was instantly shut down by Tyler, the club's Sargent-at-Arms snarling at him like a wild animal. When he drew his 9 millimeter Sten and pointed it down at RJ's face, we all snapped to attention. All that was needed for things to go sour had always been only a hair's breadth away, and none of us ever wanted to be caught unawares.

"There's no need for this." Dog stepped in cautiously. Pulling out a dirty, screwed up handkerchief he wiped the sweat pouring down his temples with it. The fatty pouches under his eyes were a muddy brown color. "True, RJ did wrong, but for harassing him the way they did ... and taking his vest. That's unforgivable. It's a disrespect that we cannot accept."

Unmoved, Tyler cocked his gun.

Deathly silence followed the sound.

"Calm down, Tyler," Snake ordered coldly. He was a man black in heart, without culture or religion, violent, and avaricious. You only had to look into his eyes to know his soul was rotten.

"Tell us, idiot. How you gonna fucking fix this?" Tyler asked

RJ, but he'd lowered his gun while a muscle high up along his right eye kept twitching restlessly.

RJ remained silent, but the rebellious glare of resentment he gave Tyler showed his complete lack of remorse for his actions. More importantly, he understood the danger was over, Snake had spoken. And he knew better than to question Snake. Especially not if he planned on becoming the Vice President of our club.

I knew Snake wanted RJ alive because of his eagerness to take on even the most distasteful tasks. Ones that even the most senior members may have had reservations in handling.

"We're going to have to meet," Snake said, moving his psychopathic stone-cold gray eyes slowly around the room. "There's a drag race down at Route 89 in two weeks. We're either going to get things resolved then, or escalate this into an all-out war."

"War. Fuck that!" Rooster swore violently. Lighting his cigarette, he flicked the match at RJ's bloody head. "If they refuse to back down, we'll just offer this piece of shit's head to them, and get the vest back."

"How about we send a message over?" Skippy suggested, his pale eyes probing. He had a surprisingly soft voice for a man his size. "I'll contact Buzzer and have him speak to his men. Otherwise, this could turn real ugly, real fucking fast."

"No messages," Tyler spat. "We'll handle this at the race in two weeks."

Cunningly, Snake allowed Tyler have the last word, as if the decision to handle the matter at the race in two weeks had always been his and not Snake's.

I didn't say a word. There was no need to. I'd learned a long time ago the less you spoke the better you fared.

Everybody agreed with Tyler and the hearing was concluded. RJ got off his knees and the men got back to getting drunk.

I made my way to my bedroom in the top corner attic of the club. The place was silent and my shoes made the wood of the stairs creak. I unlocked my door and walked in. It was small and stifling hot, but secluded enough and more importantly, it had a good escape down the rooftop if trouble ever came in a hail of bullets.

I walked around the small space to make sure everything remained exactly as I had left it. I had gone through a lot of trouble to earn this space, both in earnings to the club through arms and drugs sales, and in the house fees required of the members, so I didn't take the invasion of my space lightly at all.

Then I picked up a bunch of clean clothes and after locking the door, went for a much-needed shower. I stepped into one of the five filthy bathrooms. The tiled floor was soiled and littered with wet toilet paper.

The state of the bathroom was the thing I hated most about living here. Choosing the least disgusting stall, I stripped and stepped under the scalding hot cascade after making a mental note to have a word with Tiffany. She was Tyler's sister and, in my opinion, was way too lax in her heavily compensated duty of keeping the club house in order. Recently she had started giving me looks, but I wasn't going there. The last thing I needed was beef with Tyler.

The sound of the gushing water drowned out every other sound, and if I tried hard enough, even my knowledge of where I was and the danger outside this stall. The prisoner forgets his prison. For that instant, I felt the rough bark of a tree, and smelt the scent of the beauty who let her cheek slither against my chest and opened her legs for me. I saw her amber eyes flashing blood and moonlight as I sent her into the deepest abyss I'd ever seen a woman fall into.

Her response had been unexpected.

Her hands had grabbed my hair so hard she ripped some out. I looked down and saw the reddened scrapes her nails had made across my chest when she'd tried to grasp my shirt. I couldn't help the smile that lifted the corners of my lips. I was glad she left her mark on my body.

But she had been so ashamed she'd been unable to meet my eyes.

She made me feel things in the pit of my stomach I'd forgotten even existed over the last several years. It seemed like a lifetime ago that I'd been drawn to a woman. After the blows life had dealt over the last few years, I'd become numb. I hadn't been with a woman for years. Every one of them turned my stomach. Their greedy eyes, their grasping hands. For a long time now, I even thought I'd gone off women for good.

But this woman ... I wanted to kiss her on her soft head and whisper that I would take care of her and that child she sheltered. I thought of the little girl. It was almost like my little angel had come back to me. *One more chance for you, Daddy. Get it right this time, or I'll go away again and never come back.*

I thought of that night she died. I wasn't even at the hospital.

By the time I arrived they had pulled a fucking sheet over her head. The sight took the roar out of my lion heart. Everything I'd done since then was just another attempt to hasten the time I would hold her in my arms again.

My wife never forgave me. We broke up soon after. There wasn't too much love there anyway, so it was gone the moment the glue that kept us together left. Since then I was a dead man walking.

With Della—something wanted to be resurrected.

From the first moment I lifted my eyes impatiently in the grocery store to see what the delay was and saw her, I'd wanted her. Desperately.

When I recalled how she'd tasted, my cock swelled thickly at the vivid memory. The feel of her breasts in my hand as I'd fondled her full soft mounds, and feel of her small ass, as I cupped it hard and grinded her sex against my cock.

*"Fuck,"* I swore, as my body filled with longing. My hand fisted my cock brutally. I was convinced now that in the release I sought, I would be able to relieve this need for her.

I imagined her kneeling down in front of me. Those big, beautiful eyes looking up at me as she begged me to fuck her mouth. I saw my cock disappearing into her sweet mouth. Again and again. God above, how I wanted her sweet lips stretched around my dick. Her mouth sucking hard, milking me. The hot stream of arousal began to buzz through my veins and a groan rattled out of my throat.

"Ahhh." Blindingly hot pleasure shot through me at the force of my pumps. My knees buckled at the ripple of ecstasy that danced along the edges of my nerves, so close but still out of

77

reach. The memory of her soft body arching and the whimpers as she'd cried out into my palm came to my mind and with one last pump, I exploded.

"Fuck! Fuck! Fuck!"

I slapped my hand against the tiled wall to steady myself as my entire body strained forward with the force of the surprise release. Gasping for breath, I glanced down to watch myself explode so thickly onto the wall that I was taken aback. It had been a long time. A very long time since I'd come this hard. I stroked my cock to ease out every ounce of pleasure still coursing through me.

I lathered shampoo on my head, finished my shower, and went back upstairs. I collapsed on the bed. Sleep for me was never like the rest of the world had. For me, it was six hours spent fighting ghouls and demons in the bitter cold and the sound of my angel calling for me while doors kept banging shut. One by one.

Tonight I fell into a deep sleep. Without dreams.

## DELLA RAY

I couldn't fall asleep.

I tossed and turned. My body was dampened with sweat and my mind dazed by the lingering buzz of the orgasm from a few hours earlier.

The hours ticked by slowly as I continuously and despairingly glanced at the clock by my bedside. I knew I'd have to be up in a few hours to begin another exhausting day.

I needed the rest.

The problem was I also needed to be fucked, out of my mind … by Bone.

Filled with frustration, I sat up angrily on the bed. Pushing my hair out of my face, I glanced restlessly into the darkened room. I actually felt possessed. The memory of his kisses and his fingers inside of me, coaxing me to what I now realized was the first real orgasm I'd ever experienced in my life.

And all from three of his damn fingers.

I couldn't believe it ... I was flustered and overheated and all because of three firm digits. What would happen then if he plunged his cock in me?

I wanted to find out.

Collapsing back on the bed, I pressed my swollen clit in search for some sort of relief, but my trembling fingers seemed ineffective and hopeless. Maybe I needed something more. For the first time I started to wonder why I had never thought of buying any toys.

Nichole didn't have any either, and I wondered how uneventful both of our sex lives had been thus far, to not even having considered owning one. As I slipped my fingers into myself once again, I knew the answer to the question. We were both sexual innocents. I had most definitely never felt anything like this before and I was certain I could speak for her too.

I'd heard it was more the person than the act, but I'd never understood it until today. I didn't even know his name, so what was it about Bone that made a good fuck the only way I could fall asleep tonight?

I wished more than anything I had at least taken his phone number. I swore the next time I laid eyes on him, if I ever laid eyes on him again, that was the first thing I would ask of him. It didn't matter what he would think of me. My pride had no say whatsoever in this regard. After all, by now, he must think I was the biggest slut in town. Turning, I pounded my hand into my pillow and screamed soundlessly into it.

I froze when the door to my room creaked open.

I thought Nichole had heard me and come into my room, but

when I didn't hear much of a sound, I lifted my head and saw my beautiful baby at the door, sucking on her thumb as she cradled her favorite stuffed animal in her other hand.

I immediately sat up, alarmed. "Jess," I called, holding out my hand to her.

She came over to me and I lifted her into my arms and onto my lap. "Are you all right?"

She buried her face in my neck silently.

This soft gentle act immediately calmed me. "Did you have a nightmare?" I asked.

When she didn't respond, I laid with her on my bed and snuggled up to her warm soft body. "Go to sleep and we'll water the wild flowers tomorrow, okay?"

That always worked. She gave a small nod.

I stroked her hair and slowly, she brought sanity back to me. I almost felt a bit of shame at the thoughts and the state I had been in before she came into the room. She was just the balm I need to calm the storm Bones had stirred up inside me. I listened to the gentle rise and fall of her breathing until I joined her in peaceful slumber.

I had snoozed the alarm clock twice and consequently was running late for my shift at the diner.

Nichole had left early, Jess had crept out of bed and was quietly playing with her toys in her room, so the house was quiet as I jumped out of bed in a panic. I quickly cleaned Jess and myself up, put on the nearest clothes we could find, poured some cereal down her throat, and was out of the house as swiftly as I could manage.

Not before I saw the message Nichole had left propped up on the kitchen counter.

*Need to talk to you tonight.*

Other than the three times we had to stop, so Jess could lovingly water the wild weeds growing between the side-walks, we made good time and we arrived at her daycare on time. I couldn't just drop her off like other parents though, I had to linger while Jess clasped my hand and didn't let go with the usual fright in her eyes at being away from me for such an extended period of time. Her teacher had said once it was probably just her mirroring the concern always boiling in the pit of my stomach. I always felt terrified she would be bullied by the other children. She never was. The other children were extra gentle with her.

Eventually, I had to run and leave her to face the big bad world on her own.

I arrived to work almost fifteen minutes late, but luckily the owner, Sandy was also nowhere to be found. Sighing in relief, I got to work and tried to settle into the flow of the day. My heart however, kept jumping every time the bell dinged with the arrival of a new customer.

Then came the disappointment that it was not whom I hoped

it would be. It turned my mood darker and darker with each passing hour.

He is not meant to be in your life, I reminded myself.

My head fully understood and accepted this fact, but my heart was deaf. I became jumpy and irritable, and by the time lunch break came around, I was more than ready to take the quick rest.

Gloria came over to perch in my corner, brimming with curiosity at how my perceived theft from her had worked out. "Did you go home with him last night?"

I almost choked on the sandwich I was trying to get through before my time ran out.

She wasn't put off by the 'what the hell' look I gave her either.

"You snatched him away from me," she stated with a shrug. "The least you can do is come back with some stories."

I realized she was already over it, so I eased off and took things easy. "I didn't go home with him, Gloria. I just owed him a little debt which I have now repaid."

"Debt?" she asked her eyes gleaming with curiosity. "Wow! Did you borrow money from his club? That could get you killed if things went awry, you know."

I swallowed the food in my mouth. "Why would I borrow money from them and why would things go awry?"

"Well, you have borrowed money from everyone in this diner before, so there's nothing strange about that."

I stilled.

But she went on, completely oblivious to the insult she had so casually thrown out, "And of course, things could go cock-eyed. Don't you know how vicious these outlaws are?"

"She's right," Allan commented as he flipped a patty. "My cousin Gusto was a hang-around for the outlaws for about two years before they even allowed him to become a prospect. It's his third year and he's still yet to receive his patch."

"What's a hang-around? And a prospect? And a patch? Is that their logo?"

They both turned to me in surprise.

"Outlaw clubs are quite active around here. How come you're not the least bit aware of them?" Allan asked.

I knew they were quite active in town and had heard of the trouble they caused in certain drinking joints, but I had never had time to really consider them because my own life was in such a mess. I bit my lip and tried to sound natural. "Um ... they're into drug trafficking aren't they?"

"Drug trafficking is the least of what they do." Gloria shrugged. "They also deal in weapons. Worse, I heard they sometimes kidnap girls and gang rape them. After the girl dies from all the abuse, they bury them in the desert."

I stared at Gloria in horror.

"And they're constantly having wars," Allan added. "You didn't hear of the mass shoot out at one of the Club's parties last summer? Almost 200 members were arrested. Some of them were thrown in jail, but they have so much money, they just buy their way out."

"Jesus …" I gulped.

"That's right," Gloria said, nodding with a knowing expression. "More than twenty-five ended up dead that night."

"Oh, my God," I whispered.

"It all started about six months ago when there was some sort of explosion in one of their clubhouses," she continued. "It completely went up in flames and burned about six of their members alive. Ever since then, it's been war between the clubs."

I listened to them, terror slowly beginning to creep up my spine. "Why would they be involved in so much violence?"

"They're fucking animals fighting for territory," Allan explained calmly. "Even the cops are barely able to get a handle on them."

"That's not right," Gloria said. "One of the rival clubs harassed another club's member and took his vests from him. The club's patch is attached to that vest and to them, that patch is a badge of honor like no other. The first one to go was the club's president, Hammer. He was on his bike at a red light when a truck pulled up and he was blasted with seven bullets. Died on the spot. It was pure war from then on."

I gaped at her, frozen in place.

Gloria burst into laughter at my expression. "Still, I would have slept with the one that came in last night." Then she walked away to handle her section.

Allan looked at me with concern. "Are you okay?"

"Sure," I responded quickly.

He dinged the bell to signify a readied order.

It made me jump.

"Why are you so shaken?" he asked.

"I'm not," I retorted, embarrassed that I knew so little about life around me. Jumping up, I picked up the steaming plate from the counter and started walking away.

"Stay away from biker dudes Della-Ray," he warned in a mocking tone.

I shot him a sour look.

His response was a charming smile that did absolutely nothing to chase away the terror that had slithered up my spine and had frozen it cold.

Perhaps it was a great thing then to have had no sight of Bone. Blasts of bullets, arson, and gang-raping were especially bothersome activities that I didn't want anywhere close to my little Jess or me.

I did wonder though if he truly was involved in such activities. He didn't strike me as a bad person. Michael was ten times more psychopath than Bone. I wondered too, why he chose to live that way. He seemed mentally astute, clear minded, and particularly grounded to the things that truly mattered in life. The way he asked me to hang on to Jess were not the words of a man that did not know good from bad.

Did he become lost after his daughter died and turned to a murderous club?

## DELLA RAY

The light was on when I came back home. I took off my sneakers and socks then padded on my sore feet to the kitchen.

Nichole was sitting at the kitchen table flipping the pages of an art book. "Hey," she said, standing up.

"Hiya," I said, standing awkwardly at the doorway. It felt as if we had become strangers.

She moved towards the kettle and switched it on. "Do you want something to eat?"

I shook my head.

"How about ice cream?"

I smiled. "What flavor?"

She smiled back. "Rose and peaches."

I stopped smiling. That flavor was made by a little creamery across town. It was an hour's journey to get there. "Did you go all the way to Bennetts for that?"

"Yeah," she said, moving to the kettle that had boiled. She picked it up and poured the water into a plastic basin near the table. I could smell the bath salts from where I stood. She bent down and tested the water. Then she pushed the basin under the table. "Go on then. Get your feet in there."

I hesitated. "Nichole."

"It's okay. This is just my way of saying sorry for what I said about Jess."

I took in a deep breath. I didn't allow myself to dwell on her cruel words, but I was still hurt about it.

She looked up at me pleadingly. "I was wrong to say what I said. I'm really, really sorry. It was a horrible thing to say. I was just worried about you. I hated what your life had become, but I've accepted now that you love Jess and Jess loves you and nothing anyone can do for her will be better than the amazing love you have for her. Whatever happens we'll get through it together. I'm going to help you, Della Ray. Even if I have to get a second job to see you through this time."

"Oh, Nichole," I gasped.

She stood up, her eyes full of tears. "Do you forgive me?"

I ran to her and hugged her tightly. "There's nothing to forgive. I love you, you silly goose."

"I love you too," she choked. "I just want the best for you."

"Jess is the best for me," I whispered.

"I know that now."

Hot tears of joy were running down my cheeks. "I'm so glad

we made up. It was killing me when I thought we were drifting apart."

"What are we, icebergs? We're never drifting apart. You'll have to pry yourself out of my cold dead hands."

I laughed through my tears.

"Talking about cold things you better get your feet in the basin before the water gets cold," she said with a laugh.

We separated.

I sat down and slipped my feet into the wonderfully hot water.

She headed to the freezer and put the ice cream tub on the table with a spoon.

I opened it and peeled off the plastic covering. I never thought I would appreciate the seal so much, but with the new crop of degenerate crazies looking for fifteen minutes of fame because they licked a tub of ice cream and put it back into a supermarket freezer, it was very welcome. I scraped my spoon over the creamy surface eagerly. "Mmmm ... this is divine. Thank you so much. You can't imagine how good it feels to have my tired feet in hot water and cold ice cream in my mouth."

"No, I guess I don't know."

"Aren't you going to have some?" I asked.

She sat opposite me, her face serious. "Later. I want to talk to you, Della."

The ice cream in my mouth lost its sweetness. I should have known there would be more. "What about?"

"What's going on with you and that biker?"

I dropped my gaze and fiddled with the spoon. "I don't know what's going on with him, Nichole, but he affects me the way no man ever has. He only has to come close to me and my body feels like it is on fire."

She clasped her twitching hands. "What do you know about him?"

"Nothing. Not even his real name."

"Oh, my God!"

"I know what you're thinking, but he's not just a biker. He had a daughter with down syndrome. She died and I think it broke his heart. I feel as if he is in pain."

Nichole stared at me. "He had a daughter … like Jess?"

"What a strange coincidence, huh?"

"Yes," she breathed, her eyes huge.

We stayed silent for a few seconds, then she asked, "So you're going to see him again?"

"I'm not sure. I really like him, but he belongs to a gang … uh, a club and I really don't want to get involved. If not for me then at least for Jess. I have to put her before me. That life sounds violent and dangerous."

"So what are you going to do?"

"For the moment, nothing. Maybe he won't call again. Maybe he's had enough of me."

"Oh, Della Ray. You don't understand anything, do you? He'll be back for more. I'll lay my life on that."

# GAGE

https://www.youtube.com/watch?v=rMbATaj7Il8

Church was held on Saturday evening in the basement of St. Andrews church. It sat decrepit and surrounded by graves, but it wasn't an abandoned building. Sundays the members of the community that still hung around that isolated area came in through its crooked, cast iron gates to attend the simple mass that Father James put on to share the good word with them.

Today however, he was away in his cottage home while we took over his Lord's home. As long as we didn't break what little was still intact, he turned a blind eye to our infiltration of the building once a week for our extremely private weekly chapter meetings. Not that the poor man had a choice. Snake could be very persuasive when he wanted to be.

I hated attending these meets. For one, they were taken way more seriously than necessary, and the blatant torture netted out to out-of-line members wasn't what I'd consider premium entertainment.

I arrived late. I had a good excuse. I had to handle a debt that a prospect had been too afraid to stomp down on. The few prospects and hang arounds that guarded the iron gates parted the way with eager, attentive salutes as I rode into the premises. Grasping the brown grocery bag filled with fifty grand in hard cash from a recent meth sale, I walked into the dim basement.

Church was already in session.

The members sat on their makeshift pews, iron chairs that we had put in to accommodate the chapter's fifty-six member attendance.

Our pulpit was a makeshift bar, stocked with the club's most frequent choice of beverage and that was being passed around to all in attendance. Everclear, Pincer, Bruichladdich X4+quadrupled whiskey, and Absinthe flowed like the good old days of Rome.

Snake was up on the pulpit speaking, but there were also three vaguely familiar faces beside him. I studied them until recognition clicked. They were members from the almighty Durban brotherhood. It was them, who had sanctioned our club's formation half a decade earlier. I knew then that this was an especially important meeting.

I took my seat at the back, and tried to listen to all that was being said, especially when RJ was called and given a big pat on the back by one of the brotherhood members called Trunk. The name was as befitting as descriptions went. He was cut indeed like a tree trunk, with sturdy, thick limbs that could cripple a man, and completely devoid of a neck. His shaved head was spiked with white hair, but his beard was brown and wild.

"You did good this time around, son," he said.

RJ's extremely rare sense of propriety was on full display. He revered the man and around him was the only time he disciplined himself enough to behave respectfully.

"When will the shipment dock?" Trunk asked.

RJ happily supplied the answer, "In about seven weeks, but first, we'll need to tie up the rest of the strings in Dallas."

"Is Bone here yet?" Snake suddenly asked.

"Yeah," I responded.

"How did the collection go?"

I raised up the bag for all to see and received nods and sounds of approval.

"Get ready," Snake said. "You'll accompany the group to Dallas to conclude the deal with RJ's guy."

It was the perfect arrangement for me, and it was now to be expected since I'd gained the reputation of being disturbingly cool headed. When they needed a rise out of people or situations and didn't necessarily want violence to rev the engine, I was brought in.

Church went on excitedly as all the members no doubt, began to anticipate our very first and very own exclusive shipment of Meth. We would have sole monopoly of the drug at our own prices and thus, run the supply in the whole area, and perhaps even the entire state.

RJ had a friend of a friend who worked for a cartel that

manufactured the stuff, and he had managed to put together the deal just before we all completely condemned him as more of a liability than an asset. Just days ago, he was moments away from a bullet in his head courtesy of his reck-lessness, but now, he had good standing once again in the club.

You had to give it to him. He was extraordinarily resourceful and adept at keeping himself alive. It was quite impressive.

The rest of the meeting went as planned and the moment all the major business was concluded and it was time to mete out discipline, I rose for a break.

Three new patchers, Rose, Pole and Boner were being sanc-tioned for getting into trouble with an Armenian gang over some dealings. Worse, when they were arrested, Pole had been found not only high on Meth, but in possession of a Ruger LCP.

Tyler stepped forward, a baton in hand, and the three guys looked like they were about to shit their pants. Pole was first. The other men leaned forward eagerly, their expressions glittering with vicious anticipation. They would have enjoyed the Christians being torn by lions too. Before Pole could land on the floor with a cracked skull, I was already out in the fresh air.

I stepped outside where the prospects and hangers not allowed to be aware of - or involved in the inner workings of the club's business - were milling around. This was an effi-cient way to weed out undercover cops and keep them from infiltrating the inner circle. Until they proved themselves to be worthy, they just played at being bikers.

Junho, a young Korean hanger immediately ran up to me.

There was light in his eyes, and every time I saw him, it made me stop. I wondered if there was a time that I looked that way and it made me angry that he was looking to become involved with this crowd. He'd taken a particular liking to me and I suspected he had a good temperament so I allowed a level of familiarity.

"I was away this week, Sir," he said enthusiastically even though I didn't ask. "My grandma broke her foot so I was on cater-for-the-old-hag duty."

He thought it would impress me and make him appear hard, but I just wanted to smack him across the head for being such an idiot. He expected it so when I swung out my hand he managed to dodge the attack. His carefree laughter rang into the graveyard air.

I pulled out a cigarette from the pack and put it to my mouth and he had a lighter waiting. I accepted it, then tossed it back to him. I took a good long draw, and felt some semblance of calmness settle over my nerves.

"Why don't you ever carry a lighter?" he asked.

I looked out to the old, broken tombstones and thought of the dead who lay beneath. It brought to mind quite vividly the dead that lay in my heart. "Isn't it obvious?" I asked.

"Because there is always someone else around to do it for you?" he said after genuinely pondering on the response.

I sighed. "If I don't have it on me, then I can't use it."

He seemed to grow even more confused. "If you don't want to use it then why do you carry a pack of cigarettes?"

"Sometimes you need certain things to pull through." I

looked away to take another draw and that was when I noticed the vehicle.

It was cruising past the gates, a white washed up van with a faded painting of Winnie the Pooh on the side. That was my daughter's favorite character and the vivid memory of her kissing baby Winnie goodnight filled my head. Everything seemed to slow down in that moment as my memories transported me to another place and time. The silky feel of her hair under my lips, the tinkling sound of her wind-up toy, the sweet perfume of baby powder.

I stared blankly at the vehicle as hot tears welled up in my eyes at the memory. I was lost in the past as I watched it roll slowly. It was as if I was watching a movie. I knew something was wrong, but I couldn't think. My brain kicked into gear when I finally realized what I was looking at. I reached out to grab Junho, but it was already too late.

The windows had already rolled down and the doors to the van jacked open. Barrels were pointed at us. Shouts erupted all around us. It occurred in a split second, but to me it felt like it was happening in slow motion. I could feel the friction of the air against my skin and clothes as if I was underwater. Holding on to Junho, I dove for cover, the shots ringing out like explosions all around us.

I pulled out my gun, but backup had already arrived. I heard the bloody exchange from somewhere above my head and knew the club members were handling the attack. Next to me, the young boy was lying unconscious on the ground. At first, relief poured into me, that there were no wounds on his head or chest so nothing vital had been destroyed, but his blood was quickly beginning to seep out from under him.

When I gently turned him on his side, I saw that the bullet had burst through his spine.

"*Fuck!*" I cursed. I could hear the van screeching away. I gazed down at the whimpering boy as I slowly rolled him on his back and it felt as if my chest was suffocating with mixture of bitter regret and fury. Why was life so cruel to the best of its kind? Why did RJ escape every encounter and this boy had fallen on the first misadventure? I knew this was it for him. Life as he knew it was over.

"Bone!" someone yelled as he ran over. "Is he all right?"

"He will be!" I muttered. I was concerned about moving him and wanted to call an ambulance, but when he started to lose consciousness, I knew I couldn't wait. I jumped up. "Get me a car from somewhere!" I shouted.

"You're bleeding, Bone. You've been hit too."

I looked to my arm and saw a bullet had burst into one side and come cleanly out on the other. I had no horror of death, so I glanced at the red blood pouring out of my arm and felt nothing but annoyance. "I'm fine," I said and held on to my arm as I rose to my feet.

Someone's car, probably poor father James's was commandeered for our use, and Junho was transferred carefully into it. There didn't seem to be any other casualties as everyone else had been quick to respond.

His attention had been on me, and mine had been on the past.

My arm had begun to throb as I shut my eyes and rode with Junho's unconscious body. *You should have stayed a bit longer on cater-for-the-old-hag duty, Junho.*

# DELLA RAY

S aturdays were supposed to be for picnics … but we hadn't been on one for many months now. In fact, since Jess got sick and I had to work two jobs to pay the bills, there had been no time for picnics.

For the last few days, Jess had appeared a bit down and not as bright as was usual. I kept asking her if she was well but all she did was nod or give me one of her heartbreakingly radiant smiles.

I couldn't take it any longer, so I requested a break from the diner and forced both her and Nichole out to the park in Brookside. Jess and I immediately headed for the sandpit and began to build sandcastles while Nichole had lain down to bask in the sun with music blasting in her ears. At least, until a corgi ran over to her and began licking her face.

She shrieked at the sudden attack and both Jess and I fell to each other laughing. There would never exist a greater way to send a clear message to someone to join in on the fun. The corgi ran, more alarmed than Nichole, so Jess and I hopped over to her and sat together to have our lunch of the most delicious ham and tomato sandwiches.

Early evening came around too soon. It was almost time for me to start getting ready for my shift at Sinkhole, so we returned home.

Nichole immediately began to do the laundry while I put Jess to bed before quickly baking some cookies for Jess's lunchbox tomorrow.

The first batch of cookies were ready. They smelt so divine and I couldn't resist biting into one. That was the precise moment when the doorbell rang. I didn't want it to wake Jess up so I hurried to the door. I pulled it open and the chocolate chip cookie left my mouth and fell to the ground.

His gaze fluttered down to it and then back to me, while mine fluttered over to first the sling that suspended his right hand, and then the spotting of blood on it. I opened my mouth to speak but nothing would come out. So I snapped it shut and just waited for him to help me to make sense of why he was injured and in front of my house.

"I want your help,' he said to me.

"My help? How?"

"As much time as you can spare. Everything hurts. I also need to get out of these damn boots."

I looked down at the dusty leather. There was blood on them too.

"Even bending down to get at these is pure hell," he continued. Something different echoed in his voice. A kind of dumb pain.

99

My eyes flowed back up his body to his face. I noticed how pale he looked.

"Will you help me? I don't want to be alone. A kid nearly died in my arms today."

My mouth fell open in a silent gasp.

"Please," he coaxed.

"I-I- have work in an hour," I croaked.

"An hour is fine." He nodded.

"Uh," I said indecisively.

"I won't touch you. I just want to be with you for a while."

I looked into his eyes and the despair in them made me forget everything Gloria and Allan had said. "Do you have a home? Apart from your ... club house, I mean. You live there, right?"

"I have a small house," he murmured.

"Let's go there, then," I said, pulling my work bag, from the side table and took a step forward.

He looked at me as though he was shocked that I had agreed. His gaze went down my jeans and simple T-Shirt and down to my bare feet.

He frowned. "Aren't you going to put on some shoes?"

"If I go back in I won't come back out," I replied.

"I have a taxi waiting."

I closed the door and hopped past him into it. Climbing into the backseat, I scooted along to the other side to make space for him. I wanted to reach out and help him get into the car, but I didn't know where not to touch, so I just leaned back and let him figure his own way into the cab.

He was soon inside and we were on our way. Taking my phone out, I sent a message to Nichole telling her I had left with Bone and would go straight to work after being with him. Then I put my seatbelt on and buckled in for the ride. He seemed content not to speak and just sat quietly next to me so the ride passed with me looking out of the window and him laying his head against the headrest with his eyes closed.

⁓

He lived in Paddock Villas.

As the taxi pulled up in front of the apartment block I turned my gaze to his face, his eyes were still shut, the corners slightly tightened, perhaps in pain and his mouth tightened and pale.

He was beautiful, and I did feel like I had literally been set on fire when he touched me, but was it worth all this? Was Nichole right in that all I did was attract trouble?

Completely aware, he immediately opened his eyes, paid the fare and turned to me. "I'll be right back. I'll get you something from the house."

"Oh, okay," I said confused by the request.

"I'll be just a few minutes," he said to the cab driver. He slammed the door shut and walked away quickly.

I was left in the silence of the bright yellow Sedan and to the stolen glances of the aged ginger-haired taxi-driver.

"You two dating?" he eventually asked.

"Uh, no," was my response. I wondered why he was curious.

"Good. A nice girl like you shouldn't mix with scum like that," he commented.

"Actually, you've been paid so you can go now." I pulled the handle, got out of the vehicle, and he sped off in a huff.

Two minutes later, the hunk I had come with, resurfaced, a pair of huge black sneakers in hand. He placed them on the ground in front of me.

I laughed. "Don't worry about it. I like walking around bare-foot in summer. Anyway, I have a pair of shoes in my bag. How did you imagine I was going to work later?"

"Makes sense," he said quietly.

We walked together towards his apartments. Taking the stairs, we arrived on the second floor and walked along the balcony until I was ushered into an apartment, an apartment that was very sparsely furnished.

A black leather sofa in front of a television, and not much else. It was open plan, so I could see right through to the kitchen. There was a large two door refrigerator, but no dining table. I watched as he went ahead into the kitchen.

"I'll order some food in," he said to me.

My nerves immediately tightened. "Uh, why don't I go get you some groceries? I didn't come all the way over here just to lounge around and eat some free food." I had tried to make it all sound light and amusing.

There was absolutely no trace of humor on his face as he asked, "What if you bail on me?"

"If I was going to do that I would have never agreed to come in the first place," I answered, and as I said the words, I realized that I meant it.

He nodded. "I'm still surprised that you did."

"Well," I replied. "That makes two of us. I have less than an hour so let me put it to good use. What can I help you with?" His regard made me squirm with discomfort. Something about the way he looked at me made me feel completely stripped down and exposed, and that severely bothered me because I wasn't sure what he was seeing.

"Nothing," he replied slowly.

I blinked.

He ran his fingers through his hair then, his breathing heavy as he briefly glanced away. "I want to lie down. Would you stay by my side?" When I just stared on, he added. "I'll order something in so you can eat, at least. I can't send you off to work on an empty stomach." He pulled his phone out of his pocket. "What do you feel like?"

I shrugged. "Perhaps pizza?"

He nodded in agreement. "I'm getting ham and pepperoni, what do you want?"

"Ham and pineapple, please."

He winced.

"What?" I demanded immediately.

He wouldn't be drawn. "Nothing." He placed the order and ended the call.

"Do you at least need help taking off your boots? There are a lot of laces there."

He glanced down at them, then back up to me, a ghost of a smile on his tired face. "They have zippers," he confessed.

I was taken aback. "You lied to me?"

"Sorry. I ran out of ideas."

I gave him a hard look, then turned my gaze towards the hallway. "Where's your room?" I asked.

He led the way.

# DELLA RAY

His room was in the same state as the rest of the apartment. A massive bed sat in the center, and little to no personal belongings except the pile of clothes I found strapped over the imposing leather armchair by the corner. The words left my lips before I could think it through, "You must not stay here a lot."

"I don't," he replied. "Only when I need to get away … like today." He seemed to struggle to get his black t-shirt off. One sleeve had already been cut off, but his face looked severely contorted with pain and frustration when he tried to take it off.

I walked over to him. "The top is ruined, anyway. Why don't we just cut it off you?"

He nodded. "I think there's a pair of scissors, or at the very least, a knife in the kitchen. Wait here and I'll go get it."

"No, I'll get it. You wait here. Actually, sit down. You've gone a funny color."

"Next to the dishwasher. Third drawer on the left."

I ran to the kitchen, found a knife where he said it would be, then I hurried back to his bedroom.

He still sat on the bed and looked up tiredly at my arrival. "I never thought I'd be so glad to see a woman with a knife," he commented, his lips twisting with wry amusement.

"I wouldn't be so glad, if I were you," I retorted tartly. "I've been known to slip and cut things I shouldn't."

He chuckled, but didn't say anything.

When I stood in front of him, I asked, "Ready?"

"Do your worst."

As carefully as I could I cut the material, then gently pulled it upward. Just as I had it over the crown of his head, the stretchy t-shirt snapped from my grasp and slapped against his bandaged arm. He barely winced, but I knew I was making him suffer much more than he was letting on.

"I'm so sorry," I apologized. I felt overcome with remorse and a very strong feeling of inadequacy, but it was too late to back out. Eventually, I got the t-shirt off his head and only then realized how close to each other we were when his face resurfaced again.

He stared into my eyes, and faltered. In the heat of the moment, he forgot his condition and grabbed me with his bandaged arm. The resulting agony was instant.

There were no apologies that would suffice, so I got my shit together and helped him into bed. Just as the bell rang … I turned towards it.

"Don't leave," he begged, his eyes suddenly desperate.

"I won't," I joked lightly. "Especially since the pizza has arrived."

His eyes widened. "Oh, shit. I forgot that I ordered pizza."

He began to rise, but I wasn't having it. With my hand across his shoulder, I gently pushed him down and shook my head. "Don't get up. I'll go and get it."

Even in his condition, he was powerful enough to brush me aside. "No, it could be anyone."

"Oh, is that bad? Are you expecting someone other than the delivery guy?"

He lifted his pillow then and underneath it was a black pistol.

A gasp escaped before my hand could fly up to slap my mouth shut.

"No one pleasant," he responded. "Just wait here." He was out of the room before I could figure out what to say.

When he returned, it was with our boxes of pizza. He put them at the bottom of the bed and lay down on the pillow. His naked torso was now on full display and I couldn't take my eyes off the inked, sculpted, tanned body that I had imagined more times than I could recall.

"Eat something," he invited.

My voice came silky smooth and breathless as I replied, "Later, I'm not very hungry right now. What about you?"

He shook his head.

I couldn't stop watching him. He was so beautiful when he was in this state. But when he suddenly opened his eyes and caught me staring hungrily at him, I quickly looked away in embarrassment.

"It can't be very comfortable sitting at the edge of the bed," he murmured.

"Oh, I'm fine," I said, but the look he gave me was a wordless plea. I couldn't resist. I laid down on the grey striped comforter and placed both my hands on my stomach.

"I still can't believe you came," he said, as he turned his head to watch me.

"Neither can I."

"Are you regretting it now?"

"Well ... there's the pizza," I joked. "What's there to regret?"

He went silent after that.

I was too aware of him to even turn to steal a glance. "Tell me about the kid," I said softly.

"Yeah, he was a good kid. He took a bullet he didn't deserve," he said, his eyes staring unseeingly at the ceiling. "I was going to take him aside and beat some sense into him, so that he would get the fuck out of the club, but I never got around to it." He shut his eyes.

"Is he going to be okay?"

"He'll live, but he may never walk again. The bullet blasted right through his spinal cord."

"You were shot too, weren't you?" I asked, my voice small

with fear. This was exactly the reason I didn't want to get involved with someone like him.

"Yeah," he replied. "But I was lucky. It went cleanly through my flesh, and only lightly grazed the bone. I'll be fine in no time."

I chose my next words very carefully, "Will you tell me what happened? How did both of you get shot?"

"We had church," he explained.

"Church?" I interjected in surprise. "Why are people getting shot at church?"

He smiled at me.

Oh, my God! Was that an indulgent smile? The kind a father would give his beloved daughter, or a man might give his … his sweetheart.

"We call our weekly chapter meetings church," he clarified. "A rival club drove by in a van and released fire."

"Why?"

"I have no clue," he replied, his brow creasing into frown lines. "A few days ago they seized a patched vest from one of our members so if anything, we're the ones who are meant to bury them all, but they came at us first and none of us know why."

"Maybe they didn't want to wait for a war," I reasoned. "Maybe they wanted to start it … on their own terms."

"Perhaps," he said, turning around to look at me again. "Do you know much about the clubs?"

"I looked yours up," I admitted. "After you mentioned it."

"And …"

"And nothing," I replied, but we both knew it wasn't the truth. There was a lot I wanted to say and ask, but I didn't have the guts.

"Michael," he began and a frown instantly dug into my forehead. "Why were you with him? What did you see in him? He's damn well repugnant."

"I really don't want to talk about Michael," I said. "It was a mistake, but it's over now and one of those episodes of my past that I wish had never happened."

"But he did happen," he countered. "And I want to know about it."

I sighed. If I didn't want our current mood of comradery not to turn sour, then I needed to talk about it. "Okay, I went out with him, because he pretended to like Jess, so I blinded myself to all the little warning clues that he was big trouble and convinced myself to go along with it. Funny thing is Jess never liked him. She wouldn't even look him in the eye."

"And me?" he asked. "Why are you going along with me?"

I turned to him then. "You're not downright repugnant."

He slightly lifted his blood stained and bandaged arm. "But I am trouble, aren't I?"

I held his gaze then and for once allowed the words to come out … so that not only he could hear them but so could I, "I'm not trying to fall in love with you, or trying to have a long-term relationship," I said. "I think I just—I think I just …"

"You just what?" he prompted.

"Forget it."

"Let me know and I'll make it happen for you," he said. "As a thank you for today."

I almost succumbed, but then I thought of something better. "Why don't you answer my question and I'll answer yours."

"Go ahead."

"Don't get offended," I began, "but why are you in an MC? You seem like an intelligent, good guy. Why would you be in something so dangerous?" I pointed to his bandage. "What kind of life is this?"

He looked away.

Had I gone too far? I quickly moved to salvage the tense silence. "You don't have to respond. I shouldn't have asked. It wasn't very polite."

"Will you tell me the answer to yours if I don't respond?" he asked.

"No." I smiled. "Absolutely not."

"Okay, then I'll tell you." He stared at me with empty eyes. "I went in because of my best friend. He was in a rival club, the Mongols. Then two years ago, he stopped at a traffic light, and someone tapped on his window. When he rolled the glass down, he was blasted with seven bullets in his head. When I saw him, I couldn't even make out his face. I've been haunted by that sight ever since."

I tried my best not to show it, but my bones felt as if they were rattling with trepidation. "So you weren't a member of a club then?"

"No," he answered in a chilling voice. "I joined the Order Of Blood because that is the only way I'm going to take care of the bastard that took him down."

The implications of his words made me go silent with sadness.

"Your turn ... why are you going along with me?"

"Before I respond, please pardon one more question." I said, and quickly went on before he could refuse me, "If you take care of this guy, you could end up going to jail, couldn't you? It is, after all, murder."

"I don't care," he replied, his face set and menacing.

"Alright," I said, my heart a little torn. "That means then that there can be absolutely nothing real between us, so I will say what I wanted to."

"Go ahead."

"I-I just want to sleep with you, at least once. Believe it or not —I've only ever been with one guy, and that was a disaster, so I want to feel the way you made me feel that night." I shut my eyes then, my hands wringing with nerves. After all, he had said I should have been running for the hills ... instead I was still here.

"I can make you feel better than you felt that night," he stated softly.

I didn't know how to respond to that. An 'okay' seemed a bit lackluster and 'thank you' was not exactly appropriate, so I remained silent. I must have been silent for a long time, because when I turned to steal a glance at him he was quite soundly, and I hoped, peacefully asleep.

I stayed watching him sleeping for a few minutes, because he was so beautiful when he was asleep, then I quietly left his apartment and went to work.

# BONE

I was torn awake from a nightmare to find myself bolting upright in bed. I was gasping for breath, my heart was pounding like an African drum, and my whole body was drenched in sweat. Just another nightmare. My breathing slowed as the red mist faded away. I cupped the throbbing wound on my arm with my hand.

I knew without checking that she had left. It was as much as a relief as it was a disappointment. I had been weak last night. I shouldn't get close to her.

She must never know what her mere presence yesterday evening did for me. From the complete senselessness of the attack to the boy whose life had forever been changed right in front of me ... it was more than I could take. The only way for me to get me through another breath was her.

And it had worked.

I looked at the pizza boxes. They were unopened. Moving forward, I opened the box. It was hers. Ham and pineapple. I

114

pulled a piece and took a bite ... and nearly gagged. I spat it back into the box ... *not even for you, Della.*

My phone was buzzing.

I turned to look for it and only then realized my gun was still hooked to my fingers. I had returned back to the room with it and hid it under the pillow as I had fallen asleep. I flung it aside and picked up the phone.

It was Snake. "Where are you?" came his cold voice.

"I needed some air," was my gruff response.

"Where?" he asked.

My brows furrowed into a frown. *Had something gone wrong?* My thoughts instantly went to the girl and I felt the hairs on my body stand to attention. "Is there a problem?"

"We have church right now. How far are you from Reno's?"

"I'll be right there." I ended the call.

I thought for a moment about what the buzzing running through me could mean, but apart from the girl, nothing else came to mind. I thought to call her, but then I realized that I didn't even have her phone number.

"*Fuck,*" I cursed under my breath. I immediately tore my bedding away and reached into the slit in the mattress for my second phone. I switched it on and got my old friend, Yuri on the line.

"Do you know what time it is?" he asked.

"Can you help me look a number up?"

He groaned. "Sure, whose?"

I gave him Della's address.

"Okay I'll look it up."

"Can you do it now?" I could feel him about to ask, so I immediately cleared the air. "It's personal."

"Uh … that puts me in a tight spot. You know I can't reve—"

"Are you going to make me go to someone else?"

With a sigh, he agreed and the conversation came to an end.

I needed a shower, but I didn't have time for it so I quickly washed. Her number was already in my phone by the time I got out of the bathroom. I pulled on an old vest, it was easier to get into than a t-shirt. Then I memorized the number before I switched the phone off, returned it to its place, and ran from the apartment. I was on my Harley and on my way in no time, navigating the chilly night with my only good hand.

The moment I arrived at the discrete midtown bar, a text lit up my phone. I stared at it in surprise. It had been so long since I'd received a text, but when I saw that it was from Volt, I froze.

I pulled it up as I disembarked from the bike and read it.

*They tailed you … Tell them about the girl.*

I reread the text again, the earth seeming to sink beneath my feet. Then, I raised my gaze to the black, starless sky.

*Fuck, fuck, fuck! Why did I go to her last night? Damn me and my stupidity.*

I kicked the dusty ground with frustration and fury at myself.

*Get a hold of yourself, idiot. Don't make it worse.*

I took deep breaths and after a while, I regained my calm. Wiping my face of all expression, I headed into the bar. It was lit with vibrant red lights and hazy with thick smoke.

The room was empty but for the club's nine executive members.

Every one of them was staring at me, their gazes piercing, questioning, and waiting.

My gun was tucked into my waistband, but it would not have done me a fucking bit of good.

I slid into the nearest booth, behind a table I knew I could use as a shield if things went out of control.

"How you feeling?" Snake asked. If he had meant to sound caring, he failed miserably.

A cold shiver ran down my spine. "I'll survive."

Snake nodded.

The bar was eerily quiet, but I knew that it had nothing to do with the somber incident that had taken place just a few hours earlier. I addressed the suspicion head on, "Who was asking for me?" I asked.

Tyler spoke up. "I was. Where were you?"

I stared at him, my face darkening at the inquisition. "What's it to you?" I asked. From the corner of my eye, I didn't miss the look the other members shared with each other. "Is there a problem?" I asked around again.

Everyone remained silent. Snake responded, "None, Bone. We just got word that you went to find a woman, then disappeared with her. We've never heard of you with any hussy before so we were just a bit curiou—"

"She's no hussy," I interrupted, my fists clenching, my tone heavy and harsh.

No one said anything.

I stared grimly at the members in the bar and over to little Rick, the bar's owner behind the counter. "So you tailed me?" I asked coldly.

"Don't take it to heart, Bone," Rooster placated. "One of the members just thought they spotted you. It was more for your own good than anything else."

Malicious bastard must think I was born fucking yesterday. "Yeah? So what's this interrogation all about then? I was with a woman. Since when did that become a crime? Like I haven't dealt with enough bullshit for one day?"

"Who's the woman?" Tyler asked, his eyes drilling into my soul. Unlike the others, he wasn't even a little bit moved by my aggressive response.

"None of your fucking business," was my furious response.

"C'mon," RJ crowed excitedly. "You've always been a loner. Imagine our surprise when we found out you had someone to go to on such a tough day for ya. Volt, you saw where she lived right?" The moment the words left his mouth, he knew he had made a serious mistake.

"You fucking moron!" Volt screamed.

More curses and hisses rang out and the bastard lowered his head in shame to take a long slug of his beer.

I lifted my gaze to Volt, who had with seemingly good intention, secretly alerted me to the fact I'd been tailed in the first place.

"You left the hospital in a rush," he explained hastily, his eyes darting around the members. "I followed to make sure you were okay. Then I saw you pick her up, but I lost both of you after that."

I kept up appearances and continued to glare at him.

"Don't get your panties in a twist. We'll look over her for you," RJ piped in.

I slowly transferred my glare to him. How I hated him. The term lowlife scum was too much of an honor for him. "Haven't you caused enough trouble already? A damn kid was paralyzed on your account today, and I was almost killed. Are you ever going to learn to behave like a fucking human being, or do I have to destroy you myself?"

Embarrassed, he smashed the tumbler of whisky he had been nursing on the ground defiantly, shot up from his stool, and glared at me with his reddened eyes. "Let's see who's gonna destroy who first," he boasted, starting to reach behind him.

Before his hand could even touch his gun, Tyler's fist had slammed into his jaw. It happened so fast RJ didn't even make a sound as he crashed to the ground.

Rooster who was sitting next to him jumped up to avoid his dead weight crushing him. Rowdy laughter rang out across the bar as Rooster bent down to shake the unconscious man. "He's out," he reported, as he arose.

Tyler reached for the gun that had flown off RJ and the meeting went on without further interruptions.

"What are we going to do about the Death's Hand?" Tank asked.

"A war is unavoidable now," Dobson responded. "I can't figure out why they attacked first? What's with these blood-thirsty bastards fucking running around?"

"I say we take them all out," Tyler declared. "With their attack today, there's no going back. It's either we deal with them, or they deal with us."

"But why did they fucking attack first?" Dobson lamented once again and the bar went silent. "I mean we were the ones they offended by snatching this bastard's vest." He kicked the unconscious man in the ribs. "It was our turn to give a response."

"We were silent for too long," Shotgun quietly explained. "They couldn't take the wait any longer. It was probably driving them crazy imagining how we were going to react."

"Shotgun's right," Tank agreed. "They probably had night-mares of us burning them all in their sleep. Better an enemy you can predict than one you can't figure out. This was to drag us out in the open and force us to take action. The sissies probably didn't even intend to hit any of us. That kid just fucking got in the way."

"His name is Junho," I growled.

"Whatever," was his response.

I rose to my feet. I couldn't stand a moment longer in the

company of these fucking beasts. "I need rest," I announced. "I'll be at the house."

Under normal circumstances, I would have been stopped, but given that I was amongst the victim count for the day, I was excused without repercussions.

I got on my bike and returned to the shit hole where I'd vowed to lay my head until I had my revenge.

## DELLA RAY

I halted chopping the carrot in front of me, and glanced towards the living room sofa where Nichole was predicting all the doom and gloom from.

"It's going to be a blood bath," she said.

"What is going to be a bloodbath?" I asked.

She turned down the volume of the news program she had been watching and turned to me. "Haven't you been listening?" she asked. "It's these motorcycle clubs. The cops say it seems like a war is brewing between them."

"Which clubs in particular?" I asked, my chest tightening uncomfortably.

"They haven't said yet," she responded, and sunk back into the couch to return her attention to the television.

I closed my eyes and took a deep breath. I wanted so much for Bone to be safe.

"Death's Hand and ... Order Of Blood?" She read from the

screen. "What kind of tacky names are these? Freaking low lives. I wish the cops would just boot them all from the county. They're so much freaking trouble." Flinging the remote aside, she rose and headed over to me.

I feigned nonchalance as she came over and lifted the lid off the pot of basmati rice that was boiling on the stove.

"Mmm … it's almost ready," she said. Pulling up her sleeves, she headed over to the sink of dishes awaiting her.

I heard the faucet come on and moments later was startled by a sudden clang. I turned to see Nichole watching me with narrowed eyes.

"Are you all right?" she asked.

I nodded. "Of course, why?"

"I was calling and you didn't respond."

I frowned at her, realizing why she had pounded the spoon against the sink.

Suddenly her face changed. "Does he belong to one of those clubs?"

I nodded.

"Oh, Della. I'm so sorry."

"It's okay. It's not like I'm in a relationship with him."

"Do you want me to go get Jess?"

"Umm." I needed the time away to clear my mind. "No, I'll do it." I stepped away from the vegetables.

I moved quickly towards Jess's room, but I stopped in front

of the door to allow my mind a moment. I needed to clear my head. If what the news was saying about the clubs was true, then it meant that he was possibly in trouble. Big trouble.

He had already been shot once ... perhaps this time around he would— I couldn't bear to finish the thought and wished more than ever that I had gotten his phone number. But even if I had it, what would I say when I contacted him? *Don't get yourself killed?*

I was nothing to him so why couldn't I get him out of my mind? Why had his wellbeing now become my concern?

## DELLA RAY

The next day at the bar was a slow night for us, so I pulled out my phone and began to Google motorcycle clubs.

As I was scrolling through, a piece of conversation trickled into my consciousness and my ears instantly perked up in attention. Two men were discussing the race and how it tied up to the damn MC brawl that everyone had predicted would leave a countless number of people dead. I listened for a moment, once again my temper rising at the senselessness of the entire situation. "Why don't they just cancel the entire damn race?" I blurted out.

Both men went silent as they turned around to gaze at me, taken aback by my sudden outburst.

I just couldn't hold back anymore. I just couldn't understand it. "Why on earth would a bunch of grown ass men get so worked up over a freaking vest?"

Henry looked surprised. "You know about this?"

"It's all over the news. They're milking it for all it's worth. Luxuriating in every gory detail and trying to find even the most tenuous connection to every shootout that has ever taken place in the country. How the hell can I possibly not know about it?"

"Whoa!" Henry's brows shot up. "You seem pretty upset about it."

I exhaled deeply. "It's just so annoying. It makes the entire county unsafe for everyone else."

"You're right," Tim, Henry's friend agreed. "I've even heard that their bar has emptied out a lot these days."

That perked my interest. "They have a bar?"

"Well it's not *theirs,* but you could call it their official hang-out. Normal folks used to go by there once in a while just for the thrill of it, but in the recent months, it's mostly been just the club itself. People are cautious now ... scared of a gunfight breaking out at any moment.

"What's the name of the bar?" I asked.

Henry beamed with amusement. "Why? Are you going to go there?"

"Of course not," I stated flatly.

Henry stared at me with suspicion. "Hmmm."

"Well, where is it?" I prodded.

"Don't tell her," Henry said. "It seems like she's planning to go there for some reason."

Tim on the other hand was of a lighter disposition. "It's over on Crow Dust Street. It's called Reno's, I believe."

I gave Henry a hard look, drained my drink, and got up to return to work.

~

The next day ... yep ... I found myself walking up to Reno's on Crow Dust Street. It was off the main road, and tucked not far off from a tire junkyard. The walls of the building were made of bright orange bricks with flame graffiti all over it. Two black and silver motorbikes were parked outside.

It was indeed a biker bar. Two men sitting outside, one attired in a bandana and leather jacket, and the other bald, brawny and with a pair of dark sunglass shielding his eyes, leered at me as I headed towards the entrance.

Now I was certain I had lost it, why else would I have willingly come to a place that everyone else with two brain cells to rub together in the county was avoiding?

Squaring my shoulders, I walked in.

Outside, it was sunny and bright, but inside the entire place was lit with dim red bulbs. The outside world beyond these walls became deeply lost in this seedy place. I strolled in to the serenade of maniac, head banging music, fortunately on low volume.

It wasn't exactly busy, but every eye in that place turned to me. The men watched me with a mixture of hunger and suspicious hostility. I turned towards the bar and a creaky old man behind the bar was waiting for me, so I hurried over.

I wanted to quickly ask for Bone, then find my way out of here, but I suddenly wondered if that would be dangerous in more ways than I could understand, so I simply ordered a cold beer and propped myself on the bar stool. My plan was to converse a little with the old guy to the point where I might casually slip in a question about where Bone was, but the moment he served me my drink he slunk away as if I was infected with Ebola.

I got the message, but I couldn't just admit that it had been a bad decision to come here on my own and leave. Nearly half-an-hour passed and my beer grew warm, but I couldn't give up. Every time the door to the bar was pulled open and yet another biker appeared, my head snapped up, my heart in my throat as I hoped that it would be him.

But it never was.

With the whole ambience of the place, the horrid music, the thick smoke making my eyes water, and the menacing stares I could feel boring into my back, I decided to give up. For my own sanity.

I was about to get up and when the back door was pulled open, and a girl came in, or perhaps she was a woman. It didn't matter. The important thing was I wouldn't be the only female present, anymore. She was obviously staff, because she took her place behind the bar. After tying up her bright strawberry blonde hair, she pulled out a thick book from the cabinet below and began to flip through it. Here was my chance to ask for a bit of info. I figured being a girl she would be easier to approach.

"Another bottle, please," I called out to her with a big, friendly smile.

With a sigh, she closed her book and came over. Her eyes were a striking green, and when I smiled at her, she sent a tight smile back.

"I'm looking for someone," I said to her. This was my last chance and I reckoned this to be as good an opening as any. "Could you please help me?"

She gave me a very deliberate once over. "Depends," she said, and popped the gum in her mouth.

"Bone," I said. "Do you know him?"

Her eyes narrowed. "You a cop?"

I was so taken aback by the question that for a few seconds I didn't know what to say. When I did, my voice was a high squeak. "Oh, no. Definitely not. I waitress at a diner and a bar."

"Then why you asking?" Her tone was now downright unfriendly.

"I uh, I have a question for him," I replied, already regretting asking her.

Instead of answering my question, she had one of her own. "How do you know him?"

I hesitated. I realized she wasn't going to give me any information and I didn't want to give her the satisfaction of thinking I was leaving with my tail between my legs so I picked up my drink and headed over to an empty booth. I began to wonder if perhaps she would have spoken to me if I had said we had met when he had come to my bar. But as I looked in her direction again, our eyes met and I caught the sullen venom in her gaze as she wiped down the counter, I knew she had no intention of telling me anything.

I wondered what her problem was. Didn't tips make up the bigger portion of her wages? Whenever I was working at the bar or even the diner for that matter, I couldn't do enough to please a customer.

My thoughts were interrupted by the deafening sounds of what I could only imagine was a very big group of motorcycles arriving outside. A new fear made me grip my bottle of beer so hard my knuckles showed white. A few leering old-timers and a mean barmaid I could handle, but a whole bunch of bikers with personalities unknown? Maybe murderers and rapists in the mix?

My heart was thumping loudly in my chest. I knew I had definitely stayed for too long and it was time to leave, probably through the back door, but still I waited. Then it was too late to leave.

The door was pulled open and a collection of the most muscled, tatted, vicious looking outlaws I had ever laid eyes upon streamed into the room.

I lowered my gaze, especially as they all looked directly at me. I understood then why this was a biker bar more than anything. If you didn't run with their club, and you came in here, you stuck out like a sore decaying thumb. The last thing I needed was anyone coming up to me and offering what I didn't ask for.

Beer held no charms for me, but I drained my drink, and glued my eyes to my phone. When I could sense that they had sat down, and had turned their attention away from me I shot to my feet. The door opened and …

Bone was standing there staring at me.

## DELLA RAY

M y soul jumped out of my body. I couldn't move or speak. All I could register was the shock in his eyes, and the tousled cascade of his dark hair falling almost to his shoulders. He had abandoned his cast, no doubt without the doctor's permission, and as I stared dumbfounded at him, I realized what had made me crazy enough to come here and wait with these hardened violent men for him. Because he wasn't one of them. What a sharp contrast he made to the rest of these men. Yes, he was tatted up, rugged and dangerous no doubt, but in a good way, like a hero. The way that made you want no one else but him.

Then the most surprising thing happened. I saw his eyes fill with … fear. But it was gone so fast I realized I must have imagined it. Why would he fear me? With a hard look at me, he turned around without a word, and exited the bar. At least he hadn't completely ignored me, so all was not lost. With every single person in that bar staring at me, I went after him. When I arrived outside, the sun was setting and he was nowhere in sight, but at the rev of an engine around the corner, I knew exactly where he was.

I headed over and stopped next to his bike.

He took his time, running his fingers through his hair and then securing it all behind his head with a tie … All the while without even bothering to spare me a gaze. "What are you doing here?" he asked.

"I came for a drink," I said flippantly.

The look he gave me was lethal. At the vein that twitched by the side of his head I realized then just how furious he was at my presence. "Out of all the bars in Arnault you chose this one?"

"Fuck you too," I said rudely, and turned around to walk away, but he caught my hand and I was pulled roughly towards him.

"Let me go," I said coldly. I felt so angry and hurt I refused to even look at him.

He shook me like a rag doll until he had forced my gaze to meet his. "Why would you come here?" he asked through gritted teeth. "Do you know how dangerous it is?"

I opened my mouth to speak but no words would come out, especially at the note of intense emotion I heard in his admonishment.

"Get on," he said, steel in his voice.

I tried to pull away from his grip on me, but he wouldn't budge.

"I'll go on my own."

"Get on," he repeated more softly.

It instantly weakened me. I didn't want to be away from him either, so I was at least going to enjoy whatever moments I still had with him until we arrived at my house. When we arrived, I would probably receive vicious instructions to never try to contact him again, but what the hell? I would cross that bridge when I came to it.

I got on, and instantly reveled in his familiar scent. I tightened my hands around his waist. Soon, we were blasting through the county roads. I allowed myself to rest my forehead against his back.

*Oh, Bone. Why can't you be mine?*

Soon we arrived at my home and I instantly let him go. The immediate absence of his warmth felt so strangely final, I began to feel nauseous. It made me wonder when my heart had become so invested in him.

*Well, constantly obsessing over a man would do that,* my mind mocked.

I honestly expected him to zoom off.

Instead, he got off the bike and faced me. "Why did you come to the bar?"

The last thing I wanted to admit was I went because I was worried about him and wanted to see how he was doing, or that I wanted him to get out of that stupid club before, God forbid … it caused his death in the damn upcoming race. "I was curious," I answered, my chin lifted.

He studied me grimly.

"Your club has been the talk of the town recently. I just wanted to see what it was all about."

"Never come by again," he said, and turned to take his leave.

I felt as if my heart was being ripped out of my body. I knew then I would never see him again. I wanted to grab him and tell him not to leave me. I watched in horror as he was about to mount his bike. Soon he would be gone. Forever. Maybe he would even end up getting killed at the big biker race.

"Alright, I will never go there again," I shouted. "But you owe me."

He stopped and slowly turned around. "Owe you? Do I owe you?"

"When you needed my help, you came here, and I went with you. Don't I get anything in return for that?"

His gaze narrowed at me.

I didn't care, my blood was already fizzing with anxiety. How would my request ever leave my mouth? What kind of emotion was giving me the courage to act this way?

"What do you want?" he asked softly.

I inhaled deeply and locked my gaze with his. Then I opened my mouth and the words I never thought I would ever say to anyone flowed out, "I want what you offered from the very beginning."

"You want me to fuck you?"

My head jerked back to hear it put so directly. I was wincing inwardly, but folding my arms across my chest with a confidence I didn't feel, I gave as good as I got. "Just once. After that, we'll never have anything to do with each other again."

He went quiet for way too long. I could even almost hear the tick of the watch on my wrist as the seconds went by. The distant sounds of cars zooming past on the major road, two blocks down floated over me, and in the house behind someone must have been cooking fish because I could smell it.

"Okay," he said suddenly, and walked past me towards the house.

It took a short moment to process what was happening and when I did I ran after him. "Where are you going?" I asked in a panic.

"You have a room, don't you?" he asked.

My heart wanted to burst out of my chest. "It can't be here. Definitely not. Nichole and Jess will be back any moment."

"We'll be quick," he said carelessly.

My mouth dropped open. Never had I felt so devalued. So cheap. I swore to myself then that I would hurt him back, somehow. "No thank you," I said. "I take back my request. You can be on your way now and I hope we never have anything to do with each other again." I walked away from him and blinking back the tears of rage, I pushed my door open. I was furious with myself and him. I felt like I would explode into pieces from the anger.

I made sure to exert all my effort into banging the door in his face, but he stuck his leg out, and forced his way in. He slammed the door behind him and began to approach me like a predator.

136

DELLA RAY

https://www.youtube.com/watch?v=O0jYMMTb0XU
-tonight you're mine-

"Your temper sways like you're out of your mind, do you know this?" he asked, his eyes glittering. It appeared he was just as furious as me.

I started walking backwards as he approached. "You can't be here," was all I could say.

"You're so easily angered and irritated. And I don't know if I like it or not."

"I don't care if you do or not, I just—" I began, before coming to a sudden stop.

I could smell his intoxicating scent and almost feel the magnetic heat from his body swirling between us. I felt hot and strangely breathless. My knees wobbled. I needed to hold onto something, or at the very least sit down. "I want

137

you to leave!" I screeched in a blind panic. "This is tres-passing and we don't have anything to—"

"You talk way too damn much," he interrupted. Without any warning, he grabbed me by the arms, pulled me forward, and captured my mouth in a hard kiss.

My knees gave way, and I was forced to grab his jacket to keep myself upright.

His tongue, his beautiful tongue … it did things to my mental state that I couldn't put into words. I wanted it on every inch of my skin. I also wanted to reject him, to pull away. Instead, I sensed my hands release his shirt and snake up his chest and lock around his neck and draw him even closer to me.

All I could do was whimper helplessly, as his tongue filled my mouth, plunging, sucking, teasing … in a rhythm that left me limp. I couldn't understand it. I had kissed guys before so what was it about him? Why did it make me want to melt into a puddle of longing and desire? Only the image of Jess's innocent face was stronger than him.

I tore myself away from him and instantly felt the loss of his flesh and flavor, intertwining with mine, feeding me the lies that we were completely one. That we were perfect together, and all that we would each ever need was each other, when it was all a big lie.

"Let's stop here," I cried out.

Instead, he tore off his jacket and flung it away revealing the sleeveless t-shirt he had on.

"Bone," I called, my chest panting as I retreated backwards. "My roommate …"

"I don't care," he rasped and came for me. "Which one's your room?"

"Let's leave," I said and grabbed his hand to pull him away.

He locked my wrist in his big rough hand and pulled me along with him. "Which one's yours?" he asked harshly. "If you don't tell me, I swear I'll fuck you right here on the floor."

I couldn't help my eyes from straying towards my door. He pushed it open and I hurried in after him into my room. It was a mess with clothes strewn across the bed. I had tried on my entire wardrobe before I decided on the simple t-shirt and jeans I was wearing. I'd never felt more ashamed of my room.

Apparently, it didn't bother him one bit, because he turned around, slammed the door shut, and pulled me roughly to him. His mouth instantly on my neck.

My back arched at the sweet agony of his touch. He squeezed my body to his as though he was unable to let go. I managed to twist the lock on the door just as my feet left the floor. He pressed me hard against him, my ass rubbing against his burgeoning cock.

I reached behind to feel what I could of him through his jeans and had to grab my own crotch to soothe the excruci-ating ache.

This would be our one time together and I did not intend to hold back. I turned around, dropped to my knees, and tugged on his belt. He let me, and I could feel his eyes sear into my skin as I worked the buckle and yanked his zipper down.

Holding the edge of his briefs and jeans, I pulled them both down just enough, so his cock sprung free.

I had already copped a feel so I knew he was big, but holy cow!

I had imagined his cock fucking me in a thousand ways over the last few days, but I never imagined it would be so perfect. With widened eyes, I admired the view of his thick heavy cock. Velvety veins throbbed and snaked up along the silky looking flesh. I held the heated length of him in my hands and I couldn't believe how hard or thick he was. My eyes lifted up to his and catching his desperate gaze, a smile spread across my face. My heart was pounding as I flicked out my tongue and let myself taste that glistening drop of seed.

He let out a soft groan.

God, I loved the taste of him so much a moan escaped my lips as I savored the flavor of him. Greedily, I opened my mouth and sucked hard on his delicious cock, my tongue licking and teasing along his hard length.

My hands covered his shaft and began to fist softly up and down his length while his hand held onto my head, his beautifully toned stomach rising and falling in rapid succession at the quickening of his breath.

First, I teased him by nicking tiny bites of his delicate flesh. I worked my way from the root to the tip of his cock. He was so turned on he started to rock his hips in desperation. And that was when I hollowed my mouth to take as much of him as I could, but given his size it wasn't as far as I would have liked. The only time he was probably be balls deep was when he fucked my pussy. I continued to fist and suck hard, fucking him with my mouth until I could taste his arousal. Looking up I saw his expression change, so I milked him hard until I felt him begin to quicken, galloping towards his explosion.

*"Fuck,"* he cursed, as he held my head and repeatedly plunged himself in and out of my mouth. "I'm going to come," he warned.

Maybe he thought I might want to move away, but I held on even tighter to him. It was that action that pushed him over. When he exploded in my mouth, I swallowed it and wanted more.

*"Fuck,"* he breathed, his fingers intertwined in my hair as his big, gorgeous body jerked to the force of his orgasm. His face was raised to the ceiling in total abandonment.

I milked every last ounce of pleasure out of him. When he looked down, I opened my mouth and showed him his own cum swirling inside my mouth. His eyes widened with pleasure. When I closed my mouth and swallowed it all, he pulled me to my feet.

"What did you just do to me?" he asked, an awed expression in his eyes.

My response was a smile. At that moment, I felt more powerful than I had ever felt in my life. Now, I knew he wanted me as much as I wanted him.

He grabbed my shirt and ripped the material apart. Buttons flew in all directions just as my breasts came into view, full and swollen in the dark lacy bra that held them.

His mouth instantly went on the swell, his kiss hard and wet as he sucked and fondled my creamy flesh.

Wafts of ecstasy coursed through me, as my back connected with the door.

That was when the sound from the outside world intruded.

The slam of the front door opening announced the arrival of Jess and Nichole.

I froze.

Bone lifted his head from my breast, his eyes connecting with mine as I put my finger on my lips to warn him not to make any noise.

To my shock, he simply pulled down my bra and covered my nipple with his mouth.

"*Bone*," I gasped and tried to get him to stop, but he wouldn't.

I had to admit though that my attempts were too feeble. I honestly couldn't find any strength whatsoever to stop him. At the barrage of flaming hot desire that burned me to my core when he began to work the buttons of my jeans, my head fell back and hit the door.

"Della-Ray?" I heard Nichole call out.

## DELLA RAY

$\mathbf{B}$one slipped his hand into my panties and cupped my soaking wet pussy.

"*Fuuck,*" I gasped at the contact. I caught his hand to pull him away, my eyes pleading with him to return some of my willpower back to me so I could salvage the situation enough to stop my friend from murdering me.

He did the opposite. He jerked my underwear and jeans off my hips and said, "Relax, they already know I'm here, my bike's in front of the house."

At the realization, my eyes widened in panic.

"Jess, come with me," I heard Nichole say, and I almost collapsed with relief when their footsteps retreated towards the kitchen. He pulled my jeans down to my feet and circled my swollen clit torturously before slipping his fingers into me. I knew then … there was no way in hell I would be telling him to stop.

My eyes fluttered shut as the force of his thrusts increased

GEORGIA LE CARRE

and I tried my best to quiet my harsh breathing. But when he grabbed my ass, pushed my thighs apart, and slammed his mouth against my cunt, I had to slap my palm against my mouth and try my best to swallow the whimpers that rushed up my throat.

My other hand slipped into his thick hair as he plunged his tongue into me. I couldn't stop my hips from twitching and jerking in response. When his tongue pulled my clit into his mouth and sucked feverishly between the folds of my sex, all thoughts of Nichole and Jess's presence became utterly lost to me.

I ground my sex into his face, and he ate me up with a wild and desperate hunger.

*"Fuck"* I thrashed wildly against the door. "Oh, fuck ... Bone." I tried, I really tried to contain myself, but in that moment nothing else mattered beyond the euphoria he was flying me towards.

When I climaxed, my entire body slammed against the door and if Nichole had any doubts as to what was going on that would have confirmed it. I began to crumble to the ground. If he hadn't quickly risen to hold me up, I would have collapsed.

Without giving me a chance to recover, he threw me across his shoulder, and deposited me on the bed.

Mindlessly, I stared at him, my hand was pressed hard against my sex. The waves of my orgasm were still coursing through my body.

He tore my bundled jeans from my feet, and crawled up to me until our eyes were level. Then he kissed me.

It was different from any kiss he gave me before. This one was full of desperation. The kiss a man might give his sweetheart before he went away to war. When he thought it might be his last. At the feel of his cock as it settled between my thighs, I reached to my left and opened my bedside drawer. There was a condom there. I gave it to him. "It's very old. I hope it still works."

"Do you want me to make it quick?" he asked.

"Fuck yes!" I breathed. "Jess and Nichole are home."

He sheathed himself.

As he slipped into me, I held my breath. "Jesus," I gasped in shock. I had never had a man stretch me so wide. To allow me to get used to his girth, he stayed still and began to trace wet hard kisses along my jawline. When he took my breast into his mouth, I felt a hot trickle of desire roll down my inner thigh. "I'm ready," I panted.

He pulled out and plunged all the way into me.

My back arched up from the bed into a bow. "Oh, my Go—"

He saved me from myself as he covered my mouth with his, eating up my words. Then he removed his mouth from mine. "Keep it down," he whispered.

I almost screamed at him in fury. "I fucking told you to take this somewhere else," I cried, digging my nails into his firm full ass.

He pulled away just as his cock reached my opening and then plunged back into me. "Next time."

"There won't be one," I shot back.

His response was a dry chuckle. "We'll see about that."

"Go slow," I warned. "Or else the bed will creak. They'll be able to hear."

"You just told me there won't be a next time," he said. "So why the fuck should I do that?" He plunged into me once more and this time so vengefully the bed rocked against the wall in a vicious protest.

From then on, he was unstoppable. My nails clawed viciously down his back in retaliation for rendering my control to dust and putting me in deep trouble with Nichole. His thrusts picked up in rhythm, and came in such hard, deep drives that I couldn't find my voice. I wrenched the sheets from the mattress, and my head thrashed about as he fucked the life out of me.

"I've wanted you for so fucking long," he snarled. "From the first fucking moment I saw you. All I wanted was to be inside your sweet pussy."

I was panting. The loud smacks of his groin against my flesh made me wish to God Nichole would take Jess out of the house and into the garden. It seemed as though the very ground was shaking beneath me. I opened my eyes to search his face and it was twisted in a grimace of otherworldly bliss. I imagined that I looked even crazier than that.

"Bone," I cried out, lifting my hips and tightening my legs around him, in an effort to take him even deeper.

His cock seemed to swell even more inside of me, the thick rod grating tantalizingly against the tender walls of my sex, as he fucked me as though he were possessed.

His thrusts became animalistic, borderline cruel even, but I wouldn't have wanted it any other way. I gave up any idea of holding on to the reigns of control as the hoarse groans spilling from his throat drove me wilder still. Tortured and on the verge of unconsciousness, I surrendered completely to it.

My orgasm was monumental.

The walls of my sex clenched every inch of him so tightly, he exploded right along with me. His shudder was violent as he held me in a tight grasp, hot, and vehement.

I held tightly onto him, my lips planting frenzied kisses all over his awe-stricken face. My heart felt as if it would burst with emotion. "Bone," I gasped repeatedly, as if it was a prayer I was offering the gods. In fact, it was … *Please don't take him away from me.*

He kissed me, deep and hard, as I caged my legs around him, refusing to let go. Suddenly tears filled my eyes and I was overtaken by the torrent of emotions inside me … I whispered words that shouldn't have left my lips, "Please don't go to the race," I sobbed, my face buried in his neck. "*Please*, I'm so terrified that you'll be killed. Don't go."

I heard myself as if from a distance and at first, I didn't give a damn, but then he stilled in my arms, and it all shattered. I refused to open my eyes, and when I felt him begin to pull away, I immediately let him go and turned away to curl into a ball of shame.

I heard him silently get off the bed, and the sounds of him beginning to pull his jeans on. I should have done the same, so I could quickly show him out of the house, but I couldn't find the backbone to uncurl myself enough to meet his eyes.

He didn't say a word as he left.

When I heard the front door shut, I wiped the tears off my face.

I sat up and looked around my room, which seemed even more than a mess than ever before. I was still dazed from all that had just happened. I looked down in wonder at my still soaking wet pussy. I looked around, but could find no trace of the condom. He must have taken it with him. I thought I heard a sound outside my window and I jumped out of bed. Making myself look as decent as possible, I stepped out of the room in search of Nichole and Jess.

She wasn't in the garden, but in the kitchen with the door closed. Jess was playing in her sandpit in the garden. She was engrossed in building her castle she didn't even notice my presence as I stood by the door. Nichole however shut the book that she had been reading, and rested a dark gaze on me.

Her question was quite simple. "What the fuck was that all about?"

Widening my eyes meaningfully, I looked from her to Jess, then back to her.

She stared at me as though I were out of my mind. "You think *that* is the worst thing she's heard today? How the fuck could you do that here?"

I sighed deeply. "It wasn't planned, I swear it."

"What do you mean?" she asked, rising as she approached me. "What's going on with you Della?"

"It is *just* today. I'm finished with him," I said, and went past her to retrieve a bottle of water from the refrigerator. I drained it all in a heartbeat.

"You're finished?" she asked, her voice dripping with disbelief. "Somehow, I don't think so. You sounded like ten men were screwing the life out of you. I thought the whole house was going to collapse."

There were no arguments there especially as I had to hold onto the edge of the counter since I still couldn't stand properly.

"And I saw him," she said. "*Fuck. I* was going to skin you alive for defiling our house with some lowlife, but *goddamn it, girl.*"

I turned to her, confused. "Are you scolding me or ..."

She grinned suddenly. "I don't know, but when my shock has settled, you're going to tell me all about it."

"I might," I said.

She frowned. "But please don't bring him to our home again," she warned, genuine concern in her tone. "If he is part of an MC, it could be dangerous for us."

"Mommy!" Jess screamed suddenly.

We both turned to see that Jess had finally noticed my presence. I looked at Jess with my eyebrows raised.

She just shrugged and gave me a no-idea-don't-look-at-me expression.

"Hey, honey," I called out to Jess and she came running towards me, her face beaming with joy. I scooped her sandy little body up into my arms. "Where have you two been all afternoon, hmmm?"

"We missed you," she whispered in my ear.

"Well, so did I," I said.

"Mommy, can we have dinner together tonight? All three of us."

I pulled a little away so I could see her face. "Jess, you know I'm not your Mommy, right?"

She nodded sadly. "Yeah, but can we just pretend?"

"Why?"

She played with my hair and avoided my eyes. "Because all the other kids have mommies."

For a second, I wanted to cry with sadness for her. Then I smiled, a big happy smile. "Okay, let's do that. It'll be fun."

She perked up. "Really?"

I tickled her tummy. "Yes, really."

"Yay," she said throwing both her arms around my neck and kissing my face with big wet kisses.

I met Nichole's gaze. I couldn't be sure, but I thought I saw tears in her eyes.

# BONE

Group trips to purchase firearms were the least strenuous duties I had as the Road Captain of the club.

Today we were riding in Snake's Silverado. The mindlessness of being a passenger in a car rather than navigating a Harley was quite welcome, especially useful given the state I was in. I was completely unable to take Della off my mind.

I knew fucking her would be extremely enjoyable, but what I'd failed to anticipate was that it would blow my fucking world wide open. She had been haunting me from the moment I looked up and saw her, but when I saw her at Reno's I almost completely lost my shit. The eyes of the other members on her made me feel like a madman. I wanted to tear their eyes out of their ogling sockets. I felt as if a raw wound had opened up in my body, and anybody and everybody could touch and prod at it.

Now they all knew what she looked like. It had compromised her in a way that she couldn't even comprehend. My intention to completely block her out of my world had been ruined by my own weakness. If only I had not gone to her that night when the kid had been shot. My life hadn't prepared me for this. I didn't know how to navigate things from here onwards.

I turned my face toward the sun. No more empty promises. I was determined not to go to her again. No matter how much I wanted to. Not until I had done what I had set out to do. Not until I was sure there would be no blowback.

In an hour, we arrived at the simple detached house in the quiet neighborhood in Woodsbrow. An elderly woman came out with a wicker tray of nuts to sort through. She took one look at the six of us, all rough-looking troublemakers, added another deep wrinkle to her wrinkled brow, and turned herself and her wooden chair away from us.

"Evening, Miss Ryder," RJ greeted loudly.

"It's Mrs. Ryder," she corrected venomously without bothering to spare any of us a glance.

I didn't blame her.

"Yes ma'am," he mocked.

"What trouble have ya'all brought with you this time round?"

"No trouble ma'am," I said quietly. "We'll be in and out in no time."

She responded with a bitter *humph*, and we continued on our way.

"One day, we're gonna have to take care of that bitc—' RJ began.

I struck a blow on the back of his head - before he could complete the statement - that sent him sprawling into the house straight on his face.

He immediately shot to his feet, ready to pick a fight, but at the look that Tyler sent his way, he just glared at me and dusted off the front of his t-shirt.

Rugrat emerged from the bright green kitchen of the homely house, bare chested, his gut so round and shiny he looked like a blossoming pig. His beard, his hands, and his lips were stained and glistening with whatever he had been eating. "What is this?" he roared. "Y'all said you'll be here at three-thirty."

"So what? We're thirty minutes early." RJ tapped him on his man breasts. "We're forced to be spontaneous these days ... in case you haven't heard, there's a hit out on us."

"What's that about?" he asked. "You all haven't even launched an attack and they came calling?"

"That's not why we're here," Tyler snapped impatiently. He never was one for gossip and chit chat. "Get to it."

"Yes sir," Rugrat said, wiping his stained hands against his sagging mustard corduroy pants.

We ushered ourselves through the small door as we'd done countless of times in the past. The narrow stairs led down the basement. The dimly lit space was thick with the stink of some sort of barbecued meat from a pile of half-eaten wings on the floor.

"Where are they?" Tyler asked.

Rugrat pulled out the string of keys he kept around his waist and walked to one of the freezers. After unlocking the massive padlock that secured it, he threw it open to reveal duffel bags of weapons.

RJ and I unloaded the bags and put them on the ground to take stock of their contents.

There were almost a hundred weapons in total. Ten machine guns, handguns, shotguns, and rifles. RJ counted them aloud excitedly, confirming the numbers for me and I took careful account of them.

Once the payment was complete, we were on our way.

"Hey, have some wings before ya'll go," he bellowed, as we walked away.

Tank and Rooster only tapped his hanging breasts and stomach mockingly and we were on our way.

Only RJ for some reason deemed it appropriate to overturn his plate of wings, cackling excitedly as it tumbled onto the floor in a spicy mess.

"Fuck you, RJ!" Rugrat cursed.

I shut my eyes briefly to dissipate the cloud of irritation I felt. The man was such a fucking liability. One of these days ...

I took my place in the car and my head filled once again with Della.

The way she'd screamed out my name, the recollection of the mischief glinting in her eyes as she blew my cock, the way she whimpered when she came, and the way she begged me not to ...

"Bone," I heard my name being called.

I turned to see the others eyes on me.

"Where's your mind man?" Tank asked, amused.

Tyler watched me through the rearview mirror as he drove.

But it was RJ who became more excited than anyone else. "It's the girl, isn't it?" RJ asked. "God damn, she sure was tasty. Did you guys see that ass on her, man? Heck with an ass like that she wouldn't need toilet paper, I'd lick her hole clean for her. You must have had a feast." He gave a crazy laugh.

I knew he was trying to get to me.

"Can I have her too ... after you're done with her, of course? C'mon man, sharing is caring."

I held myself back from reacting so they wouldn't think I attributed any sort of importance to her whatsoever, but I could feel my fuse quickly burning up. I tightened my fist against the door's handles and swore that one more word from him and he wouldn't be able to walk in the upcoming week

"Shut the fuck up, you stupid piece of shit," Tyler snarled.

RJ grunted, but he screwed his head back on and kept his loathsome, stinking trap shut for the rest of the trip.

As we sped through the highway back to our storage base, I thought on how best I could keep Della as far away as possible from this whole fucking mess.

## DELLA RAY

I was at work when Nichole called to tell me that Jess must have caught a cold in her daycare. If she had been a healthy child I wouldn't have worried, but with her weak heart it made me fearful and anxious. So when I emerged back into the bar, I was in the lowest of moods.

Lena came up to me then with a tray in her hand. "Someone is looking for you."

"Who?"

She quickly ran her gaze around the bar. "Her. The blondie over there."

At first, I couldn't place her, but when she turned towards us, I instantly remembered who she was. Halting my steps, I regarded her and wondered what this visit could possibly be about. But by the time I headed over and took my seat beside her, I was ready to handle whatever trouble she had brought along.

She looked me over, from my cheap dark sneakers to the

short black skirt and T-shirt I was wearing. There was very little trace of makeup left on my face, and my hair was pulled back into a ponytail high on my head.

"You look different," she scoffed, and drained her glass. It was hard liquor too. Hanging out with so many rugged men all the time must have toughened her up for it. "If I had known you were this plain perhaps I wouldn't have bothered making the effort to come here. Has Bone seen you this way?"

I stared at her in surprise. "Did you come here just to insult me?"

"No," she said with a mocking smile. "I just came to see what was so special about you. Apparently nothing. Bone must have truly meant it then."

I knew I shouldn't ask, but I couldn't stop myself. "Meant what?"

She turned her wide eyes to me. She was wearing purple lenses today. "He said you were just a fuck, but you couldn't get over it. You had started to stalk him." She placed her claws of blood-red finger nails on my shoulder as if in consolation. "It's okay, I get it. When he fucked me I too, almost lost my mind, but I got real. After all, he's racked up quite the reputation around town. Take it from me. Your best bet is to just relish the memory and leave him the fuck alone."

I don't know how I knew, but I knew she was lying. Bone would never have told her something like that. I slapped her hand off my shoulder and lifted my chin proudly. "Is that why you came here? Are you that insecure?"

"Nope," she responded. "I was sent by the club to find out what was going on between you two. Let me tell you this.

Keep away from the man. He is vicious and cruel. Not worthy of the trouble."

Well, she had changed her tune, and in the bat of an eyelid too. I watched her smile grimly as she rose from the stool and walked out of the bar. My gaze blurred at the force of the hurt I felt. Not because of what she had said, but because I wanted Bone so much while it was becoming clearer and clearer that I would never be able to adapt to the life he lived and the people he ran with. I felt the tears trickle down my cheeks, but I brushed them roughly away and went back to work.

I couldn't have Bone and that was that.

# BONE

We pulled into the speedway south of Arnault. I had been cleared out for the race. Not all of the members were present yet, but the crowd had their eyes on all ninety of us as we rode on our bikes into the already buzzing commotion. I expected most civilians to avoid this race, but there seemed to be a great deal of ordinary folk watching attentively beyond the track's barricade.

That worried me.

Most of us present were attired in bulletproof vests and a few of us who could find our way around the authorities were armed with the needed weapons, but these civilians were to all intents and purposes … naked. It was pure speculation on their part to think that nothing bad would go wrong since there were police everywhere and it never had in the past, but it took only a second for someone like RJ to lose his head.

One dumbass could get two dozen killed in an instant.

We were set up some distance away from the strip so we

took our place and posted our eyes and ears on every movement around the event.

On our way here, we had sighted police cars on high alert, and amongst the crowds were undercover cops with their eyes peeled for trouble. The press was present but a safe distance away. You couldn't blame them, who wanted to be the recipient of a crazy outburst from a bunch of outlaws. I took a seat on one of the chairs underneath our canopy and watched the glistening machines ready themselves on the tracks.

The race was set to begin anytime now.

This event was hosted by the Hells Angels since theirs was the club with more than half a century of existence. Their various chapters in the state all deemed it important to show up at the event to establish their presence and strength in the area.

Tyler hung out on his motorcycle with RJ in his line of vision, in case he lost it, misbehaved, or there was an attack on him. My eyes were on our rival club, Death's Hand. They had been positioned strategically and quite a distance from us, but that wasn't enough to stop whatever trouble anyone wanted to cause in the arena.

The races began while I watched as the riders set out from the strip and zoomed into the distance. I suppose it would have been entertaining if we weren't in fear of our heads being blown off at any moment.

Forty-five minutes into the event and I spotted a few members from the Death's Hand club heading over to our stand. Our members were scattered strategically to ensure we had at least two members of their club in our sights to attack if tensions got too high. There was no alarm as the president of the club, Warden, and their sergeant at arms, Vice, headed over.

Snake and Tyler went to meet them, but I remained in my seat and kept my eye on them.

They spoke for a while, before they turned and called out to me. I didn't want to go, but neither did I want to be the dumbass that cost the others their lives, so I rose and headed over to the meeting. My sunglasses were over my eyes to shield my gaze from them all.

"They just explained," Snake said to me in his calm voice. "The attack was an impulsive offense from three of their members. They've since been severely punished. You were directly affected in this. What retribution do you want?"

I transferred my gaze to the two men. "I'm fine," I responded. "One of our members however is now paralyzed in the hospital. How are they going to pay for that?"

"We heard he wasn't a member, but a hanger," Vice said. "The matter then isn't too severe."

"He was a fucking member," I growled.

Both men hardened their gazes on me.

"Take it easy," Snake cautioned.

"And even if he is not a member, isn't he a fucking human being? He was the sole provider for his grandmother."

"What do you want then?" Warden asked. "Cover his grand-mother's bills?"

"And the kid's financial needs. For the rest of his life," I said harshly.

Tyler turned to me. "That's fucking insane, Bone. Where's your head at? Are even our financial needs assured?"

"I don't give a fuck," I stated. "Either that or we break the legs of all three of your members."

"Your man's insane," Vice spoke up.

I took my sunglasses off to glare into his eyes just in case he thought I was joking.

"He's speaking his mind," Snake responded.

His voice sounded so still and cold, it even sent a shiver down my spine. Of the members of the club, Snake was the only one who caused a reaction in me.

"Then how about we speak ours too," Warden shot back. "That bloody moron RJ. He was fucking disrespectful on our own turf. How are you planning to deal with him?"

Both Tyler and Snake shared looks with each other. The immediate and appropriate decision would have been to ban him from the club, strip him of membership, but he was the source for the huge deal we had in the works for the upcoming meth transaction. None of us could afford to lose him, or let anyone know why we couldn't.

"You know he's a bit of a nut head," Snake said mildly. "We're still thinking of what w—"

"Let me help you there," Vice cut in. "Take away his patch, and send him over to us. And we'll settle the score of his offenses in our bar directly with him."

"We can't do that," Tyler answered instantly, his voice warned them that the issue was not up for discussion or negotiation.

"Then how do you suggest we solve this then?" Vice asked, his voice low and threatening.

Just then, I heard a vehicle drive up and turned to see a pickup truck a few yards away from us. It was pulling into the arena. Four members of the rival club jumped out of it. Then the driver jumped out and began to put on leather gloves and I was instantly on guard. "What's that bastard over there doing?" I asked.

We all saw the corners of the driver's mouth lift in a sick smile. I could see that Tyler had also noted his gloves.

"Tell him to move away from that truck," Snake said. "We want to see what's behind him."

"It's no biggie," Warden said. "Calm yourself, man."

"If he makes one wrong move, this entire arena will turn into a grave site," Tyler stated as a thick blue vein was already ticking on his temple. It was throbbing with the thirst for blood. He bared his teeth at the men around the truck in a humorless smile that rattled my bones.

"May I remind ya'all that this place is packed with cops? One wrong move and we'll all be spending the next decade in jail," Snake said.

"We definitely won't be joining you." Vice laughed. "Our support gear is bringing in quite the buck so the best attorney is not a problem. Your club however, I hear is still ... struggling. How many of those shirts have you all been able to sell this month?"

Flash fast and before any of us could even react, Tyler's fist swung into the air and smashed Vice squarely in the jaw.

The big man staggered backwards before falling heavily into the grass. It was as if the very earth under our feet quaked. In that moment, I could feel the entire air of the arena change as all eyes left the race and turned to us.

"The fuck." Warden turned to us.

Snake also turned to Tyler. "Calm down," he immediately intervened, his hands raised. "You both know how quickly this can get out of hand."

Vice, red with embarrassment jumped to his feet, but before he could pull out whatever he had in his pocket, his president crashed into him to shake him to his senses.

I noted the moments as they passed, my hand was just within reach of the gun I had tucked into the back of my jeans. *Come on. Don't fucking do it.*

"I'm gonna fucking kill him," Vice roared out his anger. He was furious at being hit in front of all these people.

I noticed then that some top-ranking members of the Hells Angels, Durban brotherhood, and the Mongols began to approach us from every side. Vicious looking men, most with protruding bellies and wild beards, their glares hidden behind their small framed glasses. My attention shifted from the brawl in front of me to the president of the Mongols club as he approached along with the pack.

As I stared unblinkingly at him, whatever civility I had nursed through this entire debacle dissipated quickly and was replaced by the vicious thirst for blood that had driven me into this life in the first place. Two years ago, he had shot and killed Mace Herald the only true friend I had in this damn world. Barely an hour after I had spoken to him, he was gunned down by the monster who was now approaching me.

He held my gaze too, as he neared. No doubt, he was perplexed as to why I always had my gaze fixed on him anytime we came into contact. He didn't look away and kept his equally unblinking gaze on me.

The Hells Angels President, Leroy Dawson spoke, "Y'all need to take this somewhere else. This whole place is crawling with bugs and they're looking to take us all down. The war is not going to be between just you two anymore, if that happens."

Snake stepped up to the Deaths Hand president. "One more time, what are you going to do about the boy who lost his legs through your attack?" He looked between the leaders and his still fuming sergeant of arms.

"We can't solve this today," Warden said. "Let's tackle this another time."

"He needs his medical fees covered." I growled. "Today. What are you going to do about that?"

"You should have fucking restricted that dog you call a member to behave then. And we don't fucking owe—"

My gun flew out at the speed of light and pressed right against his forehead.

"You fucking moron," someone swore as the entire gathering around us stiffened, their hands going to their own weapons in alarm. The race forgotten.

"How do you pick em, Snake?" Vice mocked.

Snake narrowed his gaze at me, surprised at my move. "We'll handle all of this next time. Bone, put your gun away."

A few seconds ticked by before I could calm myself sufficiently to tuck my weapon away. I turned and stormed away from the gathering.

I was standing at the edge of the canopy when Tyler and Snake walked up to me. They were both clearly annoyed.

"What the fuck was that all about, Bone?" Tyler roared. "You losing your mind now like RJ?"

I kept silent, but I knew I wasn't going to be able to get away with it.

"You'll be punished," Snake spat.

I couldn't have cared less.

## DELLA RAY

"Hey."

I was brushing my teeth so I could head into the shower when Nichole popped her head into the bathroom. When I saw the look in her eyes, something hit hard against my chest. "What is it?"

"A video surfaced from the race," she said. "It's everywhere online and on the news. A fight broke out, but there were no guns involved. Only fists. At a point though, it seemed like they were going to go at each other's throats."

"Why are you telling me this?" I mumbled, turning the faucet off.

"I thought you'd like to know if he got hurt."

"I don't care." I replaced my toothbrush and snatched the bath curtain aside so I could get in for a shower.

"Okay," she responded and left.

As the hot cascade poured atop my head, I felt the knot in my heart start to loosen, but then the moment I remembered the girl's words in the bar. I tried to remind myself that it all meant nothing ... him, her ... them. All of it was of no consequence whatsoever to my life and wellbeing.

Why then was my heart breaking?

～

"Hey, I think we saw your guy on the news," Gloria said as I arrived into the diner's kitchen.

I ignored her and retrieved the supplies I needed to replenish my section. I really didn't need any more aggravation this evening. I was already like a cat on a hot tin roof. Then at that moment, my phone rang so I slammed down the thick jars of ketchup and mustard on the table and pressed it to my ear. "What?" I barked.

"That's how you answer your phone," came the response.

I couldn't breathe. I really couldn't breathe. The fire that had been charring my chest over the last few days blazed like someone had poured a jug of kerosene on it.

"How did you get my number?" I snarled.

He went silent. Then ... "I need to see you, Della."

I scoffed in disbelief. "You're out of stories to sing to your buddies? You want some new ones now?"

"What are you talking about?" he asked.

I hated how cold and calm his voice was while I sounded like I was running on coals. It wasn't fair. I was always the one suffering. He always took what he wanted and went on his way. No more. No more. "We agreed not to contact each other ever again. Why are you calling me?"

"It was a rough night. And through it all, I couldn't stop thinking about you. How do I get you off my mind, Della?"

I could feel myself start to soften. God, how I wanted to believe him. To be with him. But I couldn't. I had Jess to think of. If I had been single, perhaps I could have seen a life with him as an adventure, but with Jess, no way. I could never do that to her. I took a deep breath. "Well for starters, delete my damn number."

"I need to see you, baby."

I hated myself for asking but I couldn't hold back. "Are you okay?"

"I'm not," he said. "You have your shift at the diner, right? I'll come over."

"Please don't!" I snapped.

Silence.

"Why not?" he asked quietly.

"I don't want anything to do with you, Bone. I've got my life and you've got yours. This is what we agreed on, remember?"

"Yeah. You're right," he said, and the line went dead.

For the longest time all I did was hold the phone, the beep singing of endings and death in my ear. The door to the diner dinged open and at the sight of our manager, I put my phone away and went on with my job. I think I worked on autopilot. Smiling, pouring coffee, carrying plates, ringing up the register. All the while I could hear him saying, *I need to see you, baby.*

I was exhausted by the time I took my apron off. When I went back home, I held Jess in my arms, and I knew it was worth it. "I would do it all again for you," I whispered in her ear.

"What did you say, Mommy?" she asked innocently.

"Nothing, sweetie," I said, holding back the tears. Any sacrifice would be worth it for this little angel.

"Mommy, can we have dinner together tonight?"

"No, babygirl. I have to work, but Nichole will have dinner with you."

"Can Nichole work and you have dinner with me for once?"

I started crying then. I couldn't help it. Everything was so messed up. When Jess asked me why I was crying, I told her I had dust in my eyes.

"Poor, poor Mommy," she said sadly.

## DELLA RAY

I was an hour into my shift when I received a call from an unknown number so I watched it ring, fighting with all my might not to pick it up. It stopped and I sighed with relief. It would all be fine.

Just before I took the first step away from it, it began to ring again. I pulled it out of my pocket and placed the phone to my ear. "Hello?" I hated how breathless and eager my voice sounded.

"Della-Ray," my sister's voice came through and my heart sunk into my stomach.

"Denise?" I hadn't seen her in four years. Ever since Jess was born.

"I'm at your home with Nichole," she responded. "I hear you're at work."

The hair on my arms stood on end. "What are you doing there?"

She ignored the question. "I just saw Jess. You've done a great job with raising her. Can you get home a bit earlier today, though? My boyfriend and I need to be on our way in about an hour."

"Can I talk to Nichole please?" I asked.

There was shuffling and movement as I waited for her to be put on. I placed the tray down on the nearest table and focused on my call.

"Hey," she said, her voice unnaturally bright.

"How did Denise know where we live?"

"I told her. She wanted to see how her daughter is doing. Umm … can you ask for the rest of the night off? They need to speak to you."

Nichole sounded strange and my heart began to pound in my chest. I knew something was very wrong. I ended the call and hurried over to Henry, my suspicion about what was going on becoming too nerve racking for me to remain. He gave me the rest of the night off, and I was in a taxi and on my way home in no time.

There was a small beat up Honda in our driveway.

I hurried into the house and burst into the living room. Jess was asleep in Nichole's arms. Her mother and my sister were seated on the adjoining sofa. She was looking much, much older than was normal for her age of twenty-six. Beside her was a man in a fedora whom I assumed was her new partner.

I ignored the both of them and immediately hurried over to Jess. "Is she okay?" I asked.

Nichole nodded. "Talk to them," she said. Then she rose to

her feet, with Jess's head on her shoulders and headed back to Jess's room.

I turned towards my sister. My question was simple. "What are you doing here?"

"We're here to take Jess with us."

"What?"

"We're here to take Jess with us," she repeated.

"What do you mean?"

"We're taking her to the orphanage down at Cuyahoga. It's about two hours away from here. I signed her up for admission when she was born. I gave them a call just now and they say they can immediately start looking for a family who would—"

"You must be out of your mind!" I yelled before she could finish her ugly sentence.

"I'm not, Della-Ray and I'm not joking either."

I started to walk away from her. When I heard footsteps behind me, I hurried on and as soon as I arrived at Jess's room, I shut the door behind me and locked it. Nichole was sitting on Jess's bed and patting my baby's stomach.

"What's going on?" I asked Nichole. I felt like a hunted animal. No matter where I turned, there was danger.

She opened her mouth to speak, then shut it, guilt filled her eyes, and I understood what she had done. Denise began to knock on the door but I ignored it. I directed my fury at Nichole. "You called her?"

"No. She called me. She just wanted to know where we had moved to and how you were coping. I told her the truth."

"Why, Nichole? Why? You know what she's like."

"She's Jess's mother."

"I'm Jess's mother!" I screamed, tears streaming down my face. "I'm Jess's mother. Me. I'm the one that loves her. How could you, Nichole? How could you?"

"I'm sorry, okay. At that time, I really believed it was better if she was with a family that could afford her medical bills."

There was a stronger knock on the door, and I knew it was the man who had come with Denise.

"We don't have time for this," his deep voice came through, and when he banged on the door impatiently, both Nichole and I jumped.

"Della-Ray, she is my child," my sister said. "And I have the right to decide what is best for her. Let her—"

"You have absolutely no fucking right!" I yelled back. "I've cared for her since the moment you gave birth to her and abandoned her. And now you want to make her life a living hell? What fucking family will accept a child like her and love her more than I will? She's no fucking orphan, she's mine and I'm not letting you take her. I'm going to take care of her."

"Della-Ray, you can't give her all that she needs," she yelled back.

"And a stranger could?" I roared back.

"Yes! Listen to me, I've already spoken to the orphanage

director, and she says she will find the best home possible for Jess. She will have all she needs and you'll be able to move on with your life."

"She is my life!" I screamed back at her, "and you are going to take her away from me. You lost that right when you abandoned her."

With all the noise, Jess came awake with a low cry, and I instantly rushed over to take her into my arms. "You're not going anywhere," I promised as I rocked her in my arms. "You'll be perfectly fine with me."

The moments went by and the pounding continued, and it terrified me, especially when Denise got fed up and yelled, "I'm going right now to call the cops. This is fucking kidnapping."

"Della-Ray," Nichole began. "We should let her in. Calm her down. If she calls the police, we're done for. She has a legal right over Jess."

I raised a wide-eyed haunted gaze to her. "She's never taken care of her. Not even once since she gave birth to her. And now you want me to hand my baby over to her?" Does Jess even mean anything to you?"

"You're not thinking right. We need to diffuse this situation before it escalates out of control." With a frown, she circled the bed and headed towards the door.

But I couldn't think rationally. "Don't you dare open that do — No, Nichole!"

She twisted the lock and the door swung open to reveal the man waiting at the door.

Impatience was written all over his face. He came into the room and I shot to my feet, a scream erupting from my throat. "Don't you fucking touch me, or her!" Jess began crying once again, and I rocked her against me. "If you dare touch her, I swear to God I'll kill you."

With a heavy sigh, he turned around and exited the room, leaving Nichole and me clutching Jess. There was sadness in Nichole's eyes. I hurried straight for the door, banged it shut with my free hand, and twisted the lock, leaving only both of us in the room.

"They're going to call the cops Della-Ray!" Nichole said.

"For fuck's sake, Della," Denise called from outside. "Don't be such an ass. She's my child and I'm taking her. You can do it the easy way or the hard way."

"Don't hand her over," Nichole said suddenly.

I looked at Nichole in surprise. "I thought you wanted me to?"

"I did, once, before I realized no one can love Jess more than you. Denise doesn't care about Jess at all. I didn't tell you she was coming because she said she wanted to surprise you. She had a new man she wanted to show to you and she also wanted to look in on Jess and see how she was doing. Everything was going so well for about fifteen minutes after she arrived. She never said anything about an adoption agency until she heard Jess call you Mommy. It's just pure jealously that's making her take Jess away from you, even though she doesn't want Jess and she can see how much Jess loves you."

Even at that tense moment, I felt a surge of joy that Nichole hadn't betrayed me.

"What do we do?" she whispered. "Do you want me to call my boss and ask him to come help us? He has a lawyer and everything."

"No." I pulled my phone out of my pocket, as I rocked Jess to buy her silence and began to scroll desperately through my call log for the day. I found his phone number and prayed to God that it would ring when I called him. It did, but he didn't pick up and it rang until it disconnected. I wouldn't give up. "Pick up you bastard," I whispered, and tried again. And again. Until finally, there was a response on my fifth attempt.

"Della-Ray?" he said, surprise and urgency in his voice.

My knees almost gave out in relief. "I need you!" I cried out to him. "They want to take Jess away from me. Please. I need you right now!"

"Who wants to take—"

"I'll tell you when you get here. "Please ... please just come over right now as fast as possible. I'm in Jess's bedroom, opposite from mine. I'll owe you for the rest of my life, I swear it."

There was no hesitation in his voice as he answered, "I'm on my way."

# BONE

I had never ridden so fast through the night.

In fifteen minutes, I was at Della-Ray's door. A car was parked outside in the driveway, but to my relief it didn't belong to anyone I knew from the club. I pounded on the door and it was pulled open almost immediately by her roommate. I spotted her as I left Della's bedroom the last time I was here. She was sitting in the kitchen and our eyes met, but not a single word had been exchanged between us.

"Where's Della-Ray?" I demanded.

She jerked her head towards one of the doors. There were two others sitting on the sofas and staring at me, but they weren't my concern. I headed straight for Jess's bedroom, and they both jumped up to come after me.

"Hey!" the woman called.

"What the—?" the man said, grabbing my hand and pulling at it, as I reached her door.

I was in the worst mood I could possibly be in so at the rude contact, I looked from the place on my arm that the scrawny brute who was holding back to his face.

"Who the hell are you to just barge into someone else's house?" he asked.

I then noticed he took a step back at the icy look in my eyes. "If you touch me again, you're going to lose that hand," I stated quietly.

His hand dropped off as if I had electrocuted him. Calmly, I turned to tap against the door. "Della-Ray!" I called out.

"Bone!" she answered immediately. The relief in her voice was palpable. "You're here."

"Yeah, open the door."

I could hear her rushing to it, fumbling with the key before she was able to pull it open. The state she was in made my heart slam against the walls of my chest. Her eyes were red and her face was streaked with tears. Even her hair looked disheveled as Jess was asleep in her arms.

"What happened?" I asked, taking a step inside. "Did anyone touch you?"

She shook her head, but gave the audience behind me a dark look. Carefully placing the child on the bed, she came to the doorway. After ushering me out, she locked the door behind her, and turned to me. "Thank you so much for coming, Bone."

"What's going on?"

"That's my sister and her man. They want to take Jess away—"

"That's right. I'm that child's mother, and I'm calling the cops," her sister threatened. "You're going to be in real trouble today. The both of you!"

Irritated by the racket, I focused on her sister. I would never have thought she was Della's sister. Harshly bleached hair, heavy make-up and dressed like a slut, she was the exact opposite of Della. She looked like she had lived a hard life. "Can you not see that your sister is upset? Where's the sisterly love, lady? Can you please give her a bit of time to calm down?"

She gave me a sulky sour look in return, but shut her trap.

I turned back to Della-Ray, but the tears wouldn't stop running down her eyes. She was so visibly shaken that I wanted to hurt her sister and that excuse for a man she had brought with her. I pulled Della into my arms and held her close to my body.

"I'm so sorry," Della apologized for her outburst, but when I saw that she couldn't stop, I tightened my hold on her and rested her head on my chest to calm her down.

I rubbed her back gently. "It's okay," I said softly. "I'm here now."

She settled into my embrace and I ran my fingers through her hair. I turned to her friend whom I found watching us with deep interest and surprise. "What's going on?" I asked.

She immediately snapped to attention to explain, "She wants to take Jess away with her and dump her in an orphanage."

Della-Ray started sobbing again.

"It's nobody's business what I do with her! I'm sick of fucking do-gooders and busy bodies trying to tell me what to do with my own daughter."

"What makes her your daughter?" I asked. "Where have you been for the last four years? As far as anyone with a brain can see, Della is more of a mother to her than you've ever been. So how dare you barge in here unannounced and attempt to just take her away? How can that be good for your daughter? Della is all she's known since the day she was born."

She was shocked and wide-eyed at my accusation. "Who the hell are you?" she asked.

"That's none of your business and not what should concern you tonight," was my response.

"Wow," she went on. "Della-Ray, you have someone to fight your battles for you now? I suggest you be careful. He looks like he could slit your throat in the middle of the night."

Just then, we heard sirens blasting through the air as they arrived at the house.

With a victorious glance, her sister rushed to the door to welcome the officers in.

Della-Ray looked up at me with fear in her eyes, I told her not to worry.

She still let go of me to turn around to welcome them. They had barely arrived at the house before her sister began to sing her song and I honestly couldn't believe that they were related.

The officers glanced at me as she made up accusations about my forcing my way into the house and threatening them all to which Della-Ray immediately tried to defend, but I held her arm back, and shook my head to discourage it. There was no need.

When she was done with her complaining, the officer in charge turned to me, one eyebrow cocked. "Miller?"

"I've got it all handled," was my simple response.

"Family dispute then?" his partner asked.

I nodded.

"Sure." With a polite tip of their hats at me, both men turned around and exited the house.

Her sister stared after them in shock.

So did Della-Ray. "What just happened?" she asked.

"We've had some run-ins," I explained briefly. "They're familiar enough with me. Come take a seat," I said to her and holding her hand, I led her over to the sofa. "You both need to talk about this. You love Jess and think she is best with you, but your sister is her mother after all. Talk about it." I settled her on the sofa, then turned to her sister who was still fuming at the door. "You don't want to settle this?"

The man she was with headed over to sit opposite Della. He patted the area next to him.

We all looked towards her sister, but she refused to comply. Her jaw was set in a stubborn line.

"What's the real problem here?" I asked. "Della's taken care of Jess since she was a baby. Why the sudden need to take her to an orphanage?"

"First, tell me why the hell I have to explain myself to you?" she sniped.

God, help me, I wanted to shake some sense into her, but thankfully Della's friend stepped in, "It's my fault. I was the one who originally gave Denise the impression that Della Ray wasn't coping with the financial stress of taking care of Jess's medical bills," she confessed.

I could see the outrage bloom on Della's face, but I held her hand tighter to indicate that she should let it go and calm down.

Ignoring Della's expression, her friend looked straight at me. "Jess was not *living* and it hurt me to watch her keep struggling just to make ends meet. My intention was to call Denise and tell her to make contributions towards Jess's care instead of acting as though she didn't exist, but it seems she would prefer to put her in an orphanage."

"I still can't understand why I can't do with my child as I please," her sister piped in.

"I know what your problem is," Della yelled. "You feel guilty and you're afraid that Jess will eventually come to resent you. Your pride is threatened and instead of finding ways to take responsibility for her, you want her to be abandoned all over again, and make your incapability someone else's problem."

"How dare you talk to me that way?" her sister spat, her eyes shooting angry sparks.

I understood what was going on now and knew that it wasn't my place to decide what the outcome would be. "Della," I said to her. "Let's not drag this out any further. You've heard from your sister and since she is Jess's mother, you have to consider her option."

"But—" Della began.

I shook my head at her, then turned to Denise. "What would Della have to do to convince you that she is capable of taking care of Jess?"

That threw her. It was clear she hadn't given it any thought at all. "I just want what's best for her," she said finally. "A good family. A good education. Her medical bills paid."

"True, you have the right of being Jess's biological mother, but Della has been Jess's guardian for a while now, and for abdicating your motherhood for so long, you also do not have complete right over Jess any longer. So, let's give this a month. Now that Della knows what is important to you, she can work towards proving that she can provide all those things on your list and if she can't then, you will need to inform her of how the adoption process can be made more acceptable to her."

"I like the idea," Nichole declared. "Let's revisit this again after a month."

I rose to my feet and looked at Nichole. "Do they have room and board with you for the night?"

"Uh. No. We don't have any room."

"Let's go," her sister's partner said, and rose to his feet.

"How can we just leave?" her sister fumed.

"If you don't leave, I'll throw you out right now," I stated in a low voice.

She glared at me with venom in her eyes.

Her partner was eventually able to pull her out of the house and soon the door shut in complete silence.

"I'll be on my way too," I said to both the girls.

Della's eyes filled with tears and I knew what she wanted to say, but that the words didn't seem sufficient. With my thumb, I caught a tear as it rolled down her face. "You seem tough but in the end you're just a crybaby, aren't you?" I teased.

She lightly pounded her fist on my chest, and it made me smile despite the mess around us.

I turned around to leave but Della-Ray grabbed my arm, lifted herself up to the tip of her toes, and pressed a kiss to my cheek. She hurried off then and I was left staring after her. She was so cute I couldn't breathe. Shaking my head, I turned and saw Nichole watching us. She saw me to the door.

"I misjudged you," she said quietly.

I had a few words for her too. "You're a good friend to Della. She's mad right now though."

"She's all bark and no bite," she said with a laugh.

I smiled in agreement. Then she closed the door. I got on my Harley and rode into the night, much, much lighter than I could have dreamed I would feel, given the day I'd had.

## DELLA RAY

"I'm making you breakfast as an apology," Nichole said to me as I walked into the kitchen the next morning.

I rubbed my eyes. "Why aren't you at work?"

"Remember I told you I'm going to help you. Well, I told my boss, I have to get a part-time job and he said, he could spare me two days a week. So, I'm going out to find a job today. Who knows I might end up working with you at the diner," she said with a smile.

I stopped on my way to the refrigerator and stared at her in shock. "Are you serious?"

"Absolutely. We're going to make a plan of how we are going to care for Jess. Then we are going to call Denise, invite her over, and charm her into letting us have Jess. At the end of the day, she doesn't want Jess, she just got mad because she had thrown Jess away as worthless and you had turned her into something special and she was jealous of that. When she knows it's going to be both of us at the helm, she'll slink away. I know women like that. They don't have staying power."

I smiled slowly at her. "You know, I was thinking exactly the same last night. Denise has always been a bit of a dog in the manger. She wouldn't want a toy until I wanted it, but after a while, she would lose interest anyway. A month is a long time."

"Exactly. So … have you called him?"

"Who?" I asked.

"You aren't fooling anyone with the way you're blushing."

"No," I said, and continued on my journey towards the refrigerator. I opened the door and searched through the contents. My cheeks were hot, just as they had been the moment I opened my eyes this morning and remembered the way he had stepped in and handled it all so effectively and impressively on my behalf. A sweet warmth had flooded my chest. I made sure to cool my face down before I pulled my head away and shut the refrigerator.

Nichole stabbed a sausage and put it on a plate as I remembered I had come in for a glass of orange juice. I picked up a glass, reopened the refrigerator and filled it with juice from the carton.

As I drank, she kept speaking, "You know, I think I may have judged him too quickly. He seemed so mature and … umm … hunky. The way he resolved the issue yesterday. Very mature. And that whole black t-shirt, black jacket, and black jeans vibe he had going on … Woah!" She scraped scrambled eggs onto three plates. "I thought you said it was just a one-time thing, but the way he rushed over because of you ... that shows he cares."

I shrugged, not willing to participate in this.

She turned to look at me with curious eyes. "And what's the deal between him and the cops? How could they just leave that way unless they knew him? But how? They must trust his character, but how? And why? He's a freaking outlaw biker. He even made the news yesterday."

"They could be dirty cops," I suggested.

She considered the idea. "Oh, my God! Yes, that would explain everything. I saw a program on TV sometime back and they were saying how all these small police departments were all under the thumb of the Mafia or the Biker clubs. That's how they get their drugs into the state."

I had heard enough. I didn't want to hear anything else negative about Bone. He was a hero in my eyes at the moment and I wanted to keep it like that for a while longer. "Your bacon is burning," I pointed out.

She scrambled off to the stove while I exited the kitchen. I helped Jess into her pink blouse, pink skirt and pink shoes.

"Is Denise coming to visit again today?" she asked, carefully tying her shoelaces.

"Um ... no. Not today. She might be coming in a month's time."

"That's good. Because I like her. She's nice."

"Jess, you know she is your real mother, right?"

"Yeah." She looked at me and flashed me a brilliant smile. "But I still want to call you Mommy."

"But not when your mother is around, okay?"

"Why not?"

"Because she wants you to call her Mommy."

"Why?"

"Because she loves you."

She looked confused. "She does?"

I nodded.

She was silent as she thought about it. "So what will I call you when she's around then?"

"Call me Della."

She made a face. "Oooo ... I don't like that."

"Well, you know we all have to do things we don't like, right. I have to go to work even though I'd rather stay at home and play with you, but ..."

"You have to," she finished.

"Exactly. You don't like eating broccoli, but ..."

"I have to," she sang.

"I don't like eating spinach, but ..."

"You have to," she sang even louder.

I held back my laughter. "That's right. You don't like going to the dentist, but ..."

GEORGIA LE CARRE

"You have to," she screamed.

"Well done," I said then squashing her face to mine, I kissed her sweet, innocent mouth with a smacking noise. God, I loved her so much I would become a fugitive of the law and run away with her rather than let Denise put her in a home where she would be so frightened and lost. "Alright then. Let's go have some breakfast. Nichole is making a full English breakfast for us."

Her eyes lit up. "English breakfast?"

I grinned at her excited face. "Yup."

"With sausages?"

"Yup."

"What about bacon?"

"At least two slices per person," I said with a grave nod.

"And eggs too?"

"Eggs too."

"Scrambled?" she asked, her hands clasped in front of her.

"Scrambled," I confirmed.

"What about toast?"

"That too."

"And orange juice."

I giggled. "Of course."

"Oh goodie, Mommy. We're really having a big English breakfast!" she cried clapping her hands with glee.

And that was what we did. As I watched her and Nichole eating, I felt happy. No matter what it took, even if it meant groveling at Denise's feet or paying her money, I was determined to have Jess. By hook or by crook, I was keeping my baby.

# DELLA RAY

As I went through my day I couldn't stop thinking about Bone, but I also didn't want to call him. I had shunned him so thoroughly the previous day and yet, he had come through so completely for me that I felt a deep-seated sense of shame about the way I had treated him.

But by midday, I couldn't take it anymore and I went out to the back of the diner and placed a call to him. My heart was racing as his phone rang. All morning, I had mentally rehearsed everything I wanted to say.

Six rings in, when I had already decided to take the coward's way and hang up, he picked up. My heart skipped a beat. "I'm not a crybaby," I said.

He went silent for a few seconds. "Della-Ray?'

Immediately my paranoia went into overdrive. Hell, the man didn't even remember who I was. I tried to laugh it off. "Ha, ha, you go around calling everybody crybabies?"

"No, I only know one," he said.

I wrinkled my nose at the tease. "I uh ... I wanted to call to say thank you for last night."

"Sure."

What do I say now? What do I say? I say the stupidest thing I could, "Uh ... okay. So ... I'll see you around?"

"Have dinner with me?" he asked abruptly.

"Sure," I replied, releasing a long, pent-up breath of pure relief. It was a quiet night and I was sure Henry wouldn't mind if I didn't turn up. Most of the time I was aware they were giving me shifts because they knew I needed the money, anyway. I would miss the money from this shift, but maybe I could just cut back on something else.

We agreed on a time and the call came to an end. I looked around the bare alley as I felt a surge of excitement and anticipation. I caught myself doing a little skip as I returned to the diner. And no matter how hard I tried, I couldn't put a halt to the foolishness.

There's nothing to this, I reminded myself.

It was just a polite prelude to sex, but even though I had turned into almost a bodily function mode, I couldn't restrain the buzz of excitement coursing through my veins.

But an hour before the time he was supposed to pick me up for dinner, I was seated on the floor of my bedroom surrounded by clothes none of which was good enough for my dinner with him and feeling frustrated. I didn't want to wear jeans again, but I had nothing else that was nice enough. I couldn't even get into some of my old dresses because of all the weight I had lost.

Nichole pushed the door open and came into my room. "What are you doing? Aren't you supposed to be at the bar 7:30."

"Yeah, but I don't have anything to wear … oh, my God, what's that?" She had a transparent garment bag protecting the most beautiful frilly chiffon dress I'd ever seen in my whole life. It was a pale pink with grey roses and delicate ruffles.

"This is what I spent two month's worth of a paycheck on," she explained, twirling the hanger tantalizingly in front of me.

As I watched her I knew that she was about to offer it to me and I couldn't understand why. My eyes widened. "Are you letting me …"

"It's a Zimmerman dress," she said, carefully pulling the zipper down. "I haven't worn it yet, but you have absolutely nothing else to wear. Wait, that's not true." She revised her statement. "You have absolutely nothing to wear that would make you feel amazing, especially given the major hunk you're going to meet."

"That's the big issue," I mumbled.

"What?"

"He's a hunk, but he's not someone I can be with … long term."

She put a hand on her hip. "I thought you just wanted to get laid. Why are you overthinking this?"

"That's what I can't figure out. If I'm so sold to there being anything deeper between us, then why am I on cloud nine about seeing him again?"

"Because you like him," she said and went to lay the mid-thigh dress across the bed. "And that's okay. You're not a robot. You have feelings. I mean, I started to love him after what he did last night. Just take this for what it will be, and when it's time to part ways, then do that and be grateful that you were lucky enough to have someone that hot even temporarily. Have fun, be safe, and have a great story to tell your grandchildren."

"Well, how come you don't follow your own advice? I don't see you having fun with random guys."

She looked me in the eye. "I haven't found that special man … yet. But trust me when I do, you will see me out there having the time of my life."

"But what about marriage before sex?"

She waved her hand and winked at me. "I changed my mind last night. If I had a guy like Bone …" She let her voice trail away before continuing, "Now go out there and have fun, but don't do a Monica Lewinski on my dress or you'll owe me $750."

I found myself blushing.

"And don't bring him back to the house," she continued relentlessly. "Go to a hotel or something and thoroughly let go there. Scream the place down if you have to."

I couldn't speak. I just jumped to my feet and threw myself at her. "Thank you, Nichole. Thank you!" I whispered.

"It's okay. It's okay. We'll figure it all out. Step by step. Now get ready and I'll go see what the little munchkin is up to."

I got into the Zimmerman and I thought I looked okay in it as I came out of my room with my make-up done and my only good pair of shoes.

Jess had her head bent over her coloring book, her concentration was such I had to call her to her attention. She lifted her head and looked at me. For a second, she simply stared at me without any recognition. Then her eyes widened and she gasped with shock. "Oh, Mommy. You look like my Barbie," she said.

Now I knew I looked good, but not that good. It was the highest compliment Jess could ever give to anyone.

Nichole shook her head. "Oh, my God. You look better in my dress than I do."

"No, I don't," I said quickly.

"Yes, you do and I'm glad. Go knock his eyes out."

## DELLA RAY

I got myself out of the house thirty minutes later, and arrived at the fancy downtown restaurant. I was more than fifteen minutes early, but I had deliberately done that so I could have a drink on my own at the bar to settle my nerves. I took a seat, but even before I could place my order, I received a text message from him.

*I can't make it.*

I instantly went numb. I reread it again. And again. Just as I rose to my feet to take my leave, another one came in.

*I'm sorry.*

I slipped the phone into my tiny purse and got in the first taxi I could find. I gave the driver my address and settled into the seat. I knew I had already received the blow, but the pain however, was yet to set in. I was in shock or in such an acute state of disappointment, I stared out of the window and saw nothing. I thought about Nichole and Jess, and the dress I was wearing, the make-up I had put on, the excitement I had felt in my belly all day long.

I stared out the window as we drove past the rest of the world without seeing anything. My mind remained blank until Nichole's words began to once again play in my head.

*Just take this for what it will be, and when it's time to part ways, then do that and be grateful that you were lucky enough to have someone that hot even temporarily. Have fun, be safe, and have a great story to tell your grandchildren.*

My mind hooked on the last part of that last sentence.

*Have a great story to tell your grandchildren.*

The words were out of my mouth before I could stop them. "Excuse me. I need to change the address," I told the driver.

I gave the new address and he changed the direction of the taxi. Less than ten minutes later, I was standing outside his apartment door. I knew he was at home because his Harley was parked outside, and I was about to knock when my hand stilled a few inches away from the wood. I decided to go another route. I sent him a text.

*Bone, I'm in trouble at the restaurant. Could you please come to me?*

I sent the text knowing that what I was doing was bonkers, but for me to go on to obtain the great story that I could tell my grandchildren I needed to be certain of something first.

His call was instant, but I had anticipated that and put my phone on silent mode. I watched it light up three more times.

All I wanted to do was see if he would come find me, or ignore the call.

A few seconds later, his door flew open and he came rushing out. At first, he didn't see me waiting by the side, so I called out his name, the closest thing to his true name that I knew of so far, "Miller."

He froze and turned around. Confusion flashed across his face but at the look in my eyes, he came to a pretty decent conclusion about what was going on.

I could see he didn't like it one bit that I had tricked him. Without saying anything, I coolly strolled into the apartment and straight for his kitchen before he could throw me out. There was a bottle of water in the refrigerator so I opened that and downed a healthy portion of it. I knew he was standing right behind me, watching. My feelings were beginning to return. It was an unsettling mix between panic and endearment.

"What was that?" he asked.

I took my time in settling my breathing before turning to face him. "You said you couldn't make it."

"That wasn't a funny stunt," he said.

"I know," I replied, "and I'm sorry, but what you did wasn't funny either. Anyway, I needed to confirm something."

He remained silent and showed no curiosity as to what I needed to confirm, instead his eyes were hungrily roving over me in my short flirty dress. It was then that for the first time I noticed what he was wearing. He wasn't in his usual black attire but had instead a pair of blue jeans on, a white crisp dress shirt tucked into it. His hair was nearly combed back and for the first time since I had met him there was no air of menace surrounding him. I realized why he was dressed this way. "You were going to come to the restaurant, weren't you?"

He continued to glare at me.

I was unfazed. "Why did you change your mind when it's obvious you care about me?"

"I want nothing to do with you," he said.

That was so clearly a lie, it made me smile. "Then why were you rushing off to my aid. You could have just called the cops on my behalf."

He shrugged. "Anyone would have done that."

"Please, Bone. I just need to know why you changed your mind. And please tell me the truth. Otherwise, I'll be inclined to think that you're scared of me somehow. Why else would you lie?"

He turned around to walk off, but I stepped in front of him. "In the future, if there's something you're not comfortable with, please reject me straightaway, rather than go along and make a fool of me. I was already at the restaurant bar when you sent your text. See I don't need you to wine and dine me. We could have just fucked here in secrecy and ordered in some food. That is what you want, isn't it?"

Something flashed in his eyes.

DELLA RAY

https://www.youtube.com/watch?v=foGkU6x3eSE
-If I close my eyes forever-

I stared at him. He was breathtaking, in ways that made me wonder how he could simply just exist amongst the rest of us. His face was perfectly handsome, his nose, a perfectly strong Roman thing, sat just above his soft full lips. I recalled what it was like to taste them, and I couldn't believe how long it had been since I had.

And his hair ... right then it was all in place, but the memory of the dark mass, tousled and falling around the sides of his face as he'd fucked me mindless was a sight I wouldn't ever be able to forget.

It was understandable why I was pushing my limits with him.

Throwing all caution to the wind.

For him, I would even throw away my pride and reservations because I was certain that he would be my once in a life time kind of experience.

Slowly, I pulled down the zipper of Nichole's very expensive dress and let it slide down my body. The floor looked pretty clean so I knew Nichole wouldn't mind. I intended to dry clean it before giving it back to her, anyway.

I shut off that irritating voice in my head and I took off my bra. I let my breasts spill out for his full perusal. I was quaking inside, but I hoped to God it did not show on the outside.

I stood now before him in just the lacy peach thong that had matched Nichole's dress.

His eyes were eating me up alive.

I couldn't move one step further. "I really don't want to do all the work myself here," I said, my voice shivery with excitement.

He gazed at me for the longest time, his eyes greedily savoring every single inch of my body. He looked like a man who hadn't seen a nearly naked woman for years.

I let him consume me. It felt good to have a man so completely mesmerized by me.

Wordlessly, he began to walk towards me. From then on, I couldn't breathe properly. I watched his big hands go to the buttons of his shirt and slip them out of their holes.

It reminded me quite vividly, of when his fingers had been inside of me, and it made me ache with anticipation. He was as beautiful as a Greek God, and it seemed like an eternity since I had last kissed him. In that moment, I wanted nothing else than to have his lips on mine, his tongue in my mouth.

He shrugged the material off his shoulders to reveal a perfectly sculpted body. By the time he reached me, I was already holding onto the edge of the counter behind me. He hadn't touched me yet, but I was already breathless. I knew when he did ... I would combust. So I had to get some answers before he did.

I wanted to break him open, to figure out what was holding him back and keeping him so far away from me, and why the only thing he wanted to give was his body. I couldn't take my mind off the fact that he had been dressed this way for me. I needed to know what had made him decide not to come to the restaurant. "You're always in black ... Why did you want to look different today?"

He didn't respond. Just kept a tortured predator's gaze on me, as though he blamed me for something I could not understand.

If it had been any other man, I would have said he was playing games or he wanted to keep me from expecting too much, but those mundane reasons were impossible to pin on him. The man approaching me wasn't playing a game. The way his hot blue gaze roamed all over my face and body was as if I was the thing he had been looking for all his life. The roll of his muscles beneath that glistening olive skin made me swallow painfully.

Hell, I wanted to taste every inch of him. "You're really fucking gorgeous," I breathed.

He flung the shirt aside and my hand went to my breasts. I couldn't stop myself from filling my hands with the mounds that were mine, but only ached and responded to him. I massaged them and my nipples became hard and inviting. I was hot, ready and brimming with anticipation.

When he reached me, he buried his face in the nook of my neck and tasted me with the tip of his tongue. I shut my eyes. I was ready and willing to submit to all that he wanted to do to me. I shuddered at the softness of his lips. The heat of his breath traced my taut flesh all the way up my neck and towards the corner of my lips.

I couldn't wait any longer. I turned to capture his lips with mine and felt his smile at my urgency. His taste was precious, as though too much of it would do more harm than good to me. Even so, I was unable to stop. I threw both of my arms around his neck, ground my breasts against his chest, and sucked lustily on his tongue.

Like a blue-eyed demon, he matched my tempo, his hand tangled in my hair to keep my head in place as he ravished me, ruggedly drinking me in, as though he had been even more starved than I had thought. It turned me giddy with joy at the realization that in our desire for each other, we were equally and ferociously eager.

The moment he placed his other hand on my stomach and began to slide it down to my tormented, throbbing pussy, my whole body tensed with anticipation.

He palmed my dampened panties and then slid the sheer material aside to obtain full access to my wet silky folds. He slid his fingers into the delicate cleft. I drenched him. The sound of his finger squelching echoed loudly around us.

He plunged another finger in, and I bit down on his shoulder at the delicious intrusion. My hand tore the tie on his hair away as I needed something to claw at to keep me sane.

He slid his fingers expertly in and out of me, his thumb stroking my swollen nub.

It felt so freaking good, my heels lifted off the floor. *"Bone,"* I breathed as I ground my hips into his big, callused hand. I was on fire. All I could feel and breathe in was him. My head fell back as I entered into an entrancing state of mindlessness.

His mouth joined the attack as he sucked and pulled on my rock-hard nipples. I was overwhelmed, and as his tempo increased on both pleasure stations of my body, I flew closer and closer to the edge.

When I climaxed, it was so hard for a few moments I forgot where I was. All I could feel was the rush and heat of my release as it spilled over his hand. My core was so taut it reverberated with the powerful orgasm. Even then he didn't stop. He continued to work his thumb against my clit milking every ounce of pleasure he could.

My hips thrashed wildly and he had to lay his palm on me to provide the hard relief that I needed. I sagged against him, spent and awed.

## DELLA RAY

He lifted me, his hands gripping the underside of my thighs and pulled at them so my legs would go around his waist. I obeyed, my face buried in his neck as I tried to gather my wits. The next thing I felt was my ass on the cold counter.

"Hold on to the edge of the counter," he ordered as he jerked my hips forward. Without waiting for my response, he buried his face between my legs. Covering my entire pussy with his mouth, he began to suck ferociously.

"Bone," I gasped, my hands scurrying for some support as my body threatened to slide off the counter.

He never lifted his head until I found another climax on his tongue. I was panting heavily when I looked down to find him still meticulously licking my wet folds. His eyes were like blue fire when he stood and pulled a condom packet from his pocket. Then he began to unzip his jeans. His cock was swollen and throbbing.

My breath was shaky as I brushed his beautiful tousled hair out of his face and covered my mouth with his. I tasted myself on him and the mingling with his delicious flavor, struck a chord of intimacy within me like nothing else I'd ever known. I moaned into his mouth when I felt the wide head of his cock slipping and sliding between my folds. He teased me with that rock-hard rod until I leaned forward and grabbed a hold of it myself. I fisted him eagerly, wishing I could also have a taste of him, but I'd have to wait for that. I knew he couldn't wait anymore. All he wanted was to be inside me.

He saw the blade of hunger in my eyes and with a nip at my chin, he took control and positioned himself at my entrance. With his strong grasp on the flesh of my hips, he lifted me slightly off the counter and slammed into me.

I cried out breathlessly at the sudden penetration. Oh, God. As he filled me, my walls convulsed around him. It was the most satisfying thing to be so utterly filled, so utterly stretched. I reached down to grab his ass, my short finger-nails digging into the tightly clenched flesh.

He began his rhythm, his mouth on my neck. It muffled the animalistic groans that tore out of my throat as he began to thrust in and out of me. I gave as good as I got. I rocked my hips feverishly to meet his as he pounded himself into me.

He worked hard to completely possess me and drive me out of my mind. And he succeeded. Sweat drizzled down my back and my words became mumbled and senseless as the rush of ecstasy rattling every inch of my body. I heard my cries as though from a distance.

"Fuck me!" I cried. *"Bo-ne*. Oh, fuck … Yes. Just like that. Ohhhh, *goddddd* …" I screamed and felt the ache in my throat. Suddenly however, he halted but I tightened my hips around him, shaking my head in abject refusal. "No," I panted, "What the hell are you doing? You can't."

With a devious chuckle, he carried me over to the wall. "Look at me," he ordered.

As he brushed my hair out of my face, I caught the expression in his blue gaze, and knew he had just signed me up for a wilder ride.

He slid his dick back into me and began to rattle me alive, my ass slamming viciously against the wall. The smacking sounds of our groins slamming into each other, raw and primal, and the force of his thrusts, reached into a part of me that I didn't even realize it was possible to get to. I was whipped almost unconscious by mind blowing pleasure.

I thrust my tongue into his mouth and held tightly to his neck as I exploded in a daze of disbelief. Tearing my mouth from his, I sunk my teeth into his shoulder to keep myself from completely losing it. The pain I caused, I was certain, was what sent him over the edge right behind me.

His roar reverberated through my soul as he released his thick bursts of seed deep inside me.

He continued to pound his hips into me and I kept on climaxing until it felt like I would fall unconscious. By the time he drew in a sharp breath to signify his finale, I was long gone. All the strength in my body was lost. No strength was left in my limbs to even cling to him. I collapsed on him like a rag doll. I must have lost consciousness too, because I felt myself come awake to a lazy sweetness that buzzed through my entire body.

A euphoric calm hung over me as my eyelids fluttered open to meet those of Bone. He was watching me with such possessiveness, I felt my heart skip a beat. My fingers brushed his hair aside in an attempt to tuck it behind his ears so I could see the rest of his face. But as soon as I moved my hand the silky strands came cascading back down.

With a shaky laugh that tugged a smile out of him, he lifted me into his arms and carried me to his bed. He put me down on the bed and lay next to me.

I got onto my elbow and softly brushed his eyebrows. I thought my heart would melt when his eyelids fluttered close tiredly.

"I think I nearly passed out," I murmured.

"I think you actually did." He grinned.

My heart did somersaults in my chest. "I must have been quite starved," I explained.

It was his turn to brush my hair out of my face. "It wasn't because I almost fucked you to death?"

"Cocky much?" I scoffed, but my cheeks were no doubt crimson red.

"Apparently," he said dryly.

I couldn't contain my laughter. After the bout of amusement had subsided, I returned to his face and began to trace my finger down the bridge of his regal nose, down to the gentle rise of his upper lip. I was committing every curve and arch to memory. "You're fucking beautiful, you know," I said.

He rubbed the tip of his nose against mine. "Me? You're the beautiful one. I almost keeled over when I saw you in that dress. But now you need to eat. What do you feel like?"

"Something quick. I want more of you. I saw a can of tuna and a bottle of ranch. I could make us a sandwich."

"You don't want to eat that," he said with a smile.

"Why? It's expired?"

"Maybe."

"Fuck food. I didn't come here to eat. I want to be on top of you," I said.

With a chuckle, he obliged me and moved. Moments later and I was sprawled on top of him, our naked bodies glued seamlessly together. As I deliberately wriggled around, his enormous cock began to protrude between the folds of my sex. I grinned down at him. "Another round?"

"Can't have you fainting on me again. Food first." At the expression on my face, he added. "I insist. How do you feel about a Chinese takeout?"

"Sounds great," I said and he stretched out his hand to retrieve his phone from the bedside table. It reminded me of the gun that I suspected was still under the pillow we were using. It kinda cast a shadow that felt as if it would never go away over our euphoric sexual bliss.

As I listened to the magic of his deep voice while he made a quick order, I traced circles around his pale pink nipples. I leaned forward to nip at it and it made him groan.

After he ended the call, he caught my mouth in a deep bone melting kiss that left me completely limp and useless against him. He lifted me into his arms and took me to the shower, then turned the faucet on, tested the temperature of the water, and moved us under the shower.

I clung to his neck as the water cascaded down on the both of us. I kissed him feverishly, my body quaking from the torrent of emotions that he'd stirred inside me. Being with him this way, just the two of us without the burdens and harshness of the real world beyond, was like a beautiful dream, but at the back of my mind, it seemed to be ticking into a nightmare. Still, I pushed the notion away and allowed his body to make mine sing.

"You feel so fucking good, Della. I can't even believe how fucking good," he grunted as he rammed his hips repeatedly into mine.

He was still deep inside of me when the doorbell rang with the delivery of our food. I didn't even hear it as he pummeled me against the tiled wall, my hand splayed on the steam frosted glass. Surely, we hadn't been fucking for forty minutes. He wanted to hold out till my energy was replenished but being naked with me in such a confined space had turned him wild.

"Stay," he said and left the shower stall.

It seemed as if it was forever before he came back, but when he did, he found me rubbing my own pussy seductively. "Oh fuck," he said, flinging away the towel around his hips.

When I came, it was as if I flew away and left my body. Throughout it all, he held me solidly in place, his hands underneath my thighs to ensure that I had a solid lock around me. Without that, we both knew that I would have melted to the floor like wax. He rinsed us both off then and I was deposited once again on the bed.

"I'll be right back with the food," he whispered into my ear.

But I registered nothing. I curled up into a ball, and went straight into one of the deepest and most peaceful slumbers of my entire life.

# BONE

https://www.youtube.com/watch?v=sP-ub5wF-_0

L ike some kind of creepy deviant, I watched her sleep.

At first, I had cradled her sleeping body in my arms, but after a while I had become so consumed with worries I had to get up and pace the floor restlessly.

I thought about my pathetic attempt to become one of the normal folk. How I had switched out my black attire, so I would be as far as possible from the world that I had embroiled myself in. To be just another man taking his woman out for dinner.

I'd been just about to step out of the house, when the reality of who I was hit me. Who was I kidding? I hadn't come this far to let my dick do the thinking for me. The plan had been to ignore the chatter coming from my brain and completely cut her out of my life, but the moment her text came through, I became like a caged animal. I couldn't sit still. I imagined the worst. It had become impossible for me to resist her. All I could do was run to her. There was no way around it. I was a sucker for her big beautiful caramel eyes. I just couldn't push her away. Hell, I couldn't even say no. Even when I know how damn dangerous she was to me, to what I needed to do.

I walked back to the bed and lay down next to her. Her skin felt so soft and silky I wanted to weep at the sweet sensation.

She shifted then, and her eyelids fluttered open.

Our eyes met.

"Bone," she whispered sleepily. Then she blushed, a soft rosy glow spread all over her face as I continued to stare at her. Embarrassed, she hid her face in my chest.

I felt my heart melt. It'd been a very long time since anyone had touched any depth inside me like this girl had and it scared the shit out of me. Every nerve in my body became taut with panic. "I'll go warm up the food," I said and jack-knifed out of bed. Not till I exited the room, was I able to breathe.

But I didn't go on to the kitchen, I turned and watched her through the slit between the door and the wall. I saw her pull the covers up to her chest. She shuffled around a bit before settling into a comfortable enough position. I watched as she remained still in thought for a moment before softy brushing her fingers across the pillow that I had just gotten up from. Shutting her eyes, she buried her nose into it to relish my scent.

I felt real fear then. The kind that could not even be compared to the most dangerous situations I had encountered in the club.

It was the same ghost of a fear that had reared its sensible head earlier. Now, its whole body had appeared and it reminded me much more clearly of the risk I was taking and what I was once again, putting on the line. The hairs on the back of my neck were standing.

*What the fuck are you doing, Gage?*

I turned around and headed into the kitchen. While I put the food into the microwave, waited for the ping, then took them out, I practiced how I would behave with her. This time, I would not let my emotions get carried away. One day, one day when I was free, I would turn up on her doorstep. I would explain everything to her, hopefully she would understand, and we'd start again. Her, me and little Jess.

I would have to fuck this up now, but I would make it right again when the time was right.

A few minutes later we were in bed, a tray of shrimp chow mein, fried dumplings and spring rolls spread out before us as our chopsticks dug into the boxes.

She ate in the most amusing way I'd ever encountered. It was no trouble for me to eat without spilling a single thing, but with each bite she put into her mouth, something simultaneously dropped off onto the bed. She kept on apologizing, continually promising me new sheets.

I definitely didn't want her to go and buy me new sheets, especially not with her desperate financial situation. I wanted to put her at ease, so I said without thinking, "It's not a big deal. You can take them home to launder, and bring them back later."

She stopped then, her eyes softening, and I realized that I had just done one of the cruelest things to her ... painted her a picture of hope that there would be more after tonight. How could I, when I didn't even know if I would still have my head on my shoulders in a few weeks from now? A chill struck through me in that moment. For the first time in a long, long time, I didn't want to die. I wanted to live and take care of her and little Jess.

"Why do they call you Bone?" she asked suddenly.

I looked up from my meal and shrugged. "The club's president gave me that nickname. It's from the movie, A Space Odyssey 2001."

"I've seen that movie, but I don't get the connection."

"Remember that scene after the ape-men had contacted the monolith."

"Kind of."

"Okay, remember the one that sits on top of a pile of tapir bones. He picks one up and toys around with it, hitting harder and harder until he uses it to wallop a skull hard enough to shatter it into pieces. That was supposed to be the moment the ape-men invented the club. Something that allows him to strike harder than he could with his own hand. It also extends his reach and prevents the risk of injury that attacking with only his body would expose him to."

She frowned. "You're the bone in the President's hand."

I nodded and she cocked her head and studied me. Over the years, I had stopped hating the name, but with her in my life over the last few weeks, I was beginning to doubt more things than I wanted to. I was even starting to question the man I had become.

"And you're okay with being the weapon in his hand?"

"I told you I have a plan. It's part of the plan."

"You know what I think. I don't think of you as a weapon. I think of you as a great big heart hidden somewhere inside all that steel and bone."

I didn't need to tell her that she was the only one I had let close enough to even dream of suspecting something like that. Anyway, what I had wasn't a big, warm heart. It was a dead one.

When she saw that I didn't comment much on the topic, she moved on. "And what of the others in your club?" she asked. "What are their Nicknames?"

"Why do you want to know?" I asked quietly.

A sliver of hurt flashed through her eyes.

It made me want to hold her tight and rock her. Dammit, why was this so hard for me suddenly?

"I'm genuinely curious," she added. "I've always heard that bikers have very colorful nicknames. Some are rugged, others are actually cool." Another noodle slipped through her chopsticks and fell to the sheets. She sucked in air through her teeth with irritation at herself. "I was just wondering what ones your club members have."

"I don't know all of their names. There's too many of them." Once again I tried to evade her question.

"Well the ones that you know then," she insisted.

I finally conceded. "Well, we have Rose," I began.

She blinked with surprise. "What?

"He's pretty," I explained, and moved onto the next. "We have Tank because he's shaped like a tank, and his cousin Shotgun, because he once accidentally shot himself with a shotgun. And Rooster—"

She laughed. "Why because he crows?"

I chuckled softly. "He has a horrible voice. Quite aggravating."

She giggled prettily again and it felt like some kind of sweet warmth along my nerve endings as I continued, "We have Tattoo Man. He's covered in a ridiculous amount of ink. We have Tyler, he's the Sergeant at arms—"

"Isn't that his real name? Tyler? Why doesn't he have a nickname?"

I shrugged. "I really don't know. He was in the club way before me. I guess he didn't care for one, and no one dared give him one either. He's tough. We have Snake, he's the president—"

"And he's cold-blooded?" she piped in excitedly.

"Yeah," I said briefly and moved on. "We have Skippy—"

"Wait," she interrupted. "He … uh … He skips a lot? Tight ropes? I don't get it!"

I chuckled. "He puts peanut butter on everything."

Her mouth dropped and remained open.

Picking up a piece of shrimp from my plate, I put it into her mouth.

She shut it closed and chewed thoughtfully. "Wow," she mumbled. "Is that all that you remember?"

"For now," I said, and continued with my meal. She would never realize that I had already said too much.

We ate quietly for a few more minutes as she processed her thoughts and then she returned with questions. "About Rose," she began.

I narrowed my gaze at her just as my phone began to ring. I turned to retrieve it from beneath my pillow. It was Rooster. With a finger to my lips, I requested her silence, and listened to what Rooster had called to say.

"There's trouble," he said. "Tank and Shotgun attended a party last night and met some Death's Hand members. They got into a fight."

I let out a deep sigh and placed my meal on the nightstand. "And?"

"Shotgun got his skull smashed with a bottle and Tank got thrown off the second-floor balcony to a concrete floor. They're both in the hospital right now. Tank's got a broken arm and fractured leg, but the doctor says there's hope, although he might not heal the same."

"And Shotgun?"

"He's in a coma."

I cursed under my breath. "Where's the meeting?"

"It's at the house in ten minutes. We're going to attack tonight."

I killed the call.

"Everything all right?" she asked quietly.

I gave a little nod. Then I stood and headed over to the small closet by the bedroom window to retrieve a pair of dark jeans and a dark t-shirt, which I put on without a word. The fantasy was over. Real life had called and I had to go running like its little bitch. It was only when I turned around that I realized that she too, had politely gotten up and was taking the things off the bed.

"There's a little problem in the club," I explained, and we both stared at each other. I couldn't say anymore.

I moved to pull out my bedside drawer and retrieved my handgun, confirmed its safety and tucked it behind me. After grabbing the other equipment that I needed from an inner compartment in the drawer, I turned and snatched up my jacket from the armchair by the corner. "The key is behind the door. Just lock it when you leave and keep it with you. I'll come pick it up."

Della nodded.

I could see her eyes had begun to fill with tears. I wanted to go to her. Hold her and tell her everything would be fine. There was nothing to worry about. We would be together forever. But I couldn't.

What came out of my mouth sounded harsh, but it was for the best, "Don't call me. I'll call you." Then I strolled out of the room. I had just pulled the front door open when I heard her quiet call from the bedroom door.

"Please be careful, Bone."

# BONE

I nodded in acknowledgement and went out of the apartment. Putting all thoughts of her behind me to focus on the urgency of the present, I immediately placed a call to Tyler. He didn't pick up, and I couldn't wait any longer so I got on the bike and was on my way. When I arrived in the basement of the clubhouse, the executive members of the club were already in deep discussion.

I listened without saying anything. By the time they were done, my soul sunk in horror. "We're going to burn them alive?" I asked, keeping all expression out of my voice.

"Well, we're not exactly doing that, are we?" Skippy replied. "We're just burning their house down."

"And barricading the exit, so no one will be able to run out," I stated. "Doesn't that sound like murder to you?"

"And is that a problem?" Snake asked, his pale eyes glittering like shards of ice.

I stared at him.

"Shotgun is in a bloody coma," Snake stated in a cold voice. "Right from the onset, they have been the one to come directly at us even when we hadn't retaliated from the way they treated RJ. You want our club to become a joke? We need to react. Show them we're not pussies."

"Why the objection?" Tyler asked. "This is not the first time we've taken care of someone before."

"He's began to wear skirts since he started dating sugar tits."

I spun around to RJ. I would never understand how I stopped myself from charging at him and killing him myself.

"Bone," Snake called, his voice stern. "A favor for a favor, a life for a life. Shotgun is going to be deformed for life. The bottle caved in his entire skull before shattering and you know how thick his skull is. They let him bleed out without doing anything to save his life. It's over for them," he said through gritted teeth.

"And how are we going to escape after a carnage like that?" I asked. "It's going to be big and the heat is going to be all over it."

"No doubt we'll be arrested for questioning, but where's the proof? They'll let us go and keep their eyes on us in relation to this feud. Which will then allow us to facilitate the meth transaction coming up right under their noses."

Everything fell into place then. I stared at Snake. "This feud will be a distraction?"

"Exactly," he said, with a cold smile.

"Cameras?" I asked.

"The street ones will pick us up as we head over. Theo?" he called out.

Out of nowhere, one of our prospects stood.

I frowned at his presence.

"He knows his way around the wires," Snake explained.

"Not very well," the boy who was even younger than Junho said shyly. The kid couldn't have been more than sixteen years. "But I have checked and confirmed that there are only two cameras in our way if we take a different route, if we take highway 52, and then go through Blacktown. That way, it will be extremely difficult for us to get noticed. I would have shut it all down, but I'm not that skilled and I'm scared that if I poke around too long, we'll be noticed."

Snake nodded, then went into the plan. "We're going to park in the alley on Jemdo Street. The moment we do, everyone grab your bars then drill and barricade the doors and windows. We only have a minute. Then those with the torches and gasoline you know what to do. Bone, you're on the backdoor." He pointed to a house plan that someone had pasted on the wall.

I went closer to study it.

"We leave in ten minutes," Snake announced.

"The trunks have been loaded already and remember your fucking gloves," Tyler added. "Anyone who gets into trouble will be cut down immediately, so you better watch out. After the whole place is set on fire, disperse from the house as discussed and meet at the corner of Berwyck Court. Any questions?"

There were none so all fifteen men filed out and so did I. I found Dog heading up the stairs and quickly went after him. He knew I was behind him so he went into his room.

I shut the door to face him. "We're just going to go through with this?"

"What other choice do we have?"

"Countless people might end up dead."

"Stop fucking whining and just fucking go through with this. It's not rocket science," Dog growled.

There was no getting through to him, so I turned around and stormed out of the room.

"Bone!" he called out. "Bone!"

I didn't respond. I hurried down the stairs to join the men as they went through the walls of the back fence. Our bikes would remain parked out in front of the house, soundless and calm like the night, and for all who would ask we were home watching Sons of Anarchy.

The attack began the moment the clock struck 2am.

With everyone stationed like they should be and the needed equipment in hand, we began.

The door I was in charge of only needed a bar across it, and I had five seconds to drill it in. Others handling the bigger windows had a 3-man team. They were supposed to drill two huge bars into the wall. There was no way to do it silently and in no time, we heard sounds from the house as they began to stir. It was accompanied by hurried footsteps and panicked voices, but it was too late.

The gasoline was already poured around the house.

The men lit it up and it all went up in flames. Lit torches were busted through the windows on the top and second floors and it began to spread like a wild forest fire. I heard the roars, screams and curses of the men inside the house just before the whistle was blown for us to escape. We scattered like vermin, each man to his own escape route.

It all happened so fast, and before I knew it, I was vaulting over the back wall and running with the others to the house. It was the end and some of the men were high on an adrenalin rush. I bypassed the gathering of excited men in the basement and went straight to bed. I kept my eyes shut, but I did not dare fall into sleep.

Trouble came, at the crack of dawn.

Tyler busted into my room and I instantly sat up. With one glare from him, I knew I was in trouble.

"Basement," he barked and stood there while I got to my feet.

It worried me that I couldn't take my gun with me as I'd lost it during the mission, but I had gone to bed with a knife. If my life were put on the line, it would buy me a hostage.

I walked in to see sour and angry faces. This came sooner than I'd expected, but it didn't surprise or faze me. I stopped by the door and crossed my arms over my chest.

"You messed up, Bone," Rose began. "I can't believe you fucked up."

"To the fucking middle!" Tyler roared at me.

I lifted a deadly gaze to him. I wasn't to be pushed around

like the rest. "Say what you fucking need to me and then we'll go from there. Don't push it."

Snake held his hand up to halt the altercation, his gaze on me. "We got only three of them," he began, and pointed to the gigantic muted television on the north wall.

I turned my head slightly to look at the screen that showed an image of the house we had set alight. The building was covered in such heavy flames that it had colored the early morning sky with a fiery red glow. There was thick black smoke pouring out of it. It looked like a monstrous explosion, and everywhere there were firemen, reporters, medical personnel, and the police.

"Eight others escaped and it was all through the east back door." He turned to me, his face expressionless. "The door you were fucking in charge of. How were they able to burst through it, Bone?"

My response was simple. "I have no idea."

"The problem," Snake began in an almost friendly tone, "is that you're the one that fucked up. If this was anyone else, we'd see it as some kind of mistake, but you're fucking thorough in everything you do, so we can't help but think that there's something more to this story. You gonna tell us what it is?"

"I don't know what you want me to say. Apparently, I fucked up. So be it."

I could feel the aggravation of the others in the room. "We fucking risked our lives for this, man, and you just gonna mess it up like this?" Tattoo Man said. His face still black with smoke.

"You guys can pussyfoot around this bastard all you want. I'm calling a spade a spade. You're a fucking liar, Bone," Tyler snarled. "You deliberately didn't screw the bar down properly. What we need to figure out now, is why you did it?"

"We'll have to investigate this, and until we do, you'll have to be in the pen," Snake decided.

There was silence in the room as they waited for me to reject this, but I didn't bother. It would be a horrible experience as I had seen so many other members have in the past, but it was either this, or put an end to everything that I had worked for, for the last two years.

## DELLA RAY

"Do you know where he is?" the strawberry blonde asked me.

The last time we met, she had left a very rotten taste in my mouth, but now I felt as if she was delivering the news that I'd been dreading these last few days.

We were both standing in the parking lot of my diner.

"He's missing?" I asked, staring at her in shock.

She narrowed her gaze at me suspiciously. She thought I wasn't telling the truth, until the genuine concern in my gaze must have made her realize I knew less than her. She sighed and slumped her shoulders in defeat.

She was about to return to her car, but I stopped her with a hard grip on her arm. "What do you know?" I asked.

She jerked her arm out of my grasp. "Since you don't know where he is, it's not your concern."

"Have you tried to call him?" I asked as she walked away.

She stopped. "You have his phone number?"

"Yeah," I replied.

She didn't believe me. "That's not possible, I only know three other people who do. Even Tyler wouldn't give it to me and he's my brother."

"Well, he called me, so I have it."

"Give it to me," she said.

My eyebrows shot up at the order. "Tell me what happened to him first, then I will.'

She sighed elaborately and lifted her eyes to the sky in exasperation. "Don't you watch the damn news?" she spat.

"The fire incident? He was a part of it?"

"More like sabotaged it. I don't know the details, but I do know that he's under investigation by the club. He's been missing for a few days now and no one will say where he is."

I felt all the blood drain from my face. "Will they hurt him?"

"What do you think?" she asked sourly, and then pulled her phone from her pocket. "His number!" she demanded, as she got ready to tap it in.

I didn't give it to her. I turned around and rushed back into the diner.

"Hey!" she called out. "Hey!"

I barely even heard her.

She was long erased from my mind as my concern about Bone's safety crippled me. I hurried into the bathroom in the diner, and pulling out my phone, I dialed his number. I'd been a bit worried about him over the last three days, especially after I'd seen the news report about his club's involvement with the disastrous fire and I'd heard nothing from him, but I had been unable to allow myself to call him. I was scared that I would be pushing my bounds, especially since he'd warned me not to call him.

Now, I could no longer hold myself back. When the unavailable message came up on my phone, my heart sunk. I spent the rest of my shift in a terrible state. The moment I was done, I rushed over to his apartment.

I still had the key with me so I opened the door and found my way in. I walked around the bedroom, living room, and the kitchen. I opened the trashcan and saw all the takeaway boxes inside it. Everything was exactly the same way I'd left it three nights ago. It looked as if he had not come back here at all.

I dialed his phone number again and when it still didn't go through, I realized then that there was nothing I could do but wait until his return.

But what if he never did?

Perhaps seeking the help of the authorities would stir the pot, but whether it would bring him to the surface or cause even more trouble for him, I had no clue. And neither did Nichole. Her advice was to wait. Bone was a smart operator and there was a reason he told me not to call him until he called me. Maybe he even knew he would have to disappear for a few days and that was why he didn't want me calling and worrying.

Before I left for the Sinkhole, I thought to leave the key

somewhere he would be able to find it, but there was nothing in front of his door to hide it in, not even a plant. I was reluctant to send him any text messages in case he was in serious trouble, and he didn't want much known about him by the members of the club.

Bone had been so tightlipped, I wasn't even certain his club members knew about this apartment so I kept the key on me and went to work full of fear and worry.

The next day, I stopped by the apartment after my shift to check again. This time, I brought with me a small potted palm plant. I placed it in front of his door, dug his key into the soil, and left. The following day I returned again, and all was still as I had left it. I watered the plant and placed some noodles that he could quickly make on the kitchen counter. If he was in a hurry. I don't know what I was thinking, but it was the only thing I could think of doing for him.

Just before I left, I stood just inside the door and mourned for him. Tears ran down my face. All day I had to pretend I was fine, but here I could let the tears come. It had been a week now and there had been absolutely no word on him. What haunted me was the look of urgency in his eyes as he had exited the room in a rush. Perhaps he had been killed by his members and his corpse disposed of.

The pain at this thought was horrendous. I dropped to the ground with it. It couldn't be. It just couldn't be. I knew he wasn't dead. I would feel it if he was. There was more between Bone and me than just physical. We were connected at some other level. It took me all this time to realize it, but to me, it was true.

That night at the bar, I found myself unable to go on without some sort of consolation. So I called Henry aside and asked, "These clubs. I know they usually have bloody fights with other clubs, but what about between themselves? Can they just hurt their members at their own discretion?"

"You're joking, right?" he asked. "Of course, they hurt and even kill each other. When it comes to their affairs, they're their own law. I mean I've heard of them throwing members off balconies and causing paralysis, busting their skulls open, even death." At my horrified expression, he stopped. "I'm sorry. Didn't mean to freak you out."

"No, no. It's fine," I said, but in fact, I was sick to my stomach with fear.

I had Jess to think of and I needed the money so I went on with my work, a ghost of myself. When I went to bed later that night I was haunted by nightmares. I shot up from bed and pounded my own chest for air, barely able to breathe. The sound of blood dripping into a pail from the slit throat of a body hanging in a dank basement still resounded in my ears.

## DELLA RAY

The next morning, I found myself at Reno's bar. I was quaking in my shoes, especially since Bone had warned me from ever returning here, but I needed them to know that someone was aware of his absence. Someone cared and would go to the authorities if he didn't turn up.

That they weren't going to get away with it if they were planning anything nefarious.

The bar was empty, which was to be expected since it wasn't yet midday. I called out the old man I had met the last time as he came out of the door behind the counter.

He scowled disapprovingly at me, but I ignored it and spoke up, "I'm looking for Bone."

He cocked his head at me. "Why would you be looking for him here?"

I was a bit taken aback by the question. "Their club ..." I went on. "The Order of Blood. They hang out here do they not?"

"Miss, do you see anyone here right now? And this is Reno's

bar and grill, not the Order of Blood. If you want them, I can give you their address."

I gazed at his faded green eyes and the deep lines on his face. I didn't know what to do. There was absolutely no way I was going to head over to their clubhouse. Even meeting them in a public place would be a scary event. I squared my shoulders. "Well, I have a message for the club's members."

His gray eyebrows shot upwards with surprise.

"Let them know," I said firmly. "That all of Bone's friends know he is missing, and if he doesn't turn up soon, then we are going to send the cops to them. We knew exactly when he left, and that he got a call to come to the clubhouse, and since then he hasn't been seen."

I didn't know what else to add after that, so I shut my mouth and looked at him sternly.

He folded his arms across his chest. I was sure I saw a glimmer of something in his eyes. Either amusement or respect, but I couldn't be sure. Not that I cared. I just wanted Bone back.

"You came to threaten an outlaw MC?" he asked.

I swallowed hard and he shook his head. "Missy, don't you have a job or something? It's too early to be doing things this stupid."

"I mean it," I said through gritted teeth. "I won't let this go until I hear from him."

He lifted his hands exhaustedly in the air. "Sure, I'll pass on your message. Who should I say left it?"

"Bone's friend ... and family," I said immediately.

He studied me quietly. I felt like he pitied me. "Got it. Now please leave."

"How will I know you've delivered it?" I asked.

"Well if I deliver it and it spooks them enough to release Bone like you hope, that'll be proof won't it?"

"And if I don't hear from him?"

"Then you can go to the cops like you've promised. Just leave me out of it. Good-day."

"I'm giving them one more week, no, four more days. If Bone does not resurface in four days, then I *am* going to the cops."

He shook his head and went back through the door he came in from, slamming it shut behind him so loudly, I jumped at the unmistakable note of conclusion.

With my heart heavier than it had been before I arrived, I made my way out of the bar, and felt indeed as stupid as he had perceived me to be, but still I'd done the only thing I could. I'd let the club members know that Bone couldn't be disposed of without the cops becoming involved.

I would wait, just like I'd said, but two days later and I found myself filing a Missing Person's Report at the County police station.

I realized I wouldn't get far when the uniformed officer started asking me the most basic questions about someone I had called a friend, and I didn't know the answers.

"Um ..." the officer sat up. "Who exactly is the victim to you again, Miss?"

My voice was small. "A friend."

"Whose name you know as just Bone. You don't know his real or last name."

"Miller," I said. "His last name is Miller."

"Um, Okay," he responded as he scrolled through his computer. "We have quite a number of Millers here but ... no Bone. You don't know his age or ..."

"I told you, I'm sure he is in his early thirties."

"Okay," he said. "And once again, you're certain that you don't have a picture of him?"

"I can describe him though."

"Does he have any social media accounts that we can employ? Residential address, job or occupation?"

I stared blankly at the officer who was now looking at me as if I was some kind of time waster or I was well out of my mind. "Forget it," I said. "Just forget."

"Don't worry, he'll turn up when he's good and ready," he said mockingly.

The moment I got out of the station, my mission fruitless, and my person labeled mentally unstable, I pulled my phone out of my pocket and drafted a furious text over to Bone.

*What the hell is your fucking name?*
*You're fucking missing and there's no way for me to even fucking find you!!!!!!!*

I sent the text and hurried back to work in the diner. Somehow, I managed to put Bone into a box in my head and close the lid. I didn't allow myself to think of him at all.

Three hours later, I walked into the kitchen to see Gloria staring down at my phone as she sloppily munched on a burrito. I had left it on the counter to quickly use the restroom. I was prepared to give her a mouthful when she turned, her face full of teasing fun, and asked me the words that made me stop in my tracks.

"Who is Gage Miller?"

I felt as if the breath had been knocked out of me. I hurried over to pick up the phone and unlock it to see the text from the number that had been ingrained into my head over the last several days. The message simply read:

*My name is Gage Miller.*

## DELLA RAY

https://www.youtube.com/watch?v=rfSN_lJ7cuw
-when I need you-

I held onto my chest, as the relief poured in. The tension had been like an elephant on my chest. Brutal. Tears rushed to my eyes as I looked around with the desperate need to be out of here. "He's back," I muttered, my voice shaking. "He's fucking back."

"Are you okay?" Gloria asked.

It was only then I realized that I was the object of intense attention of all the staff. "I'm fine," I replied, and hurried out of the kitchen. The crawl towards 5pm was the longest most excruciating wait of my life. The moment it struck, I was out of the door and on my way to Gage Miller.

When I arrived at his door however, a small scream escaped my lips. The door had been kicked open in a fury, its frame

SAVING DELLA-RAY

destroyed and the lock dangling in the air. My eyes widened in alarm as I crept into the apartment. It was eerily quiet. There was no one in the living area, so I ran to his bedroom ... and found him.

On the floor, just a few inches away from the bed. It looked as though the bed had been his goal, but he had been unable to make it. With my heart in my throat, I instantly hurried over to him. When his full state came into view, I had to cover my mouth with horror.

He was covered in blood, but that wasn't what was most horrifying. It was the fact that parts of it had blackened with age, which insinuated that he had been in this state for quite a while. The sides of his head and countless parts of his body were caked with dried blood. His left eye was swollen shut with a terrible bruise surrounding it, and on the other side of his face was a deep gash across his cheek that had turned the skin in several nasty shades. The side of his lip was busted open and from his nose ran a fresh trickle of blood.

I had never seen a man or anyone in this condition and I shouldn't know what to do, but instinct took over and drove me to action. I wasn't even sure he was alive so when I grabbed to his arm and he winced with pain, I sighed with relief. "Bone," I called out. "I mean, Gage."

He muttered something unintelligible.

"We need to get you to a hospital."

He was too heavy to move even an inch, so I rose to my feet and reached into the purse slung across my shoulders for my cell phone. I was so intent on what I was doing I almost jumped out of my skin when his rough hand closed around my ankle. He mumbled something, but it was too low to

239

make out so I quickly lowered myself to the ground and placed my ear close to his lips.

"Don't," he whispered.

"Why the hell not?" I cried. "If you remain in this state any longer you're going to die!" I couldn't even imagine how a man could still be alive in the state he was in. I started to rise to continue with my plan stubbornly but he pulled strongly on my limb and even in his injured state, it was strong enough to send me tumbling down to the floor.

"You'll make it worse. Don't. Someone will be here ..." He trailed off probably in exhaustion and unfathomable pain.

My chest tightened with helpless frustration, but I had no choice but to obey him. I understood so little about the rules and regulations he must submit to and I didn't want my defiance to make things worse for him.

"Let's get you up," I suggested, and went to grab his hand, but he shook his head ever so slightly. To my distress even that tiny movement caused him to grunt with pain.

Beyond worry and wait, I couldn't say or do anything else. I dare not even put a pillow under his head lest I cause more injury. I called Nichole and told her what was happening and warned her that I didn't know when I would be back. She said she had everything covered and I was to only come when everything was fine. She could even take Jess to day care tomorrow if necessary. I thanked her and sat down on the floor next to Gage to wait. It was the most excruciating ten minutes wait of my life as I watched his battered bloody state and waited for whoever it was he was expecting to come.

After what seemed like a lifetime, I heard footsteps as they came through the door. I couldn't help the fear that coursed through my blood as two men appeared at his bedroom door. The first man had a gun and my first thought was … he had come to finish the job and kill Gage.

Thankfully, the man behind him had a black medicine bag in hand. They immediately hurried over when they spotted us.

"Hurry," I said. "He's been beat up bad."

I stood and backed away so they would be able to at least lift him up onto the bed.

It was the most agonizing sight to see him groan with so much pain. It made something freeze over inside of me. The man that had the gun began to inspect him while the other turned to me. "Would you please wait outside, Miss?"

"The hell I will. I'm not going anywhere!" I declared and folded my arms across my chest to monitor them closely.

To my surprise, he just made an exasperated noise and returned his focus to his examination of Gage's injuries.

"How is he?" I asked, five minutes in.

"Badly battered but he'll live. Could you please get me a bowl of hot water so I can wash and dress his wounds?"

"Be right back," I said and rushed to the kitchen. It felt good to be able to finally do something.

"I'm going to get someone to fix the door," the other man said.

A little while later, Bone had been given a sedative. Whether he was conscious or not, through the grueling process of the doctor treating his wounds, I didn't know, but I heard only the occasional hiss of pain and even those tore at my soul.

When the doctor came into the kitchen to wash his hands, I asked him what kind of food would be best for Gage to consume at this time. He recommended soup. I quickly ordered some. Then while I was in the kitchen sorting out a grocery list, I heard the pound of tools. The sounds relieved me greatly. The door was being fixed.

Nichole called me. Jess was feeling restless because she hadn't seen me all day.

She put her on and she was sniffing a bit. "Mommy, why didn't you come and pick me up today?" she asked in a small voice.

"I had something very important to do."

"What was it?"

"Someone was hurt and I had to help them."

"Oh dear," she said, her voice changing. "Was it like that time we helped that baby bird?"

"Yes."

"Where do you think he is now?"

"Well, with his Mom and Dad, of course."

"When will you come home, Mommy?"

"I don't know, honey. But I promise to come as soon as I can, okay?"

"Will you come in time for us to water the wild flowers tomorrow?"

"I think so, but if I'm not there, Nichole will do it with you."

"Oh."

"You'll have to teach her what to do because she won't know where the plants are or anything."

"Yes, I can do that," she said brightly.

"That's my girl. So anyway, how was playschool today?"

She launched into a story about her best friend, Mike. He was a little boy who had a speech impediment. No one else would befriend him, so Jess decided to make him her best friend. As I was listening to her both men came into the kitchen and I turned around to meet their gazes. I knew Jess's story would go on for a long time so I told her I would call her back in five minutes and ended the call.

"He'll be fine," the doctor said to me. "He just needs time to heal."

"Do you have anyone who can stay with him?" I asked. "I need to be at work."

"We don't," the other man said. "But he should be okay. After a proper rest, he should be able to move around, at least a little. I'll be back soon to check on him."

"Instruct me on his medicine and care," I said to the doctor.

Both men turned to gaze at each other.

"I owe him," I explained. "I'll help Gage the best way I can until he gets better."

Now they looked at each other worriedly. Then the man who had come in with the gun spoke, his voice harsh, "Don't ever call him Gage again. Call him Bone. And don't tell anyone else his name either. No one. Do you understand?"

"Okay," I said quickly.

I was given a key for the new lock and then the doctor produced a few packaged drugs from his bag. He instructed me on his food and doses, then they were on their way out.

I'd been hoping to return to work after Gage's treatment even though I was already late and I worried that I had been absent too many times already. However, when I got into the room and saw him lying so still and pale underneath the covers, his eyelids tightly shut in pain, I knew that I wouldn't be able to leave.

I called work and told them I couldn't make it and received an earful from Henry. It was going to be a busy night and they were counting on me. All I could do was apologize profusely. "Get your act together, Della, because you're starting to slack," Henry said as his parting shot.

I knew I would be in financial trouble again if I lost my job, but what could I do? I put thoughts of financial Armageddon away and carried a bowl of lentil soup into the bedroom.

I hated the idea of waking him up if he had already fallen asleep. As no doubt, sleep wouldn't come easily to him given his state. His eyes were shut so I decided to wait a bit more. I was about to tip-toe out when he spoke.

"You shouldn't be here," he said, his voice tense with pain.

My nerves instantly tightened with fear and anger that he would kick me out and for the fact that he'd put himself in this state. "I'm not here for you, but for my own peace of mind."

"If you continue to remain here that peace of mind might be permanently gone."

His voice was low but I could pick up on every strained word. I turned around then to face him. "How?"

"Why the hell did you come here? And why the hell did you go to Reno's? And the fucking police?"

For a few moments, I was struck dumb. "How did you find that out?" I felt a mix of emotions ranging from confusion, dread, and fear rampaging through me, and none of which I was willing to explore. So I focused on the only pressing matter at hand. "Eat your soup. You need energy to heal."

"Leave," he breathed. "Now, and don't come back. If you want to protect Jess and everyone else you love, don't drag them into this mess."

My heart constricted at the mention of Jess, but I couldn't back down. Not when he was in this state. "Don't worry. I'll leave after you're well. You won't have to see me again."

I was about to walk out when I heard a shuffling sound. I turned around to see that he rolled on his side and was in the process of sitting up.

His matted hair was all over his battered face. Strangely, it made his hooded blue gaze all the more piercing as he lifted his eyes up to me. "Why aren't you listening to me? Do you think this is all a joke?"

I couldn't even feel the sting of his rebuke because finally he was alive, the way I always knew him. I knew then that he would heal again. That no matter how bad it looked ... Bone would beat it. The relief made tears gather in my eyes. I tried my very best to chase them away, but failed miserably.

A frown spread across his forehead.

"Eat your soup," I said, my voice breaking. "I'll be back tomorrow, but in the meantime, let me know if you need any help and I'll be right over." I left his apartment then and rushed to work. All the while, I wondered about those men who had come to help him. They must all really want revenge bad on that guy Bone had mentioned before.

Lena smiled when she saw me. "Oh, good you're here. Table nine is asking for you," she said as she passed me, a full tray in her hand.

I changed quickly and I was back at work. I smiled, laughed and chatted with my customers and felt better than I had all week.

Now, I knew he was alive.

# GAGE

I couldn't believe that I couldn't walk.

I looked at the wheelchair with disgust.

Yuri straightened from his job of assembling the darn thing. "Do you need help getting on?"

I turned my face away. "Just leave it there, thanks."

"Alright then," he said, his gaze going to the half-eaten meal by my table. "They're aware now, aren't they? That you own this place."

"No doubt," I sighed. "It's probably under surveillance. You were careful on your way in, I trust."

"Of course. I had my glasses on and was careful with my angles. Even if they get a picture they have nothing clear enough to search with."

"Well, don't come by anymore."

"I won't," he responded but then his eyes went once again to the food on the table.

"What?" I asked.

"The girl, she's—" he began.

I immediately shut it down. "I'll get rid of her."

"Don't," he said immediately.

A cold claw tightened around my stomach. "What?"

"She's good collateral for you. They still suspect you, but with her around, they'll figure anything that you do out of the ordinary will be because of her. Perhaps they'll think you're in love with her and so will want to protect her."

I stared at him like he was out of his mind. "You do know what that will mean for her, right? She will no longer be safe."

"Look who's talking about safe. You told her your fucking name, for crying out loud."

I dropped my head. I shouldn't have done that. I was half-dead and I just wanted her to know in case I died.

"She's already attached to you," he continued. "So you might as well just ride it out. If we plan it well, your death at the end can release her of any relation to you. They will never come after her and she'll be free then to live her life as she sees fit."

Anger at his words nearly blinded me. "I don't want her involved." I growled.

"Don't be stupid, Gage."

I smacked the lamp by my side. It flew across the room and crashed into the wall.

He lowered his voice, but still went on, "Get as mad as you want, but you shouldn't have gotten with her in the first place. I've seen how she is with you that first night we came. Her attachment to you is not ... ordinary. I don't think she'll walk away from you even if you told her to go."

"She's not going to be a part of this," I repeated, and my word was final.

He just shrugged. "Up to you man. If you want to get your man, I suggest you start thinking with your head and not your dick."

"Get the fuck out!" I shouted.

"Call me if you need me," he said as he walked away.

I lay back on the pillows and cursed out loud. I looked at the clock. It was five. She would be finished with her shift at the diner now. I thought of her. How she made her ugly uniform look like it was something right off the catwalk. And even in my broken state, my cock stirred. Yuri was right about one thing. I was a fool who'd been thinking with my dick. And I had to stop doing that. I had to find a way to protect her.

Twenty minutes passed with me staring at the minute hand of the clock slowly ticking my life away. Eventually, I rolled over to the kitchen. I needed food to get my strength back. I was no good to anyone like this. I was reaching up for a pan when I heard the sound of the key in the door.

In spite of everything I had said to myself, I felt my heart leap with joy.

With the help of the counter's edge, I leaned up a bit from the chair to reach for the handle of the saucepan on the top shelf, but it toppled over and the entire set of metal pans came crashing down upon me.

I collapsed back into the chair just as she came into view. "Bone!" Della cried and hurried over. "You're in a wheelchair?"

"Yeah." I picked up the pan I needed from the floor and slammed it on top of the stove.

She stopped just before she reached me. She could see that I was in a bad mood and she didn't know how to proceed.

I let her know. "I told you not to come back." I dumped the contents of a can of soup into the pan.

"There's no need to eat that," she said to me. "I got you better food. Steak and fries."

I wanted so much for her to stay that I became angry with myself. To hide my face, I bent and began to pick up the pots and pan within my reach on the ground, but she instantly came over to help me.

My hand reflexively shot out not to shove her away, but to stop her from coming any closer to me, but to my horror, the force of my hand caused her to fly backwards and almost slam into the wall. I stared at her sprawled on the floor. My hand trembled as it instinctively reached for her.

She got to her feet, slowly and quietly.

I couldn't speak. I was afraid. I kept pretending to myself that I wanted her to walk away, but the idea of losing her permanently terrified me.

She didn't meet my eyes as she walked away.

I knew this was my best chance of letting her go. If she walked away now, she would never come back, but suddenly I couldn't breathe. I pushed my chair forward, grabbed her waist and pulled her to me. Turning her around, I leaned forward, buried my face in her stomach, and refused to let her go. I was filled with remorse.

She remained still, then she spoke very quietly, "Apologize."

"I'm sorry ..." my voice shook. "I am so, so sorry. I would never, ever hurt you. It was an accident. A pure accident."

She loosened my grip from around her then and began to pick up the fallen utensils.

I stayed still and didn't dare meet her gaze.

She placed them on the counter, turned off the gas, and then returned to the meal that she had been unpacking.

I turned the chair around to face her. "I don't want you to be in danger Della-Ray," I pleaded with her. "Please listen to me."

"I don't want you to be alone. Not at this time. And I've told you, it's not for you. It's for my own peace of mind."

"Why does it bother you so much if I'm hurt or not?"

"How the hell would I know?" she yelled, finally turning to me. The sudden outburst surprised even her. Della turned around and leaned against the counter to catch her breath. "I'll be out of here when you can stand on your own."

# GAGE

She didn't know it, but I understood exactly what she was talking about. My safety rattled her peace of mind just as hers did mine. But neither of us wanted to acknowledge it because that would solidify the dilemma in a way that couldn't be resolved without a painful ending.

"I'm in a position right now where all I can tell you about myself, is that I care about you. Is it enough?" I asked

She halted. "Enough for what?"

"Enough for you to put your life on the line to be with me. Because if it is not enough, then you better leave right now."

She stilled once again, then left the counter to retrieve a plate from the cupboard. Her answer when it came was strained and filled with desperate hope, "Are you saying that you want to be with me?"

"I want to try, I'm not sure I'm capable of being the man you need."

"What does that even mean?"

"That it's the wrong time ... for the both of us. I'm still filled with wounds that haven't healed. I don't want to make you become another. And I can't walk away yet. I've got something I have to do. So please trust me, and give me time. If I ... if it's meant to be, I'll come back to you."

She dropped her gaze and clasped her hands tightly. "I'm not asking for—a future with you. All I know is you're terribly injured right now and I'm not going to leave you to handle it all on your own. I owe that much to you."

"Okay," I said softly. "That's a good starting place."

She still couldn't look me in the eyes. "I only stopped by to bring you food. Why don't you go sit on the bed and I'll bring it to you?"

"Okay ..." I rolled the chair towards the bedroom.

## Della

I was longing for a future with him. It was my dream, the thing I prayed for, but I was too afraid to believe that it could even be possible. A haze of doubts and fears regarding his safety, mine and Jess's made any thoughts of a life with him seem like a fantasy. And I never was one to believe in fantasies. I knew there was no Santa Claus before any of the other kids at school.

I didn't want to be late for my shift at the bar so I quickly popped his still warm food on the plate and seconds later, I was walking towards his bedroom carrying a tray of food and drink.

He was sitting by the window. It looked out to an empty field. There was absolutely nothing to see, but he was admiring the scenery.

I knew somehow that he was no longer in the room, but in some private hell of his. "Why don't you eat it while the food is hot," I said placing the meal on the nightstand.

He turned and looked at me. Something in his expression made my heart bleed. I wanted to go to him, but I was afraid he would reject me. My greatest concern was that he would confront me and ask for the new key to his door that his friends had allowed me to hold onto.

He said nothing, just stared at me.

I stood there awkwardly, shifting from one foot to the other. It seemed impossible to think that we were lovers. To think how wild we became when our skin touched. I hugged myself. "I should go. I don't want to be late again. I'll be back tomorrow with more food."

"Goodnight, Della," he said softly.

"Goodnight to you too," I said, backing out of the room.

## DELLA RAY

For the rest of the night, not a single real smile could I
rustle up. I handled my usual duties, but for the first
time, I felt truly dissatisfied. I had never really thought of
anything beyond my current engagements, my constant and
immediate need to get through the work I needed to do to
ensure my paycheck at the end of each week.

That paycheck would go towards what Jess and I would
need, her medical bills and our living expenses. We were
always in debt … we were always lacking, but I had truly
never felt dissatisfied until today. I felt tired and used up.
When was the wanting going to stop?

When I got a moment's break from serving, I tossed my tray
to a nearby table, then sat down and glanced around the
room I had spent most of my nights in over the last three
years. I was wasting my life, but there was nothing I could do
about it really. And soon I would have the worry of Denise
trying to put Jess in an orphanage. I sighed with despair.

Henry was passing by at that moment and I guess he noted

the darkness on my face. He pulled out the chair in front of me and sat. "Hey, hey, what's going on?" he asked.

I didn't even want to speak. I just slightly stretched my lips into a passable smile.

"What's wrong?" he asked.

Where to start telling him about the mess of my life. "What's right?"

He sucked in air through his teeth. "Is it serious?"

I was never one to complain. It solved nothing. I straightened my spine. "Don't mind me. I'm just sulking. It's just today. I'll be as right as rain tomorrow."

"One of those days then, huh?" He smiled.

I nodded.

"You know what I told you about not pulling your weight around here?"

"I know. I'm sorry."

"Hang on. Hang on. I was wrong. I shouldn't have said that. You are one of the best workers we have here. When you're slacking off is the only time when one of us can rival you."

Suddenly, I felt all emotional. At least someone appreciated me.

He knew I was fighting back the tears so he turned away to gaze at the fairly busy bar, his hands linked together behind his shaved head.

Time to change the subject or I would start balling my eyes out. "Do you have any plans?" I asked. I'd never given his life outside the bar any thought. "Beyond this bar? You've been working here even longer than I have."

He glanced back at me. "Of course. I've been saving for a bit to open a mechanic workshop. I spend my days fixing up cars, then hop over here for the night. You do the same don't you, with the diner?"

"Yeah," I replied. "But I'm definitely not saving towards anything."

"Well, you can't do that too easily." His voice softened. "You have your niece to take care of. Her bills must be very expensive. Are you feeling burdened?"

"Never!"

"So what's the problem?"

"I don't know," I lied. "I used to always feel satisfied, but not so much now. Maybe it's just tonight."

He peered into my eyes. "Did something new happen?"

"Not really."

"Hmm ... that means that something did and whether good or bad it means that you need a change. Even if it's of jobs and goals. Don't ignore it." With two taps on the table, he rose and went back to work.

I did the same, with his words echoing in my head. There was nothing new about what he had said, but I could feel my resistance to keeping the past as it was - beginning to melt. For the first time in a very long time - I wanted more.

# GAGE

I was seated in front of the television, a soft plaid blanket that Della had brought, over my jeans when a strong knock sounded at the door.

"Bone!"

I'd been expecting trouble and in a way, it was good to finally meet it head on. I rolled the wheelchair over to the door, turned the lock, and pulled it open.

Tyler, Rose, and Volt stood in the corridor.

Their uninvited visit was a big deal, especially as they were not supposed to be aware of this apartment's existence, but they were past pretending. We all knew that bridge had long been crossed.

Without a word, I turned around and headed back to the place in the living room where I had been. I had a gun hidden on my lap and was grateful for the foresight to have kept it underneath the blanket as I'd settled in for the evening with the news on.

They came in and the racket began.

"You're living large, Bone," Rose bellowed, his eyes sparkling with excitement as they roamed around the apartment.

The other two took their seats on the sofa.

I turned towards them.

"How you holding up?" Volt asked.

I glared at them both.

Tyler folded his hands across his chest and leaned back into the sofa. "We're here for further investigation," he said. "You're not off the hook yet."

"Don't take offense, Bone," Rose said and came over to stand by my side. "You know how things are. Jump these last hoops and you'll be in the clear soon enough."

"We need your fingerprints," Tyler said.

Volt immediately began to dig into his backpack for what I supposed was a kit.

"What for?" I asked, my tone cold and unforgiving.

"It's an added measure," he replied.

I turned away from him. All these checks had been done before I was patched into the club two years earlier but now it was all being re-done to see if they had missed something. Thus far, they had re-obtained my social security number, all addresses, and needed background information in a bid to review if I was a rat.

"You screwed up big time," Rose said. "But if all goes well, especially with the drug deal in a few weeks then we'll petition Snake and the rest of the club. You'll be re-instated and all will be back to normal."

I didn't bother informing him that a month from now, I intended to be dead. I didn't need reinstating into their stupid fucking club.

Suddenly, there was movement at the front door and we all looked up.

"Expecting someone?" Tyler asked.

I glanced towards the clock on the kitchen wall. It was only four o'clock so it shouldn't be her, but I knew it was her. I felt chills go down my arms and the hair at the back of my head stood. My hands nervously gripped the chair, but I stopped myself before I could overreact and put us both in deeper suspicion.

She walked in and froze when she saw the full house.

Suddenly, I heard the cock of a gun from behind me and saw fear flash in her eyes just as she let out a scream of terror. She shot down to the floor, her hands to her ears, the plastic bag she had brought falling to the ground.

My gaze briefly noted the bell pepper that rolled out of the bag before I turned around to see that Volt was the one who had a gun pointed directly at her. "Put that damn thing away!" I growled. I hoped that for his sake, he didn't think I was joking.

He didn't respond. Instead, he shared a look with Tyler, and began to move towards her.

The blanket across my lap flew off and in a flash, he was staring down the barrel of my own gun.

The entire room went very still.

For what seemed like a lifetime, no one said anything.

Then Tyler rose slowly. With his gaze on me, he went over to Volt who was also staring at me in surprise. With his hand on Volt's hand, he lowered the gun.

I refused to lower mine. "Go to the bedroom, Della," I ordered.

When she didn't move, I turned to glance at her.

She was trembling. Her lips parted to speak, but the words wouldn't come out.

"I'm fine," I assured her. "Now go to the bedroom and close the door."

With a brave glare at the other men that quite surprised me, she picked herself up from the floor and left the room.

I returned the safety to my gun, picked up the blanket from the floor, and spread it across my lap.

"I wasn't going to hurt her, Bone," Volt said, his tone dipping with a hint of hurt at my reaction.

"Well, I was going to hurt you," I stated clearly. "If I had my full strength, you would be unconscious by now."

"Whoa, Bone," Rose complained. "Take it easy man. You're the one who messed up. Everyone does from time to time, and they pay for it. Why are you so sour about it?"

"Get your fucking questions done and be on your way!"

## DELLA RAY

I hugged my knees and I waited for Bone. The whole time, my ears were cocked, listening carefully for every bit of movement or trouble.

My hand was on my phone, ready to call for help if he needed it, but even then I knew it would be too late. When the door was suddenly pushed open, I jumped up from the bed, my knees almost giving out in relief when Bone rode in with his wheelchair.

"I'm sorry he startled you," he apologized.

I watched him, my heart breaking at the state he was in. I couldn't hold back anymore. I was trembling like a leaf in a storm. "I want you to leave the club." I sounded ridiculous and I knew as I had absolutely no right to request this of him, but right this minute I didn't care what he thought. I just had to say my piece. I had earned the right after that idiot pointed a gun at me for no freaking reason at all. "I want you to leave otherwise I'm—I'm not going to be involved with you any longer. And it's going to be your fucking loss. With me and Jess, you could live a better life, I swear it to you. You don't need to live in this insane MC life."

I felt as though I had gone crazy, my breathing was ragged, and out of control. I wanted to shake him awake, to pour some common sense into him. He could never benefit from the club. It just couldn't be worth the constant risk to his life.

"I'll leave," he said quietly.

I froze. I was almost too scared to ask, just in case I'd heard wrong. "What?"

"I'll leave," he repeated. "In four weeks."

I swiped the tears away from my cheeks. "What? What do you mean? What's happening in four weeks?"

He didn't respond.

I lowered my gaze from the brightness of his eyes so I could think. Then it came to me. His retaliation for the death of his friend. Something deathly cold slithered through me. "What are you going to do? What do you mean exactly by you're going to leave? Do you mean the club or …" I couldn't say it.

He looked ashen under his tan. "I can't tell you."

"You're just going to get yourself killed, aren't you?" I sobbed. I had truly gotten involved with the wrong man. I rose from the chair and looked around in a daze in search of my purse. I found it on the floor and slung the strap across my shoulder.

I wanted to say goodbye to him but I didn't have the courage to.

My heart felt like it was splitting into a thousand pieces

inside of me. But better now when I could still recover frag-ments of it to keep me moving forward, rather than later on when I would be even more invested in him. Just the thought of him getting hurt destroyed me in ways that I didn't want to even fathom. With my parents' deaths, I had known what it felt like to lose a part of your being. I didn't want to ever feel that way again.

"I've got to go to work. Your food is still on the floor. Help yourself," I said and walked out of the room without looking back.

# DELLA RAY

https://www.youtube.com/watch?v=PaKr9gWqwl4
-only love can hurt like this-

Two weeks later, and I was slowly crumbling into an irredeemable mess. Even Jess noticed. She brought out her pink doctor's bag and started taking my temperature and listening to my heartbeat using her pink stereoscope. "I think you need more vitamins," she said after a very thorough examination, which included looking into my ears with one of her medical instruments.

She wrote me a prescription and I promised her I would go to the pharmacy and get it.

Even Nichole tried to ease the burden by doing more house-hold chores, but that just made me feel even guiltier. There was nothing wrong with my body. It was just that my heart was breaking.

That evening I walked into my shift at the bar, sleep deprived, with a headache that was threatening to split my head into two, and found it already bursting with patrons. I stopped at the door. Suddenly, I felt as though I couldn't do one more night here. As I stood there indecisively at the entrance, Henry spotted me as he rushed by with a tray filled with cocktails and cried to me to come to his aid.

Pushing my mental exhaustion aside, I pushed myself into the bar and got to work. I spent the night mixing up orders and spilling alcohol everywhere.

Midway through the shift, Tim, the manager confronted me. "What's going on with you? Is something wrong with your niece?"

"No. I'm sorry, I don't know what's wrong with me," was all I could say. My entire body felt like a lump of wood that I was lugging around.

"Go home," he said.

My eyes widened at him in surprise. "It's okay, Tim—"

"No, Della. It's not okay. This has been going on for a while now," he said. "You used to be my best employee, but now you're constantly distracted and sometimes downright sour. It's costing me. Just go home and let me know when you're ready to come back to work." He walked away with a pained expression.

I realized how difficult it must have been for him to do that. I bucked up then and put all my effort into properly completing the shift.

When Henry dropped me off that night, he squeezed my

arm. "It'll be fine. Just get your head together and come back as soon as you can, okay?"

I nodded. I felt numb inside.

When he drove away, I stared at the door and didn't want to go inside. Didn't want to go to my room and toss and turn for the remainder of the night in remembrance of how it had felt to have him there with me. It was all driving me out of my mind.

Releasing a heavy sigh, I stared up at the moon. It was full, creamy yellow and beautiful, but all I could think about was how he was faring and if he had healed by now.

I glanced back at the tree where he had once ravished me. In a moment of weakness, I pulled my phone out of my bag. I even called up his number with my heart pounding in my chest. But just before I could make the grave mistake of calling him, the sound of an approaching car attracted my attention. I turned around to see a glistening SUV pull up by our sidewalk. No way could Nichole be expecting a guest at this time. Especially since, she wasn't even home now. She'd taken Jess with her to visit her parents for the night. Jess loved going there because her parents had a big German Shepherd that simply adored her.

Uneasily, I turned fully to watch to see who got out of the car. A shadow rounded the vehicle, but when he came into the light of the evening, my mood plummeted into hell.

"What are you doing here?" I spat at the slime that had come to pay a visit.

"Della-Ray," he called out, a sick smile across his face. "You can't possibly still be this mad at me."

I couldn't believe this. "You're unbelievable. You can't possibly still think you're in any way still welcome in my life. What is wrong with you? Why do you keep showing up?"

His response was a dry, grating chuckle. "I heard you were done with Bone! So I was hoping I'd have a chance now."

I glared at him, wondering how someone could be so dense. I didn't have the capacity right now to handle any of this so I simply said to him, "Michael, please leave, otherwise I'm going to call the cops and this time around, I'm going to press charges against you."

I turned around to leave, but he came at me and grabbed my arm. Anger like I'd never known roared up inside of me. This was the worst possible time for him to be trying something like this. I felt like I could kill him.

"Della-Ray, give me another chance," he pleaded. "I'll be good to you I promise … and your niece. We had something good between us."

"Let me go!" I screamed, and pushed him away with all my might. I could smell the alcohol on his breath and it made me feel sick.

"Awww … come on baby girl," he cajoled.

"Don't you dare touch me!" I reached for my phone, dialed 911, and placed the phone to my ear, but he smacked it away from me. The phone fell to the grass. I didn't panic, because I knew all I had to do was keep screaming, and one of my neighbors would come out and help me. In fact, Mr. Harper two doors down, who loved both me and Nichole, was also a hunter who owned a shotgun. I knew he was a mean shot. A few times, he brought us pieces of meat that he had hunted himself.

As I turned around, Michael grabbed me and pulled me into his arms.

The moment his mouth landed on mine, I roiled with the need to puke. I struck blows at him that seemed to hurt me a hundred times worse than it did him, but just when I was about to kick him in the nuts and send him reeling so I could scream my head off, he was suddenly dragged away from me.

It took me a while to comprehend what was happening as I fought to catch my breath, but when I did, I was struck with shock. I used the back of my hand to wipe my mouth as I watched Gage jam his fist into Michael's face.

Michael went flying backwards.

Gage turned to me, his hair tousled from the wind, his face had healed quite nicely.

I stared at him as if he was in a dream I was having. An indescribably beautiful dream. In this dream I couldn't speak, at least until Michael made a sound which made Gage turn back around to face him.

"Don't hurt yourself!" I warned in panic, as I scrambled to retrieve my phone. "I'll handle him. I can call the cops."

Ignoring me, Gage crouched down to grab Michael by the hair. He pulled his face towards him and after saying low words to him that I couldn't hear he pushed him back on the grass.

He then grabbed my forearm and would have dragged me with him, but I pulled back. He turned around to look at me.

"Why are you here, you sick asshole?" I asked, my tone thick with bitterness and emotion.

"You can call me any name you want, it's not going to change a thing. I'll keep on coming here every night to check up on you," he said.

My heart knocked hard against my ribs at the thought of him caring that much that he was looking out for me, but then it made me mad as hell to think he wouldn't give up his stupid club for me. "If you're not going to be with me, then why bother? I can take care of myself."

"No, you fucking can't," he said.

I could hear the furious tremble in his voice. To learn that he was probably going through even a bit of the hell that I was ... gave me a thrill of joy. I stepped forward and slipped my hands around him, holding him tightly to me as I pressed myself against his chest.

*Then take care of me properly. Get out of that damn club and choose me, I* wanted to say, but I didn't dare. I knew I would be only asking for more rejection.

"Then take me home with you tonight and show me how much you care," I said instead.

# GAGE

I turned around and she hopped up on me, her legs opening wide, so I could feel the heat from her warm willing pussy on my stomach. Jesus, it felt like it had been so long. I couldn't wait to feel her naked body against my skin again. I held her tightly then kissed her exposed neck and collarbone.

Then I swooped on her mouth. This was mine. And only mine. I wanted to kill that asswipe when I saw him kiss her. I wasn't done with him yet. But that could wait. Nothing was more important than this moment with her.

I lifted my head and in the moonlight, I saw the hurt and the sadness in her eyes. Taking her to my bike, I carried her off into the night. The wind felt good in my face. This was how it was always meant to be. Me and her riding out in the open road. I felt her rest her cheek on my back.

When we got back to my place, she wanted to walk, but I wouldn't let her. It was some romantic notion of mine to carry her to my lair and do what I wanted to her. I put her on the bed and watched her get undressed. I bent down, laid my forehead against her belly and breathed in the scent of her pussy. Like a drug … it fucking intoxicated me. I licked around her belly button. Then I bit the soft flesh hard enough to leave teeth marks.

She jumped with surprise.

Yeah, I wanted to leave marks on her body. "Open your legs and lift up your hips so I can see everything you've got, baby," I ordered.

Obediently, she spread her legs wide.

My cock was so hard and heavy, I had to reach down and rub it through my boxer briefs to relieve the ache. "Now hook your knees with your elbows, baby. I want to see what I'm gonna eat."

She pulled her knees outward and exposed everything to me. Her glistening pussy opened up like a pink flower. I could see her pretty little thing throbbing and pulsing for my cock. I rubbed her dripping slit, and the tender petals, before gently dipping my finger into her hungry little hole.

Della gasped and closed her eyes.

Her scent alone was driving me insane, so I gave in to the temptation and licked the insides of her thighs all smeared with her cream. As soon as her flavor hit my brain, I lost all control. I sucked her whole pussy into my mouth like a fucking caveman.

"Gage," she moaned, as desperate for my cock as I was for her pussy.

"Mmmm … Mmmmm …" Hell, I couldn't get enough of her.

The more I drank the more addicted I became. "Come on my face, baby," I said, as I devoured her. Sucking her juicy clit hard, I felt her body bow off the bed.

"Jesus, Gage!" she screamed as she grabbed my head to climax hard and deep all over my mouth and beard.

Hearing her scream made me feel like a God. A feeling I hadn't felt for years. I lifted my head and looked down at her. She was still wide open. Even her little asshole was all wet from her dripping nectar and begging for my cock. I could do anything with her. Anything. Because she was all mine. Only mine. Every hole, every nook, every cranny, every curve—mine. The fact that she wanted me to do whatever I wanted with her made it all the more delicious.

I got my dick out and stood over her. "I'm going to go in bare tonight, Della-Ray. I want to fill you up with my seed. I want to fill up your mouth, your throat, your belly, and your pussy with my cum."

She nodded eagerly as she still panted.

I grabbed her wrists and held them over her head. She looked so beautiful like this. Her skin so creamy with spots of pink blushes and so fucking helpless. Too good for me, but I wasn't giving her up for nothing.

Fisting my cock, I put it at her entrance and thrust hard into her wet warmth. A little moan escaped her as I pushed my fat cock even deeper still. I let her feel my hunger. "You like my bare cock inside you, baby?"

Her nod turned into a gasp of pain as I bit one hard nipple.

"There's never going to be anything or anyone between us, you hear me?"

"I hear you," she panted.

I bit her other nipple and felt a gush from her pussy flow over my dick. I started sucking that nipple as I fucked her harder. She was so hot and wet it was pure heaven. Grabbing her hips with both hands, I tilted them up more, so I could get a deeper angle. I felt her pussy hot and silky, clench around my dick with every thrust. I could feel myself already hovering on the edge, so I stopped, but she started to rock her hips, and fuck herself on my cock.

I ravaged her lips with a kiss as her warm tongue swept into my mouth.

Then she bit my bottom lip still sticky with her juices and sucked it into her mouth. "I'm going to come," she warned.

I grabbed one of her legs and swung it over my shoulder. I got in so deep she let out what sounded like a cross between a yelp and a moan. I felt her pussy spasm against my bare cock.

"Come inside me, Gage," she screamed as she went over the edge.

I thrust hard and felt myself explode deep inside her, enjoying the sensation of her pussy milking my hot cock.

We lay together in a tangle of limbs for quite a while as we came back down to earth.

We rested for a bit, then I ordered a takeout. Sitting close together, we ate the food. Afterwards, we fucked again. This time it was different. I took my time and made it last as I moved slowly and deeply into her, savoring every moan and whimper from her lips. She then sobbed her heart out. I held

SAVING DELLA-RAY

her close and promised her that the next time ... I wouldn't be taking her home afterwards.

She looked into my eyes, her eyes so full of yearning I had to open her legs and bury my mouth in her pussy so I didn't blurt out things that would bring danger to her.

Dawn was in the sky when I took her back home.

There were tears in her eyes. "Please be careful, Gage. It's not just you alone in this world now. There's me too. I'm here waiting for you."

# GAGE

Altogether, fifteen of us set out in four different vehicles of varying levels of inconspicuousness on the two-day road trip to Dallas.

We looked nothing like bikers, our vests hidden away and in its place simple t-shirts and flannels that told the story of normalcy. We were still under investigation for the fire, so we had to be extra careful.

I rode in Snake's Camaro, with the owner himself at the wheel, as Skippy and Volt were squashed in the back. RJ rode shotgun with Tyler in his Range Rover by order so that he could be monitored and kept in check in case he got too … excited.

We arrived in Dallas and checked into a motel. We were the last group to get there. The rest had already logged into other motels in different parts of town.

The next morning, we went at varying times to the quiet neighborhood in Eastwood.

We were received at the door by three men from the cartel's party and led down to the basement. Another group of men patted us down for weapons or wires and when we were all ordered to leave our weapons outside, my stomach instinctively tightened.

Once everyone was satisfactorily clean, lookout posts were assigned, and the meeting began.

I went over to one corner to listen carefully. I took a mental note of every one of them and listened very carefully as Snake was introduced to their leads and of course, RJ's cousin.

The address for the shipment's location was given and I was put in charge of the shipment truck filled with tomatoes that was waiting to be inspected.

I pulled out my phone to inform the remainder of our party that were on standby, so they could confirm that the shipment was indeed there. Nobody said anything while we waited for confirmation. When my phone rang within fifteen minutes, I snatched it and Dog confirmed that it was all there. As I ended the call, the funds exchange in the room began.

Just then, a sudden shout came from above. All our heads shot up to the ceiling towards the thundering of footsteps.

Snake's gaze immediately connected with mine. "Go!" he commanded.

I turned to Volt to come with me.

We hurried up the stairs to retrieve the guns that we had surrendered. I quickly found mine while Volt did the same and we rushed towards the front to see two of the Mexicans crouching and peeping through the window.

"What's going on?" I asked.

Rose turned to me, fear in his eyes. "The cops are here. They've fucking surrounded the building. How the hell did this fucking happen?"

"Remain calm," I said to him.

"How the fuck are we going to get out of here?" he shouted.

I could see that the entire house was surrounded by almost a dozen Dallas police cars, if not more. They were all stationed out of their cars, their guns at the ready. I gave Rose the only answer that would be suitable, "It's going to get bloody."

"Fuck!" he screamed.

I hurried back down to the basement to inform the rest of the men of the situation.

Panic instantly broke out.

"What the fuck!" RJ's cousin Marcus turned to Snake in fury. "Did you fucking do this?"

Snake was immediately triggered. "Have you lost your mind?"

"Then how the fuck is this happening?" Marcus asked. "We only sent you this location an hour ago, so how the fuck is this happening?"

"You got a fucking snitch in your nest?" one of the Mexicans screamed.

Another of his companions spat, "RJ, what the fuck is this?"

RJ's hands were on his head. He looked doomed. I had never seen him so quiet as he shook his head, wide-eyed with confusion. "I c-can't understand."

"We need to figure out how to get out of here," Snake said, his voice cold and measured as usual.

"Should we surrender?" I asked.

They all looked at me like I was insane, the previous suspicion of my loyalty flashing across their eyes, but in that moment they had bigger fish to fry. Mainly how to get out of this death trap alive.

"We don't have that much ice in here," I explained. "Perhaps the cash would be the biggest problem."

"With this much cash present, they'll be on the fucking look out for the rest of the shipment. We're going to fucking lose everything," Tyler said.

"We can burn the money," I suggested. "Without that, they've got nothing."

The room was silent as everyone contemplated my suggestion. They knew it was our only hope. Suddenly, Skippy flew down the stairs. "They're advancing!" he cried. "We need to get out of here."

We all exchanged looks with Snake, but it was the Mexican gang's boss who made the call, "I'm not getting arrested. I either walk out of here on my own two feet or as a corpse."

That ended any debate we could have had.

Snake stepped forward and we all headed upstairs. From the window, we assessed the situation.

Tyler straightened and said, "We need a hostage and it has to be someone big."

I studied the area and knew exactly who to point to. "Him," I responded, the sheriff at the back who was on the phone. "He seems to be the one in charge."

"We might not be able to get to him," said one of the Mexican dealers. "Any one of them is just as good. The moment someone gets out here and just before you're arrested, disarm someone and place the gun to his head."

"That's fucking risky," Snake said. "They might—"

"It won't be," Marcus countered. "We'll attack from here. Which of your men have clear shots? We'll use that to startle them before they put him in handcuffs. From this distance, they can't fucking miss."

The room went quiet. A few seconds later, it was broken by Tyler as he cocked the gun in his hand. "I won't miss," he said with steel resolve in his eyes.

"Neither would most of us here. The real question is who's going to take the risk and go fight for a chance for the rest of us?"

The room went even more silent, the only sound was the loudspeaker outside commanding us all to step out in surrender.

Suddenly the last voice I wanted to hear spoke up, "I'll go."

We all turned to RJ.

"I set this up in the first place, I'll be the one to end it."

Tyler immediately retaliated. "I'm not fucking putting my life in the hands of a madman like you."

"So what the fuck are we going to do then?" RJ roared.

Tyler pointed the gun at him. "Just fucking stay put. If you're itching for a bullet through your head I can help you out with that, but not at the risk of the only shot we might have of getting out of here."

The room went silent again.

"If we mess it up this once, they won't fall for it again," Marcus said.

"I'll go," Snake suddenly announced pulling his jean jacket off his shoulders.

I wasn't surprised. I kinda knew he would step up, but I was ready for him. "No. You're too important to our club. Without the head, the snake doesn't live to fight another day. I'll go."

The room went silent at my declaration. I cocked my gun in preparation. No one else would care enough to stop me since I was offering, but the quiet grief over my safety filled the room.

"You might not make it," Snake said quietly.

I tucked the gun behind me into the waistband of my jeans. "Well, someone has to go," was my response. "I'll hold onto one of them for as long as I can. Make sure that you're all able to take them."

"Stay alive," Skippy said. "They'll arrest you but we'll be able to get you out. Just make sure to stay alive."

With one last look at the men, whose world I had lived in for the last two years, I pulled the door open and with my hands in the air I stepped out towards the barrage of law enforcement officials awaiting me.

## DELLA RAY

https://www.youtube.com/watch?v=pmTiK9jp970
-there's a calm before the storm-

I was halfway through the first coat of shell pink polish on my right hand, when my phone began to ring. I was ready to ignore it, but when I saw that it was Nichole, I leaned over and tapped the call through. "Hey."

"Where are you?" she asked, her tone grim.

"Home. I just put Jess to bed. We left pizza for you. Where are you?"

"Sorry I couldn't come back on time to help you with Jess."

"It's okay. I don't start back at the Sinkhole until tomorrow."

"Are you in the living room? Is the television on?"

My brows furrowed at her strange questions. "No," I replied. "I'm in my room. Why?"

"Nothing," she responded. "I'll be back soon."

"Are you okay?" I asked again.

"Of course. We'll talk when I get back. Bye."

"Okaaaaaay," I responded and wondered at her strange tone. I went over to the living room and switched on the television. The news channel was on, but it was on a commercial break.

Before I could pay much attention however, there was a knock on the door. It was hard and immediately made me ill at ease. I went over to it and took a peek through the peephole, but saw no one. I waited, as uneasy feeling trickled down my spine. I had ordered some new shoes for Jess, but a delivery at this time? My hand reached out to lock it, when the door flew open. I fell back with a scream and Michael loomed over me. There was a sick leer on his face, but there was something different about it. It was as if he knew something I didn't. I was afraid, but I wouldn't show him. Nichole would be here anytime.

There wasn't much he could do to me.

"You're here again?" I spat. "How can you have absolutely no self-respect? I told you the next time—"

With his hand to my chest, he pushed me into the house.

I staggered back, losing my footing and landing on my ass painfully. Now, I was really afraid.

He looked around. "You haven't heard, have you?"

I was stunned and very afraid. I began to peel myself off the floor.

"Bone is dead!" he announced.

Everything in me stilled. The strength left my bones, and I collapsed back on the floor. My voice was a whisper. "What?"

He linked his hands together to watch me, and I suddenly realized why he came here. To watch me spectacularly fall apart.

He turned towards the television that I had put on, but had not yet paid attention to. They had returned from their commercial break and the red breaking news strip lined the screen. I listened to the broadcaster, her face not particularly registering, but her words striking every single chord in my shocked heart.

She was discussing with another guest about the bust of more than 3500 pounds of meth hidden in tomato crates heading across the state, discovered through the interception of the dealings between the Mexican cartel and the outlaw biker club based in the picturesque town of Arnault.

They had tried to escape, with the now deceased member simply known as Bone holding an officer at gunpoint, but the officials had been able to quickly disarm him and in the confusion, he had been killed. All the culprits were now in custody with many wounded from the resulting vehicle crashes.

Thus far, only one death had been recorded and it was the one that chased my soul out of my body.

I turned to Michael, who was watching me intently.

"I've seen it," I replied woodenly. "Could you please leave now?"

His laughter was haunting. "Not on your life."

## DELLA RAY

I left without making a fuss because Michael asked me whether I wanted to go with him alone or would I need to take Jess with us. She was the perfect bargaining chip for my submission.

He seemed quite disappointed at how easily I had given in, but at this point rather than panic, my brain seemed to have shut down. Instead, I could only look on and regard everything with a numb emptiness. I didn't even feel pain at Gage's death. That would come later.

Three men were waiting for me outside the black van parked in front of the house. I knew then that I was in deep trouble. This was not a little revenge planned and executed by Michael. This was club business.

Never mind, at least I would be getting away from Jess first and then I would figure out the rest once she was out of the equation. I was bundled into the back and the doors were shut. There was nothing in there, except some old pieces of cardboard. I sat on them and let my eyes get used to the darkness.

We drove through the night, much farther than I had expected. A couple of hours later or perhaps it only felt that way to me, and we arrived at a cabin in the middle of nowhere. The doors opened and the only thing I could see all around was shrubbery. Behind them, tall giant trees hid the cabin from the rest of the world. It felt like we had travelled to the ends of the world. There would be no one here to save me.

I wondered then if this was where it would all end for me.

Was I being punished for my relationship with Gage? Well, if I was, I would have done it all again. It was worth it. No matter what happened now. It was worth it.

"Move!" One of the three men pushed me forward and I stumbled into the cabin. I heard one of them say something to the others and it was followed by laughter that howled into the night. They wouldn't dare do this if Gage were alive.

I felt my chest constrict with the first cry of despair, but I refused to think about him. A plethora of horrible emotions were bubbling up inside me. The worst of them was anger. Such anger at him that I wanted to destroy everything in my sight. I would never forgive him. I told him. I told him to walk away. Did he listen? No, he had to go and die.

And all for what?

Bastard. How could he leave me to suffer this?

I was thrown into a room like a captured animal and the door was locked behind me. I had seen from a small oil lamp set, which they took away with them that the room was small and there was a window, but it was nailed shut with planks. I didn't bother looking for a main switch. I knew without looking there would be none. In the darkness, I prayed for the sun to quickly rise so some light might come into the room. I sat on the bed, and waited for my eyes to get used to the dark. Then I began to scan the space for anything I could use as a weapon.

A few hours passed, and through a small slit in the wood, I could see the new day had arrived. By now, Nichole would have realized that something was terribly wrong. I had never once disappeared without telling her where I was going. Maybe she would call the police, but they wouldn't do anything until forty-eight hours passed. So, I couldn't put too much hope that anything was going to happen that way.

A few more hours must have passed before the door was pushed open and I looked up to see Michael had appeared bringing with him his nauseating scent of tobacco and alcohol and a wooden chair. His grin was wide and smug.

It made me sick to my stomach. I knew he had brought me here to break me and rape me, maybe even gang rape me with all his friends, but I refused to cower or to be intimidated by him. Even if it all ended in my death, he would never get an ounce of whatever satisfaction he sought from me. I would never beg him to spare me. I was ready to die without giving in to him.

"I can see you're deep in thought," he said confidently as he dragged the wooden chair with him and set it in front of me. "I hope I'm in there somewhere." He sat on the chair and leaned forward to stare into my eyes. "For once. Granted, it's not under the best of circumstances but hey, I'll take it." He reached forward to brush my hair out of my eyes.

For a moment, I thought that I'd let him to show him how little he meant to me, but the very thought made my skin shrivel up. I jerked back as his fingers brushed my skin.

"You're fucking beautiful," he said, leaning back. "Too beautiful for your own good. Maybe it made you stupid, otherwise how else would you have been with a fucker like Bone?" He suddenly swung forward and yanked on my hair.

A wince escaped my lips at the pain.

"You've humiliated me quite grandly in the past," he said, tightening his grip. He kept pulling and pulling until my face was positioned in front of his smelly crotch. "Now is the time to pay for it."

When I immediately lifted my head, he struck a blow across my face that was so hard I saw flashes before my eyes. Tears misted in my eyes, but I shut my lids and ordered them away. I thought of how they had tortured Gage and he never once cracked. I used him as my model. I would be strong like him.

He began to unbutton his jeans then lowered his underwear and his cock sprung out of his jeans. Grabbing my hair, he dragged me so I was stuck between his legs. "Now," he said, his voice thick with lust. "You can do this the easy way or the hard way. Either you suck my cock like a good girl or I knock out every tooth you have and you still have to suck my cock. Only difference is you'll be eating baby food for the rest of your life. You decide."

I gazed at the already hardened cock and lifted my haunted gaze to his. I spat on his face and gave my response. "Over my dead body."

At the sudden attack, he wiped the saliva off his face and

gave me a look that froze my soul over. He rose to his feet and grabbed my hair roughly. From then on, I wasn't even sure what happened. I felt my feet leave the floor and then my body crashed down as I was thrown to the ground like a ragdoll.

The breath was knocked out of me and I lay there gasping like a stranded fish, but he wasn't finished. He tossed me onto my back in fury and sat on my face. I thrashed my head about like someone possessed and tried screaming at the top of my lungs as I fought with all my might to get him off me, but all that came out of my mouth was a muffled sound.

I stopped struggling and let my limbs go limp.

He raised his crotch from my face.

"All right. All right. You win. We'll do it your way," I said.

"I knew you'd see the light." He shoved his cock into my mouth.

I almost choked at the disgusting intrusion. When it was all the way down I bit down as hard as I could, determined to cut it off. His roar was agonized enough to wake the dead. He began to pummel my head with blows. I heard the thundering of footsteps then the door flung open. Three men had come to his rescue. I could feel the salty taste of blood run down my throat. The sensation of drinking his blood was so disgusting I opened my mouth to spit it out.

He was pulled up and rushed away from the room.

A fist pummeled into my jaw and blood spewed from my mouth.

"Fucking bitch," one of the men hurled over his shoulder as they left the room.

I crawled away to one corner of the room. It felt as though my face had been struck in a thousand ways and I didn't know if my nose had been broken. I spat out blood and using my pajama top, I wiped his blood from my face and mouth.

To my surprise, none of them came back for more freak show hour from me.

## GAGE

"Are you ready?" asked Joel Lee, the detective that I had become quite familiar with over the last six hours.

I looked up from my coffee cup. "I am." I rose to my feet and followed him.

The Dallas Police department was bustling with activity, officers, detectives and staff. All hurrying from place to place, as they handled a seemingly endless stream of offenders.

Outside, an irritating mob of press was camped, hoping for any juicy bit of an update from the bust earlier in the day so they could breathlessly update their networks with it. To all I was still proclaimed as dead and it was to remain that way.

"I suppose you'll never want to hear of Arnault again?"

My mind instantly went to her. I had to go back, I left my heart there. "Not in a hurry," I said softly. "I already handed over all my reports and sorted through the paperwork before I left."

"That's where the doom is," he said with a chuckle. "Infiltrating the clubs seems like a piece of cake when it comes to those damn papers, doesn't it?"

My response was a smile.

He pulled the door open and ushered me into the monitoring room. We met three other detectives there, all waiting to listen in on the interrogation. I was decently acquainted with them so we exchanged handshakes.

Almost immediately, the detective in charge walked into the interrogation room and took his seat. He slammed his folder of files on the table. "He's a tough one, isn't he, that Snake?" he commented. "All the others gave up the one they called RJ, and pinned him as the orchestrator to save their own heads, but he's refused to say a word till now. I've always wondered what motivates these guys, beyond the money, of course? Especially him? In a different setting, he would have been a decent leader or the CEO of a Fortune 500 company. Why the hell would he be on this path?"

I watched Nathan Snake, the cold brutal man who had led me over the last two years, through the one-way mirror. Suddenly, he turned to the one-way mirror and looked at it. For a second, it felt as if he was looking right at me, but of course, he wasn't.

A knock sounded on the door, and we all turned towards the officer who'd come into the room. He had a phone in hand. "Lee," he called. "Miller needs to take this. He has an emergency down in Arnault."

My eyebrows met. "What emergency?"

He handed the phone over to me.

"Hello?"

It was Yuri. "Where the fuck is your phone?"

I was taken aback by the hostility in his tone. "It's been submitted. It's evidence." The nerves in my gut tightening with dread. "What is it? Is she okay?"

"She's not."

"What happened?"

"Jeremiah just called," he said.

I almost doubled over from the implication. I walked out of the room despite the calls of the other detectives.

"You know him, right?"

"I do, he's undercover in Deaths Hand. What did he say?"

"Michael. Do you know Michael? He's the main dealer for their club."

I stopped then and shut my eyes. I wanted to punch my fist into the wall. My voice was a croak of disbelief. "What happened?"

"He contacted a few of them from the club to help him with something so Jeremiah tagged along. He mentioned some beef you had with Michael over Della-Ray so when they went to her house last night to kidnap her, he figured out what was going on. They have her captured now and moved to some cabin in Sugar Groove. Looks like he's going to …"

"He's going to what?"

"What do you think, Gage? They already think you're dead."

"Going to what?" I yelled.

"He told them he was going to have her then pass her off to them to use at one of their orgies."

"Miller!" one of the officers called behind me.

I was already storming towards the exit. "Send people over to that cabin right now," I shouted urgently.

"You know I can't do that Gage. It'll put Jeremiah in danger. It's not possible for anyone beyond the four of them to have known about this plan."

I turned around and smashed the phone on the ground. As it shattered, I stared at it and fought to breathe. It felt like I was going to collapse. I felt the tears fill my eyes.

Just then, two of the detectives I had abandoned in the room came running out to me.

"I need to go back to Arnault now. Right now!"

"It's not recommended that you return so quickly unless it's an emergency. Why don't you give it a few days?"

I curled my hands into fists. "I need to fucking leave right now! My family is in trouble."

One of them retrieved his keys from his pocket. "Got it. Come on, man. I'll order a copter, right now. It'll be ready and waiting by the time we get there."

## DELLA RAY

T he room I was in smelt like death.

Or perhaps it was just the way I felt.

I was still huddled in the corner by the bed, stained with my own blood, my face and arms throbbing. My only hope now was that perhaps I had injured Michael enough for him to stay away and not attempt to put his stinking cock in my mouth.

So many times during the night, I had thought of my baby. I buried my head between my knees to hide my tears as the realization dawned on me that I might never be able to see her again, and if by some miracle I did, I wouldn't be the same loosey-goosey person. How could I after these monsters brutalized me. Perhaps they would hurt me so much that I would never be able to find whom I once was before tonight.

Bone's image came into my mind and I immediately pushed it away. I couldn't handle that grief now. Turning my head, I wiped at the tears on my face and turned toward the window by my side. I needed to survive for Jess's sake. Maybe I could try to pry some of the planks away.

At the sound of the door, I rushed away from the window, my heart in my throat that Michael had returned. It was not Michael, but one of the other men. This one was as bald as an egg and tattooed with the image of Gollum holding the ring. He shut the door behind him. He let his hand make a crude stroke of his crotch and when I jumped to my feet with fear, a sick smile spread across his face with excitement. "Time to play, bitch," he called mockingly.

I plastered my back to the wall. If only it would swallow me up. "Don't come any closer to me," I warned. "Michael will be very angry. I'm his woman. He wants me for himself."

"Well, not so much after the way you attacked him. He was gonna share you with us when he was finished, anyway. You're going to be sucking a lot of dicks, sweetheart. So you better get used to the idea. Me, I just can't fucking wait anymore."

"I'll hurt you," I snarled. "I swear."

"Try that same wildcat shit on me that you did to Michael and watch me dig your pretty eyes out." Out of nowhere, he produced a knife and held the shining blade in the air. "I will carve my initials on your face and kill you myself if even your teeth graze me. Get on the bed, bitch."

He was no Michael. I realized now that it had all come to an end for me.

# GAGE

https://www.youtube.com/watch?v=EYyarcp5LtU
-I will be there, I will be there-

After a short copter and car ride that seemed to take forever we arrived at the agreed upon meeting point.

Jeremiah met us down the road from the house. The moment I jumped out of the car, he appeared from the trees and hurried up to us.

"Where is she?" I asked.

"She is locked in one of the rooms. One of our members, Bull has his eye on her, but it looks like the men are starting to get restless. They haven't had fresh meat like this for a long time. What's your plan?"

I felt as if my brain was on fire. Without answering him, I began to hurry forward, but he stopped me. "What is your plan, Gage? Otherwise, I'll be in deep shit."

"You fucking left my girl alone with those monsters."

"Yuri!" he said through gritted teeth.

Yuri locked his hand around my wrist. "Gage, we have to do this right or we could implicate him. He's spent four years in there. I'm not giving him up for anything. Not even your girl."

I forced myself to calm down, my gaze on the cabin in the distance as they conversed.

"Michael and Tav will be back any moment now from his treatment," Jeremiah said in low tones. "You both need to either be gone by then or—"

Suddenly, her high scream pierced the afternoon air.

I tore Yuri's hold away and sprang into a dead run. I readied my gun the moment I arrived at the house and kicked my way through the front door. There was only one closed door in the whole room so I rammed myself against it. The wood gave away immediately on impact with my bulk and I burst into the room.

At the sudden intrusion, the beast that had been on top of her turned around in shock.

His pants were around his knees with his dick out and ready for the assault. My gaze fleeted over to hers and I felt something in my chest shatter at the bruised and battered woman that I was supposed to protect.

"Gage!" Yuri called in warning as I aimed my gun, but I was past reason.

"What the fuck is going—" The first shot blasted into his

crotch and an agonized scream tore from him as blood splattered everywhere.

"Get her!" I yelled.

Yuri hurried over to help her off from the bed.

Without blinking, I pointed my gun at his chest and blasted two more bullets into him. He had a leg in death's door but he wasn't dead like I needed him to be. I could feel tears rolling down my face as I blasted one more, straight into the middle of his forehead.

I could hear her cries and screams as she was pulled out of the room by Yuri, and soon I was left with only Jeremiah as he gazed at the carnage of human flesh before me. I couldn't move ... I didn't know how I was ever going to face her.

"What the fuck, Gage? How are we going to explain this one?"

Shutting my gaze, I reigned in my ragged breath, and put the gun away.

She was standing outside the cabin. She looked numb. No expression showed on her battered face.

I stopped in front of her.

She raised her head to gaze at me.

The ache I felt for the state she was in was soul deep. I couldn't understand how she could ever forgive me for bringing her into this danger.

The moments ticked away, her ragged breathing the only sound she made. Then she lifted one hand and touched my face. "You're not dead," she whispered in awe.

"I don't know how to express how sorry I am," I whispered back.

"They said you were dead," she said slowly, almost in a dream like state.

"I'm an undercover agent with the U.S. Bureau of Alcohol, Tobacco, Firearms, and Explosives," I explained immediately. "I am so sorry that I couldn't tell you the truth … and I am even more sorry than you could possibly know that I wasn't here to protect you. I—" Words failed me and my heart broke all over again at how inadequately I had protected her. I would have given my life to take back all the pain she had suffered in this ordeal. There were no words enough to tell her this. I held her gaze and didn't stop the tears as they rolled down my face.

She wiped them with her fingers. "Don't baby. Don't. A few slaps doesn't count for nothing. You're alive and that's all that matters," she whispered.

God, I loved her so fucking much. I actually felt insignificant in the face of her quiet strength. Before I could tell her, we were interrupted.

Jeremiah burst out of the cabin. "Michael and Tad are on their way," he announced.

It struck me for the first time, who the man he was referring to was. "Tad? The Mongol's secretary?"

He nodded.

"Why is he with Michael?" Yuri asked.

"I don't know." Jeremiah shrugged. "He was with him when he stopped by the clubhouse to get Bull and me."

I rose to my feet then and turned around to face the both of them, the saddest smile on my face.

"I think you should leave, Gage …" Yuri said.

"Not without Della-Ray."

"You can't take her," Jeremiah protested. "She has to call the cops right now and say that she has been kidnapped and assaulted. It has to be on record. Otherwise, no one will be able to explain how they got here."

"And what about the body?" Yuri asked.

"That's for you to clean up. Speak to your superiors," Jeremiah stated. "He threatened you both with a gun, you reacted to protect yourselves."

"Then what about you?" Yuri asked.

Jeremiah stopped then and sighed in exhaustion, his fingers running through his messy head of ginger hair. "I don't fucking know."

A moment of silence ensued and then I spoke, "Let's go to the kitchen."

Both men came with me and soon we were in the adjacent room. I addressed Jeremiah, "How important is completing your assignment to you?"

He kept his gaze fixed on the wooden floor deep in thought before finally responding, "I've put four years of my life into it," he said. "I don't want to throw it all away."

"Okay then," I replied. "It means that you cannot have been here."

Yuri turned to me his brows brimming with anger. "Does

that mean that you're going to take care of Michael and Tav?"

"I'm not going to let Tav go." I growled.

He shook his head. "Not like this, Gage."

"All of this is because of him. I joined the program to get him …"

He shook his head. "No, not this way."

"I'm sorry, but I'm out of time and patience and frankly, interest. I wanted him to rot the rest of his life away for killing Mace, but now I just want him gone. He cannot exist in the same world that I do. You can report me if you choose to."

Silence.

I knew they wouldn't.

"What about Michael?" Jeremiah asked. "Are you going to take care of him too?"

"What do you think?" I scoffed.

"Gage," Yuri called.

"I think you should leave, Yuri …" I said.

"Nah, don't do it," Yuri tried again.

"He's a piece of scum. I'll be doing the world a favor. He put his hands on her. If I don't take care of him today, he's going to turn up dead before the week ends."

"How are we going to fucking explain all of these?" he complained.

"We turned up to save her … they acted up. We defended

ourselves," I said.

The room went quiet for the longest time and neither of us moved. My mind was already made up ... no matter what happened, these three had written their sentence the moment they touched that sweet, innocent girl who had never harmed a soul.

"When do I make the call?"

Her voice was so sudden that we all jumped.

She was standing by the door, her gaze boring directly into mine.

I wanted to call out to her, but my mouth couldn't form the words.

"Will this get you into trouble?" she asked.

My response was simple. "I don't care."

"I do," she said.

An all-consuming fire started in the pit of my stomach. "Will you disappear with me?"

"Gage," Yuri called, but I was unable to drag my gaze away from hers or to even respond for that matter.

Finally, she broke her gaze from mine and turned to him. "I'll make the call. I don't need a reason stronger than Gage's supposed death for me to move out of the county for a fresh start."

I couldn't breathe.

Yuri pulled his phone out of his pocket and she went with him as they returned to the cabin's living room.

# GAGE

I heard the car crawl to a stop and waited for Michael to come to me.

The first thing they noticed as they walked into the room was the body of their colleague sprawled across the bed that had now turned a bloody red.

"Holy Fuck!" Tav roared.

Michael staggered away in fright. They were both completely speechless for the first few moments before Michael darted his head around for lingering danger. His eyes instantly connected with mine at the opposite end of the room, where I was seated while calmly waiting for the both of them.

All the color drained away from his face.

"Isn't this …" Tav stuttered. "The fucking biker from Order of Blood?"

"Aren't you meant to be dead?" Michael gasped. A crazy laugh escaped Michaels lips then as he shook his head in realization. "You tricked everyone. You're the fucking rat."

I wasn't interested in him … yet. Instead I looked at Tav.

He had begun to slowly retreat away from the room.

The sound of a cocking gun came from behind him. He froze, his hands in the air. When he glanced around and saw Yuri behind him, he shut his eyes with defeat. He knew it was an ambush. The game was up, but he didn't know why. "What the fuck is going on?" he asked.

"Do you remember Mace Herald from the Black Angels club?" I asked.

Not even an ounce of recognition flashed in his eyes.

I went on, "Three years ago, on June 15th, you knocked on the window of his van at the Maple Canyon intersection. And when he rolled down the glass, you put five fucking bullets into his head. His wife couldn't recognize him, you lowlife. He had two kids. Babies. But you don't care, do you? Nah …"

His eyes widened with the memory. "Joker? Are you talking about Joker? What the fuck does he have to do with you?"

"He was my best friend."

"How the fuck is that possible? He was a fucking agent … he was working for the ATF and that's why the club—"

"You only found that out a year later. You killed him because he found out about the funds you stole from the club's merchandise. He called you out on it and told you to report yourself to the club, but you killed him to save your own fucking neck. It's taken me a long time to catch up to you, and here I am. I swore to avenge him, so time's up for you, I guess."

"So what now?" he asked. "You're going to off me too, do the same to me as I did to him? You can't, can you? You're the law." He had the audacity to smile.

I pulled out my gun and pointed it straight at him. The smile dissipated from his face at the realization that I wasn't joking.

I cocked my gun and his hands flew up in a useless warding off gesture.

He was gunned down straight through the heart, and then through the abdomen to throw off the precision of the hit when they ran their investigations. Being hit in an attempt to attack us would be his end story.

As he dropped down to the floor, breathless and bleeding out, I placed the gun on my lap and turned to Michael.

He instantly dropped down to his knees, his hands together in a panicked plea. "Bone, I didn't mean to harass her. I swear to fucking God. I was just going to scare her a little bit ... but never hurt her. I have feelings for her too. I was just a bit angry at how she had treated me ... She chose you over me, man and that hurts. You know how it is ... Just please. There's no need for this—we can just go our separate ways. I swear, I'll never tell anyone, or even cross your path again."

"We need to wrap up and get out of here. We have a lot of explaining to do," Yuri said.

I gazed down at Michael as he covered his head, his entire body trembling with fear.

I sent two bullets into him. One in his left arm and the other straight through his lungs.

After wiping my prints, I handed the gun over to Jeremiah and walked out of the room. I then sat with Della-Ray as she made the call to say she'd been kidnapped.

When she was done, she turned to me, tears in her eyes. "Will everything be okay now?"

"I think so. But even if it's not, I promise you that I'll never leave you to face anything alone again."

A very long silence followed, as I waited for the response that would determine our future with each other.

"Were you ever going to come back?" she asked with the blanket tightly around her and her gaze on the floor.

"I was never going to leave you. It was going to take a few weeks, but I was always going to return, to ask you to come back with me."

"But in those weeks you were going to leave me thinking you were dead?" She turned to me.

Dammit, I couldn't take the tears in her eyes. I placed my hand softly on her face and delicately wiped her tears away. "I was, but only for a little while. Only until the news around my death became stale, because you would have been watched closely by the club for any foul play. And if they suspected that something was wrong, you would have been the one to be harassed in order to get me to reveal myself. I regret involving you in any of this. It was never my intention but—"

"I tied your hands, didn't I?" She rose to her feet and just then, the sounds of sirens in the distance announced the approach of the cops. She turned to glance at me. "I don't regret it," she said. "Do you?"

For the first time since we had gotten to the house, I breathed easy. "Never," I replied. "Never. How can I, when I found you? I love you, Della Ray. I love you the way I've never loved another human being."

She turned to me then. "I love you too," she said. "With all my heart, Gage Miller."

Her warmth and touch melted me in a way that I couldn't believe was possible. I couldn't hold back. With my hands on her face, I took her mouth with mine, and kissed her from the depths of my heart. At the delicious heat that consumed me, I felt the tears roll down from my eyes at this woman who had somehow become mine. "I will heal for you," I promised her. "Thank you for giving me another chance to come back to life." I let her go.

Then I sprinted out through the back door.

# DELLA RAY

https://www.youtube.com/watch?v=-59COFjB6Sk
-lean on me-

"Shouldn't you wait until your face heals a little before you go to see Denise?" Nichole asked.

"I want her to see me like this. The only good that can come out of getting battered is that she will pity me and let me keep Jess."

Nichole rubbed her palms together. "I never realized you were that Machiavellian."

I grinned at her through swollen lips. "I never needed to be before."

"Okay. Good luck and take care of yourself," she whispered.

"Thank you for taking care of Jess for me while I do this."

"I'm Jess's godmother. I'll always be here for you and her."

The next morning, I took the long flight to Ohio. During the trip, I gazed out of the window and thought of Gage and what we did to those men. I always thought of myself as a good person, someone who would never hurt another human being, but yesterday I found out that was a lie. I was more than capable of hurting another human being. I even took joy in seeing that bald monster blown to bits. Now I knew I was only good because I had never *had* to be bad.

Denise lived with her boyfriend in a tiny house in a horrible part of town. She was drinking Gin and coke and the TV was blaring in the living room when I arrived. The place was a mess. It stank of cigarettes and sweat. I felt sad to see her like this. I remembered her the way she had been when we were children. I never thought then she would end up like this. She was so brave and strong.

"What happened to your face?" she asked, moving into her living room.

"Long story," I said.

"Sit down," she invited carelessly, as she resumed her seat in front of the TV.

I moved some pizza takeaway boxes and sat down next to her. "Can I turn the TV down a bit?"

She took a drag from her cigarette. "You think you're better than me?"

I shook my head. "No, of course not."

"I was raped when I was twelve. I was raped," she said fiercely.

"I know," I whispered sadly.

She grabbed the remote and turned off the TV. "That's my favorite program," she said bitterly.

"I can wait. Watch it first. We'll talk afterwards."

"No. Say what you have to say and go."

"Do you ever think of Mom and Dad?"

She took a swallow of her drink. "What's the point? They're dead."

I had a clear image of the police officers that come to take us from our home that day when they were killed in a freak car accident. I saw again the expression on my sister's face before she began screaming at them to get out of the house.

"I think of them all the time," I whispered.

"I don't," she said harshly.

"Do you know Dad always loved you best? No matter how hard I tried to make him love me more, he always loved you best."

She killed her cigarette in an ashtray overflowing with cigarettes and looked away from me. "I don't want to talk about the past."

"Why? Are you afraid Dad is looking down on you?"

She whirled her head around. "If you have come here to ask me whether you can keep Jess, you're going about it the wrong way."

"Jess is twenty-five percent Dad, Denise. If he is looking, he would have been proud of her. He would never ever give her up for adoption. He would have said, she's the child of my child. My favorite child."

GEORGIA LE CARRE

"You're so full of bullshit," she said, but her voice sounded odd.

"Do you know, Denise that Jess will probably never have a boyfriend, never marry, be in and out of hospital all through her childhood, and she leaves this world before she's thirty."

She stood up and started pacing the small space.

I went on, "I just want to give her what we never had. I want to give her a home. I want to protect her so she won't be raped by a stranger the way you were while she is moving through the care system. Do you know how many children disappear while they're in the care system in this country, Denise?"

She ran her hands through her badly bleached hair distractedly.

"She's our flesh and blood, Denise. Part of Dad and Mom and you and me. She belongs with us."

"You can't afford to keep her."

"I'll manage. I've managed so far."

"How?"

"The same way we all have to. One way or another, we manage."

"Are you on food stamps?"

I shook my head. "I work two jobs."

She sat down and dropped her head into her hands.

"Please, Denise. Don't let her go into the same system that caused you so much suffering."

She turned to me. "I let him rape me so he wouldn't touch you, you know."

I crouched next to her and touched her thin arm. "Oh, Denise. I'm so sorry. I'm so, so sorry. You can't begin to imagine how sorry I am."

"Every fucking night," she howled. "I protected you."

"I know you did and now it's my turn to do something for you. Let me protect and take care of your baby the way you did for me. It's only right. No one will hurt her while I am alive."

She nodded fiercely and I knew she was trying to stop herself from crying. "All right. You keep her. You keep her safe, you hear? I protected you. Now you protect her."

"I will. I promise I will protect her with my own life."

"I'm such a mess."

"You know how I remember you? I remember you climbing higher up the tree than anyone else. Even the boys."

A small smile played on her lips. "I was fearless, wasn't I?"

"That's still inside you, Denise. You can be that again. Nobody can take that away from you. No one."

She sniffed. "What happened to your face?"

I grinned. "You want the long version or the short one?"

"I want the long one, Della-Ray."

315

So I told her about the kidnapping and the bikers.

Then for the first time in years, she reached out and touched my face. "I'm really glad you came today," she whispered.

"I'm really glad I came too."

"I'm gonna make some changes in my life, Della-Ray. I'm gonna make some changes."

My eyes filled with tears of joy.

## DELLA RAY

One month later
https://www.youtube.com/watch?v=vUSzL2leaFM
-you look wonderful tonight-

"Okay, that's the last thing unloaded," Nichole said. "Great. I'll start unpacking Jess's stuff first."

"No, you won't."

I looked at her curiously. "What do you mean?"

"I mean. You are going on an all-night-dirty-stop-out date and I am unpacking and babysitting Jess."

I put my hands on my hips. "What are you talking about?"

"Come on. We got to get you ready. We only have an hour."

She looked so full of mischief I followed her into the room

that was going to be my bedroom. She opened the box marked *Date Night* and to my surprise, the chiffon Zimmerman was in it. She pulled it out. "Remember this? Gage called me and asked if he could buy it off me. I had no problem saying yes because A … you look so much better in it than me and B … how can you say no to a man that is being so freaking romantic."

I stared at Nichole in shock.

"He wanted you to wear this tonight. He said he wanted to show you off in the dress because the last time he missed it and he has regretted it ever since. He also said you looked so beautiful in it and it was what kept him alive through the pain and heartache. Oh, and he said can you please do your hair exactly the same as the last time and wear the same shoes too?"

I stared at her speechless.

She went around my back and prodded me along. "Well, come on. Jump in the bath. You don't want to ruin the fantasy for him by smelling of sweat and dust."

I laughed then. It took less than an hour to get dressed. I did my hair like the last time and wore the same shoes from before, not that I had anything different.

I looked at Nichole nervously. "I still look the same, right?"

She shook her head. "Not really."

"What do you mean?" I asked worriedly.

"You look ten times better. You have the glow of love and happiness on your face now."

I smiled gratefully at her. All these years, she had truly been the wind beneath my wings. It seemed as if the more troubles came our way, the stronger our friendship grew. I would miss her like crazy, but she had to finish her art apprenticeship in Arnault. After that, maybe she would move here to join me. Until then, we would just have to speak everyday on the phone.

The doorbell rang making both of us jump.

She laughed. "Stay here and just look pretty. I'll play the part of your butler."

I felt too anxious to giggle. I hadn't seen him in a month and my mouth felt dry with anticipation.

She went out and I heard her say, "Please come in, Mr. Miller. Your date awaits." Then she was coming into the room again, a huge smile lighting up her lovely face.

Right behind her Gage followed. He was clean-shaven and looked so goddamn handsome I almost passed out with sheer excitement.

He just stood there all six foot four of hard muscle. He was wearing his blue denim jeans, and the same crisp white shirt open he had worn that night when he didn't turn up for our date. He looked at me with a sexy grin on his face and his eyes were eating me up. As if it was all a grand dream on the radio Eric Clapton's *Wonderful Tonight* started playing.

"OMG, Gage, you look so hot!" I blurted out. I rushed to him, threw my arms around him and hugged him tightly.

"You ready to go, baby? Because we have unfinished business," he said.

"I am."

"Your taxi awaits."

We walked up to the taxi.

My hands were trembling with emotion. I slanted a glance upwards at his face and could hardly believe this was my man. That I actually got the hero. Little ole me ended up with the hero!

"Where are we going Gage?" I asked.

"It's a surprise."

I liked surprises, especially such exciting ones, so I quietly got into the seat.

Gage closed the door and came around the other side. He slid in and I could feel the heat from his thigh. I put my hand on it. "Don't start that now, or we will be going straight to the hotel," he warned.

I pulled my hand away and he chuckled.

A short while later, we pulled up outside Dolce Vita. I always believed that I was an independent feminist, but I felt a thrill of delight when Gage came around and opened my door. Feeling like something infinitely precious, I got out. Gage paid for the taxi and I turned to face him. "We're having dinner here?" I'd read about this exclusive Italian restaurant. It was the haunt of celebrities and the rich.

"Unless you don't want to?"

For a moment, I hesitated, feeling slightly guilty, as I knew dining here would surely cost an arm and a leg.

He understood. "Hey. It's okay. It's a treat. We deserve this."

I smiled up at him. "Yeah, you're right. We deserve this."

He took my hand and led me up the steps.

Uniformed doormen opened the doors for us and inside, an elegant woman in black checked off Gage's name in her reservation book and showed us to our table.

I could feel the other diners' eyes upon us. I was pretty sure it was not due to me, but the gorgeous beast escorting me. When we were seated, I looked around me curiously. I had never been in such luxurious surroundings before.

"Like it?" he asked, a twinkle in his eyes.

"What's not to like? It's absolutely beautiful."

A waiter arrived with the drinks menu, but Gage told him we would have a bottle of Dom Perignon. He nodded approvingly and went off to fulfill the order.

"Champagne? Hmmm, are you trying to impress me, Mr. Miller?"

He grinned wolfishly. "Is it working?"

"Definitely. I'll show you how impressed I am later," I whispered.

The waiter arrived with the bucket of champagne. He poured it into flutes and left.

Gage lifted his glass. "To the most beautiful woman I have ever laid eyes on."

I lifted my glass. "To the most beautiful man I have ever laid eyes on."

Gage laughed. "And to our mutual appreciation society then."

I took a sip of the cold bubbles. I felt as if I was in a dream. It all seemed so surreal. So wonderful.

Another waiter in a suit came to take our dinner request.

Gage ordered a large steak, oddly enough, a T-Bone steak.

"Missing being Bone?" I asked, with a happy giggle.

"No. But I'll always love Bone, he brought me to you."

As the waiter left, I caught Gage just staring at me. "What?" I asked.

"You look so fucking beautiful," he declared with such intensity. "You can't imagine how glad I am to be with you tonight, baby." As he said it, I swear he blinked away tears.

The words and the look in his deep blue eyes made my heart skip. "I'm deliriously happy you're alive and here with me, Gage. I don't know what I would have done without you."

He lifted his flute and held it out. "To being alive," he said.

"To being alive," I echoed as I clinked my glass to his.

I watched him tilt his head as he drank. A few strands of his beautiful hair came loose and floated back. "I love you, but I realize you're still a stranger," I told him.

His eyes widened. "A stranger?"

"Well, not to my body, but I don't really know much about you."

He looked at me indulgently. "What would you like to know?"

"Everything."

"I don't see why that can't be arranged," he said softly, as he entwined his fingers with mine. "When we have our whole lives ahead of us."

# EPILOGUE

One year later
https://www.youtube.com/watch?v=450p7goxZqg
-all of me-

I sat in the bathroom and stared at the blue line. Wow, what a coincidence that I should find out I'm pregnant on Jess's birthday!

There was a bang on the door and I jumped on the toilet seat, my hand flying to my chest.

"Food is ready! Come out, Mommy," Jess called.

"I'll be right there," I called back, and tucked the white stick into the pocket of my shorts. "It will need a confirmation," I told myself. "Don't jump to conclusions yet."

I walked into the kitchen and stopped at the sight of the table. It was loaded with a growing stack of pancakes, strawberries, syrup, and juice.

Gage turned around. He had Jess glued to his body like a baby, as she worked the sausages that were cooking on the stove.

"Wow! You guys cooked all this while I was in the bathroom?" I asked while taking the nearest seat.

"We started even before you were awake, Mommy," Jess crowed.

Gage put her down and she made a sad face, so he lowered himself to her eye level and gave her a smile that never failed to melt her or me, for that matter.

He spoke so softly to her that I could barely hear what he was saying. That was exactly the tone he used on me too. To the rest of the world he had a stern tone, but to those that he had in his heart, he was gentle, intimate, and consuming.

Jess ran off to carry out whatever errand he had sent her on.

Then he turned his searing blue gaze on me.

After all this time, I still felt my heartbeat quicken when our eyes met like this.

Strands of his silky hair fell lightly down the sides of his face. He'd gotten rid of the beard, but it always made me happy that he didn't cut his hair after his undercover assignment came to an end. Instead, he had maintained the dark cascade, but had never allowed it to go past his shoulders.

He was dressed in nothing but the pair of dark slacks that I had peeled off his body last night and the memory jostled me to where all I could think of was having my hands on him again.

He leaned against the sink, and studied me intently. "Why are you upset?"

"I'm not upset," I responded, taking a strawberry from the platter in front of me.

"Nichole is coming up from Arnault today, isn't she?" he asked.

"Yeah, she is."

"How is she?"

A smile spread across my lips. "She's fine, but she mentioned a secretive, mysterious billionaire who has come to live in Arnault. Apparently, he paid a visit to her gallery. Something about the way she described him made alarm bells ring in my head."

He frowned. "In what way?"

I grinned. "In a good way."

I saw him relax then. "Right. Good for her. About time she found someone. Is your sister okay?"

"Yup, she's fine too. She said she would call later to speak to Jess."

He came over to sit by my side. Pulling my chair between his thighs, he stared into my eyes. "Back to you. Are you worried about sending your manuscript to the publishers?"

"Nope, I've already decided that if they reject me, I'm just going to self-publish."

"So what's wrong?"

He looked at me with such concern in his eyes that I felt as if

I must be the luckiest girl alive. Who would have ever thought I would get to keep such a gorgeous man with such a beautiful, protective soul … all for little ole me. Over this last year, my love for him had dug in even deeper than I had ever believed possible. Leaning forward, I threw my arms around his shoulders and kissed him. "You've ruined me," I whispered to his lips. "You pay for everything. You take care of Jess and me. I know how expensive Jess's medical bills are. I could never pay you back."

"Repay me? Are you out of your mind? You're my life. Before I met you and Jess, I had nothing. For years, money just poured into my bank account and I had nothing to spend it on, so I'm happy to spend it on you and Jess."

I chewed my bottom lip. "How would you feel about paying for one more person?"

Before he could respond, we heard Jess's footsteps as she hurried over clutching two gaily wrapped presents in her chubby hands. "Presents!" she squealed with excitement. "Presents."

I kept my gaze on Gage as he went over to get the sausages he'd cooked. "We'll do the presents later. Let's eat before the food gets cold. I have to head in to the station in an hour." He brought the sausages over and placed one on my plate.

"You fry sausages every chance you get. I can't believe you're making us eat them with pancakes," I teased.

"I'll have yours if you don't want it," he said and held out his fork.

I put my body in the way to hide my meal … and that was when I saw it.

Jess had already opened one of the presents and inside was a small black box. She fumbled with it.

I pulled my gaze away, my heart pounding in my chest.

"Jess, you shouldn't open other peoples' presents," Gage said. "That's Mommy's, not yours."

I returned to my sausage, unable to breathe.

My little girl however, kept on fumbling with the box until she pried it open.

I didn't dare look at Gage and I would never know how the next words flew out of my mouth, "I think I'm pregnant," I said quietly. "I did a test, but it doesn't mean much. It's not accurate. You can't trust these things. I'll go for a confirmation later today."

When he didn't say anything, I still couldn't look at him, so I laughed nervously.

"Della-Ray," he called. "Look at me."

I turned to him then.

"You just told me the happiest news I could have ever received at this point in my life and yet, you're not even giving me a chance to receive it. Is that what you meant when you asked whether I could support another person?"

I nodded.

I felt him move then and in a flash, he was on a bended knee beside me. "Yes, Della-Ray I can support another person. I can support any amount of little persons you care to bring into this world. Jess, bring Mommy's present to me, please," Gage said.

Smiling, Jess thrust the little black box to him.

My gaze shot up to him in shock as he opened the box and the gorgeous heart shaped rock inside winked at me like it knew a little secret that it would only share with me. I looked back up at him in a daze as he took the ring out of the box.

"I'm not giving you a chance to say no," he said. "So this is not a question. You're pregnant with my child, so this is the price you have to pay for that."

My heart couldn't take the joy. I couldn't breathe. I covered my mouth to muffle the ugly crying sounds that were now rapidly working their way up my throat.

Still on his knee, he pulled Jess over to stand in front of me. Then he began to whisper in her ear, much to her delight.

"Mommy, will you marry Gage?" she asked. "He loves you to the moon and back."

I wanted to cry with happiness. Never could I have imagined that Gage would include Jess in his endearing proposal. I leaned forward and kissed my baby on her lips. Then I whispered in her ear, "I will."

Jess squealed with excitement. "I will," she whispered into Gage's ear then she stepped to the side so I could see him better.

Suddenly, I dove for the love of my life and assaulted him with kisses.

He landed on the floor with me on top of his chest. "I love you," he growled possessively.

"Not more than me. Not ever," I growled right back.

The End

I really hope you enjoyed Gage and Della-Ray's story.

Nichole's and her mysterious billionaire will have their story told after

Nice Day For A White Wedding

If you feel like reading a sample chapter from Nice Day just keep scrolling…

COMING NEXT - SAMPLE CHAPTER

NICE DAY FOR A WHITE WEDDING

CHAPTER 1

**Cindy**

A light tap on my office door makes me look up from my computer screen. I check the time. It's only ten o'clock. Surely we don't have trouble already? As the manager of a small London casino, I have seen my fair share of trouble over the years; drunks, bad losers, cheaters, fights, drugs – you name it, I've dealt with it.

But at this time of night? No one has lost big yet and people are at the happy stages of drunk rather than the fighting stages.

The knock might not mean trouble, but something tells me it does.

"Come in," I call.

The door opens and Stewart, my head of security, steps in. He grins at me as he comes over to my desk. So there isn't a fight then. He wouldn't be grinning like that if all hell had broken loose.

"What is it?" I ask.

"You might want to put the cameras on," he says. "We've got a live one."

That's Stewart's way of telling me we have someone winning big. Now don't get me wrong, we have big winners now and again, but this is someone who is having enough luck to raise Security's suspicions. Ninety-nine percent of the time it is someone who has found a way to cheat.

I open my top desk drawer and pull out a remote control and fire up the bank of monitors on the wall to my right.

"There," Stewart says. "On the craps table."

He moves to the bank of monitors and points to a man. The man has his back to the camera, but even sitting down, I can tell he's big. He's both very tall and very well built. If he gets ugly, he might need all four of my security staff. He doesn't look rough though. He's wearing a black suit and I can see it's an expensive one, so that's something at least.

I press another button on the remote control and the bank of monitors showing all of the public areas of the casino becomes one screen showing only the craps table from different angles. Whatever the man is up to, he's attracted quite a crowd of fans around him. It's often the case when someone is on a winning streak. Our clientele can't help enjoying seeing us taken to the cleaners. It's payback for all the times we take them there.

The man pushes a large stack of chips forward and nods to the croupier. Sasha looks into the camera before she rolls the dice and I know she's wondering if we're watching from the office. Don't worry Sasha, we're watching.

The dice land and the crowd around the table raise their arms excitedly, high five and cheer. They stop short of slapping the big man on his back. By their reactions it is clear he has won big. Again. A voluptuous woman in a long black dress moves in for her own slice of the action and slinks onto the seat next to him. He does not turn to look at her.

"How many is that?" I ask Stewart.

"I counted six in a row before I came up here," he says.

So that's at least seven wins. Probably eight or nine by the time Stewart got here and I got the monitor on. Sasha pushes a stack of chips towards the man and I have a quick tally of how many chips he has. There is a little over two hundred thousand pounds in front of him. It's a lot of money, but it's far from a cause for panic. Some of our high rollers start with more than that. And of course, he could lose it all on the next roll, but somehow I doubt it.

I turn to look at Stewart. "But he has only won about two hundred thousand?"

"I know," he nods, "and I wouldn't even have come up here if not for the fact that one of the change guys was going off on his break and gave me the head's up to keep an eye on him. Apparently, he only started with fifty pounds."

This makes me raise an eyebrow. The man's suit, his quiet confidence and the way he's throwing big money bets on the table tells me he's got plenty of money. And guys in a casino with plenty of money don't start with fifty pounds. Tourists or hen and stag parties start with fifty pounds' worth of chips. Guys like him start with five or ten thousand pounds.

Unless they know they can't lose.

I watch closely as the man lays on another bet. He pushes his full pile of chips forward and nods to Sasha. A few others follow his lead and push chips into the same box. I ignore those people. They're just small fry, pushing on a few hundred. They're not involved in whatever scam the man is running. They're just taking advantage of what they now feel is a sure bet.

I curse as the man wins again. He isn't taking a huge amount of winnings and we can easily foot this kind of loss, but it annoys me because I can't for the life of me work out what he's doing. I can spot a card counter at a hundred paces. I've seen countless devices that cause havoc on the fruit machines, but the craps table is the hardest one to cheat on.

I know of only two ways to rig the odds at a craps table. Either have the box person involved in your scam and have them use weighted dice, or attach magnets beneath the table that affect the dice. I know neither of those are happening here. Sasha has worked here almost as long as I have. She was one of my first hires and not only is she loyal, but she's also adept at spotting and reporting scams. And magnets would have sent an alarm signal to my office the second the man entered the casino, so even assuming he had managed to get them in place, I'd have known about them.

"What do you think?" Stewart asks me.

"I think our friend there has found a new way to rig the game, but I'm screwed if I can work out what the hell it is," I say, shaking my head. "Come on. I think it's time he met the manager."

I grab my keys off my desk and Stewart and I leave my office. I lock the door and we head down the corridor. I have no idea how I can prove the man is cheating, but maybe up close and personal, I'll spot something. Even if I can't prove it, this situation still needs dealing with.

If a person is winning too much I tend to discreetly convince them to try another game, or move to a table with lower stakes. That way if they are genuinely on a lucky roll, there is chance their luck will run out. Naturally if they are cheating they are shown the door and banned for life.

Stewart and I step out of the elevator and walk along the short corridor to the casino floor. I pause for a second before we go through the door. I run my hands through my straight blonde hair to make sure my hair is in place, then I smooth down my slim-fitted black skirt.

"You're going out there to ban a cheater, not go on a date, Cindy," Stewart mocks.

I laugh, knowing he'll never understand what I'm doing. Looking poised and in control is a part of my thing. I have to always look calm and unflappable, and messy hair and a creased skirt just don't give that impression.

I push my way through the doors and I am instantly assaulted by noise and activity. Although it is still early the casino is already busy. There are people everywhere and all the fruit machines are taken up. Their whirling reels and the bursts of music as they spin fill the air. Even the more obscure table games are full to capacity. Waiters and waitresses move around the floor with drinks trays. Stewart and I quickly make our way towards the craps table. A cheer comes from the direction we are heading. It sounds like mystery man has done it again.

Subtlety is going to be the key here.

I begin to make my way through the thick crowd gathered around the table.

"Excuse me. Excuse me," I hear myself saying over and over again.

Most people move aside easily at my request, but some not realizing I work here and thinking I just want the best view point for the game give me dirty looks. I finally clear the throng and come out beside Sasha and opposite the mystery man which was my exact aim.

Mystery man has his head down, looking at his chips and I take a second to study him while he is unaware of my regard. He looks even bigger in person with a full head of shiny black hair. From what I can see of his forehead, I would guess he is in his early thirties. I was definitely right about him being from money. He has that casual confidence that only seems to come from having insane amounts of money.

Which begs the question of why anyone that loaded would risk getting caught cheating a casino out of what is essentially small change.

He must have felt my eyes on him because he looks up and straight at me.

Dangerous!

That is the first thought that flies into my head. The air of danger is all around him. From the unyielding jaw line, to the chiseled cheek bones, to the scar above his left eyebrow. There is a hint of a tattoo creeping out of the collar of his shirt and meeting the raven-black hair…and those stormy gray-blue eyes…they send shivers through my body.

I find myself staring into them, losing myself in them. There is a depth there that pulls me in, a sensual, sexual charm that sends fire racing through me and makes my clit throb. I subconsciously push my thighs together and it sends a little shockwave through my pussy. It takes everything I have not to gasp out loud at the sensation.

For the next few seconds I can't even think straight. Neither can I break the spell of his mysterious eyes. I just stand there like a brainless goldfish gaping at his presence.

Dark and stormy. That's what he is. Dark and stormy and downright dangerous. He curls one corner of his sensuous lip in a mocking smile.

Being mocked can tear you out of any sexual limbo. It does the job for me. I clear my throat, suddenly hyper aware of where I am, of the crowd around me. No more than two or three seconds has passed since dark and stormy looked up at me, but it feels like he's held my gaze for hours and I feel myself blushing slightly.

I force my eyes from his and his grin widens. Somehow, he knows exactly what he's doing to me. Hell, he probably has this effect on women everywhere.

"Good evening," he says to me.

His voice is low and gravelly, the perfect voice for his looks. The accent is Russian. For some weird, inexplicable reason, I imagine him close to me, whispering in my ear. I can almost feel his breath tickling my neck, his six o'clock stubble scratching my skin in a most delicious way.

*For the love of God, get a grip, Cindy.*

I nod to him and flash him what I hope is my totally professional smile, but his next words stun me into silence.

"I was wondering when you were going to show up ... Cindy."

Preorder your book here:

Nice Day For A White Wedding

And just in case you haven't met the couple yet.

Alexander Obolensky
first appeared in

Nanny & The Beast

and

Cindy
has made appearances in

Submitting To The Billionaire
The Heir
Redemption

# ABOUT THE AUTHOR

Thank you so much for reading my book. Might you be
thinking of leaving a review? :-)
Please do it here:

Highest Bidder

Please click on this link to receive news of my latest releases
and great giveaways.
http://bit.ly/10e9WdE

and remember
I **LOVE** hearing from readers so by all means come and say
hello here:

# ALSO BY GEORGIA

Owned

42 Days

Besotted

Seduce Me

Love's Sacrifice

Masquerade

Pretty Wicked (novella)

Disfigured Love

Hypnotized

Crystal Jake 1,2&3

Sexy Beast

Wounded Beast

Beautiful Beast

Dirty Aristocrat

You Don't Own Me 1 & 2

You Don't Know Me

Blind Reader Wanted

Redemption

The Heir

Blackmailed By The Beast

Submitting To The Billionaire

The Bad Boy Wants Me

Nanny & The Beast

His Frozen Heart

Made in the USA
Las Vegas, NV
12 September 2021